EPITAPH
FOR LYDIA

VIRGINIA RATH

EPITAPH
FOR LYDIA

VIRGINIA RATH

COACHWHIP PUBLICATIONS
Greenville, Ohio

Epitaph for Lydia, by Virginia Rath
© 2019 Coachwhip Publications

Published 1942
No claims made on public domain material.
Cover image: Sand © Buddee Wiangngorn;
    Roses © Epitavi

CoachwhipBooks.com

ISBN 1-61646-484-4
ISBN-13 978-1-61646-484-4

EPITAPH FOR LYDIA

For
Kay and Gladys
in Exchange for
One Hillside Cottage

PART ONE

This is the very painting of your fear. . . .
MACBETH: ACT III, SCENE IV

Mr. Dundas took a lukewarm highball from the tray presented to him, tasted the drink cautiously, and found it even worse than he had feared. It had a very faint whisky flavor, but mostly it tasted of celery with, he decided, just a dash of creosote.

He put the glass, minus one reluctant swallow, on the nearest table and looked about for his wife. But she had been cornered by a poet; a young poet just putting forth tender little green shoots.

Men who wanted an audience were always drawn to Valerie, her husband reflected. This young man was either telling her the story of his life or reciting his own poetry. It was difficult to guess which stage he was in, since the same dramatic gestures usually accompanied both. But he was obviously fresh and unwinded and just getting well into stride.

However, Mr. Dundas did not feel called on to rescue Mrs. Dundas from possible boredom. For one thing, she probably was not bored. And if she was, her husband considered it only just that she should be, since she had dragged him, despite strong protest, away from his own fireside to the Shraders'.

Ostensibly they had come to view Mark Shrader's latest batch of paintings. Mr. Shrader had been painting for twenty years merely because he wanted to—and for ten of the twenty because Mrs. Schrader wanted him to.

Lucy Shrader often said that her soul belonged to Russian Hill and Carmel. But her body resided in an impressive mansion on Lombard Street, built by her first husband. He had also left her a very handsome trust fund. In fact, as Mrs. Shrader said sadly, he had "stifled her with material things. Bread, when I wanted white hyacinths for my soul. . . ."

Her daily bread being guaranteed, Lucy and her trust fund married Mark Shrader. He went on painting peculiar pictures while Mrs. Shrader eagerly cultivated her soul and what her first husband certainly would have pronounced peculiar people.

Mr. Dundas, after Mrs. Shrader had first explained herself to him, always referred to the majority of those one met under her roof as "the white hyacinths." He dislikes dilettanti. Mrs. Shrader occasionally captured some bona fide hard-working artist or writer and proudly exhibited him for a limited time only. But her stock company were younger editions of Mrs. Shrader herself: people who had "always wanted to write"—or paint or sculpt or "do something in music."

Somehow they never managed to find time to sit on their artistic eggs long enough to hatch them. So Mr. Dundas had not been flattered when Mrs. Shrader assured him that he would meet "many a kindred spirit at our little gatherings. For you," she added kindly, "are in your way an artist. You also serve Beauty."

Mr. Dundas, only remembering this, winced slightly. He looked about the crowded room without seeing anything he thought could be described as a kindred spirit. He sighed and considered strolling into the small salon where Mr. Shrader's paintings were on view.

Before he could decide whether boredom was preferable to nausea his eye was caught by a splash of Parma violet at the other end of the room.

Professional curiosity led him toward it. He came up with a tall girl wearing, as he had thought, one of Gisele's most expensive models.

He had intended merely to wander past her, but she faced him and asked with a brittle sort of brightness that might pass for poise:

"Do you like it? You are Michael Dundas, the *couturier*—and sometimes amateur detective—aren't you? You were pointed out to me when you came in. I've always thought I'd like to design dresses. I'm Lydia Courtney. You don't know me."

"Then you haven't a charge account at Gisele's," Michael said cynically. "Or your name would be only too familiar. And I do hope you are happy in your little frock, modom?"

Miss Courtney eyed him doubtfully and finally smiled. "You're joking, aren't you? I mean, that's what salesgirls say sometimes. But you do like the dress?"

"Naturally, since I designed it," Michael said evasively.

Privately he thought that Lydia Courtney had more money than taste. Since she was sallow, tall and angular, neither the dress itself, which was meant to be softly feminine, nor its color suited her.

She had created a flimsy illusion of good looks that fell apart under careful scrutiny. Strip off her elaborate make-up and her eyes were too light and too small, her mouth too thin and pinched in at the corners.

Nevertheless, he felt that ordinarily she was well satisfied with her own appearance. So he wondered why she was pitiably nervous. Her thin bony hands were never still except when, apparently without realizing it, she clenched them at her sides. And her next remark showed that she was not merely ill at ease because she was alone here.

"I wandered away from my friends and can't seem to find them," she said. "They are probably in the dining room. I'm afraid the boys only came to eat. I haven't looked at Mark's paintings yet. Have you?"

Michael hesitated too long and was lost. He found himself escorting Miss Courtney to the salon. Her inspection of Mark Shrader's latest contributions to the world of art was punctuated by a glib patter in which the words "line," "brushwork," "perspective," and "significance" recurred frequently. Until, that is, she, turned and saw Michael's derisive smile.

"Don't you agree with me?" she said defensively.

"I stopped listening some time ago," Michael said pleasantly. "I never step into this room when it's hung with Mr. Shrader's paintings without paying his predecessor the tribute of a sympathetic sigh."

"His predecessor?"

"Mrs. Shrader's first husband, who accumulated the money that maintains her and her second spouse. This was once his study, you see. And somehow I doubt that his spirit has ever returned to this room—more than once."

"Oh. But he was only a moneygrubber," Miss Courtney said loftily. "Of course only a few people really appreciate Mark's work now. But the day will come when collectors will scramble for it."

"Quoting Mrs. Shrader?" Michael murmured.

"I mean, look at—well, look at Van Gogh. And—well, just look at this!"

Michael studied the picture she indicated. "Where," he inquired, "is the poached egg?"

"The—the what?"

"Oh, I beg your pardon. I see now that it is entitled Rooftops at Sunrise. I had thought it was a plate of corned-beef hash. And I see that what I took for a heap of spinach is really a cypress tree at midnight. However, I'll say one thing for Shrader. He may lay eggs, but at least he does lay them instead of merely talking a great work of art. He— Well, who let this in?"

He backed away to get a better perspective on a painting that had been given grudging space in a poorly lighted corner. It was a simple, straightforward, and effective study of sand dunes in the purple light that follows sunset.

"Shrader must have done that in a nostalgic moment to prove that he can still draw," Michael commented. "I wouldn't have supposed he—"

He turned at the strangled gasp behind him in time to see Lydia Courtney throw an unsteady hand over her eyes and sway back on her heels. She stumbled blindly toward the nearest chair and sank down in it.

"I'm afraid I—I don't feel very well. It's—don't you think it's close in here?"

"No," Michael said flatly. "Would you like me to find one of your friends and—?"

"No! No, really, I'll be all right. It's just that I haven't been sleeping well or eating. And—"

She glanced furtively toward the painting in the corner, looked away, and pressed her lips together tightly. But in an instant the words burst out:

"And that's a horrible picture!"

"Horrible? It is only a very good painting of sand dunes."

"Sand dunes at midnight," Lydia Courtney muttered.

"Midnight?" Michael looked at the picture again. "Not midnight, Miss Courtney. A very short while after sunset, I'd say."

"What? Oh, I was thinking of—of the painting of the cypress tree at midnight. You know, we were just talking about that one. It's a very natural mistake. To make about the sand dunes, I mean. Isn't it? Well, isn't it!"

Her voice rose hysterically. She clapped a hand over her mouth, and her eyes searched the room swiftly, lingering on its two doors.

"I'm—I'm sorry," she whispered. "I mean, some-one might come in and— Is there anyone in the hall? Where does that other door lead to? There might be someone—"

Michael opened the closed door. It led into a small living room, gay with chintz and flowering geraniums in bright pots.

"No one here," he reported. "And as the door into the hall is open and people are passing by constantly, there's not much point in my looking there, do you think? Do your friends know you aren't—well? That is, are you anxious that they shouldn't be worried about you? I know," he add-ed speciously, "that too much solicitude is rather trying."

Lydia grabbed at this suggestion eagerly. "That's it. I don't want to spoil their evening. I'm—I'm afraid I'm too high-strung," she said with a ghast-ly sort of coyness that set Michael's teeth on edge. "I don't want to be coaxed to go home just because my silly nerves play tricks on me. I wouldn't sleep and—and I really can't help the way that painting happened to impress me. I just see so many things differently than other people, that's all."

She fumbled with the zipper closing of her purse and, when she finally managed to open it, made great show of searching for her lipstick. Michael watched her calculatingly.

"Of course," he said at last, "many people find sand dunes depressing. I sometimes do myself. 'There is no kind of death to kill The sands that lie so meek and still. . . . But Man is great and strong and wise. . . . And so he dies.'"

The quotation had drifted into his mind, and he tossed it at Lydia, hoping for some reaction. He found himself in somewhat the position of a fisherman who baits his hook for a shiner and catches a shark. This time Lydia did faint.

II

Michael caught her as she sagged, at almost the same instant as he heard his wife's voice in the hall.

"I'm sure they came in here, Miss Bond. And I'd like you to meet my husband and— Well!"

Valerie had reached the doorway to the salon and stood regarding the tableau there with an air of mild curiosity.

"Is that a swooning female in your arms, Mr. Dundas? Surely Mr. Shrader's paintings aren't that overpowering this year? Oh, this is Marcia Bond. I've spoken of her frequently since—"

Marcia Bond's fingers were over Lydia's wrist in a practiced and almost automatic movement. She said, while Michael scowled helplessly at his wife:

"She's really fainted. She—did she say something?"

"Meek," Lydia mumbled. "Meek and still. Wise. No. Not wise. Foolish. The wind shall blow. . . . And many shall—shall make— I've forgotten."

"What on earth is she talking about?" Valerie said.

"I have no idea. Will you please open that door over there?"

Michael carried Lydia into the little sitting room and deposited her on a flounced chintz couch. Marcia Bond promptly made sure Lydia's feet were higher than her head, and Valerie unexpectedly produced smelling salts from her purse.

"I bought these just in case," she said with a fleeting smile. "But I've never needed them and apparently never will."

Lydia opened her eyes, saw Michael looking down at her, and closed them quickly.

"Marcia?"

"Right here," Marcia said crisply. "You'll be all right. Lie still and don't try to get up yet."

"If you want some brandy—" Valerie began. Marcia shook her head.

"No!"

It was a very decided negative and an unnecessarily forcible one, Michael thought, unless Miss Bond took for granted that the Shrader brandy would be as unpalatable as the Shrader whisky.

"I fancy you've sampled the liquid refreshments and found them not fit for man or beast," he said casually. "But I have heard that Mr. Shrader has his own private stock."

"Has he?" Marcia said inattentively. She was rubbing Lydia's hands, thin hands almost as transparent as ice. "I don't know the Shraders. And I haven't sampled the drinks. We don't—I don't drink."

"Oh?" Michael said.

In his hands the monosyllable expressed complete understanding and sympathy, though Valerie was uncertain what he understood or with whom he sympathized. He might be—and probably was—only bluffing, but it was a good bluff. It jerked Marcia Bond back to a hostile awareness of him.

"If there had been any brandy immediately available I'd have used it," she said sharply. "But since there wasn't—"

"You have decided that Miss Courtney would be better off not to take brandy on an empty stomach," Michael said pleasantly. "She told me she hasn't been sleeping or eating well, and I gathered she hasn't patronized the buffet here this evening. And of course a nurse's word is law."

"N-nurse?"

In one instant Marcia lost her air of calm capability and became the Miss Bond Valerie knew: the girl who talked to you pleasantly, interestingly, and, you felt, entirely by habit.

"N-nurse?" she said again. "I run a rental library, Mr. Dundas, as your wife was starting to tell you when we came into the salon. I've—I've come to know your taste in reading pretty well though you've never been in my library."

"Of course I know who you are now," Michael said. "Valerie has spoken of you frequently since she began patronizing your library."

He couldn't say that Valerie had remarked: "I don't know why I feel there is something odd about Miss Bond. So often I get the impression she's looking past me at something I can't see and that only part of her is in the library."

And he had said facetiously: "Well, my love, since her heart's not here, perhaps it's in the highlands, a-chasin' the deer." Which had, naturally, resulted in an indignant "Oh well, if you aren't interested," from Valerie.

But he was interested now. Marcia Bond was not pretty—or perhaps, Michael thought, it was only that she was not pretty this year when, she might be twenty-five or -six or even thirty.

Her face would always have been too square, but she need not always have been too pale and too thin and too indifferent to her appearance to trouble with make-up. Her dark brown hair was flecked with gray and casually combed. Her eyes were the color of sherry held to a light, and she had a beautifully shaped mouth.

She was as thin as Lydia, but she escaped angularity because she was small-boned and not more than three inches over five feet. Nor did her dress escape Michael's attention. It was exactly what he would have chosen for her: a severe dark green wool with touches of eyelet embroidery.

He was professionally pleased to see how well it stood the test of time, for he had designed it— three years ago. Since then its side seams had been taken in, though it still did not fit Marcia tightly.

These reflections were not merely professional. On them were based several suppositions: that during the last three years Marcia had grown much thinner; that three years ago she had had cash in hand to buy one very expensive dress which she was still wearing.

"And," he went on, "I believe I owe you some thanks for seeing Valerie gets the books I want to read very promptly. I'm sure you are an excellent librarian. But," he added in what Valerie disrespectfully terms his "velvet-glove" voice, "I won't apologize for supposing you are, or have been, a nurse. Your manner of taking a pulse is very professional. Even your voice, a while ago, was professionally soothing. And that's a workmanlike job."

He indicated her left wrist, neatly bandaged below her three-quarter-length sleeve.

"Nothing serious, I hope?"

Marcia moistened her lips slowly and carefully. Lydia lay perfectly still, eyes closed, and, Michael guessed, concentrating all her strength on remaining so. Then:

"It's just a slight burn," Marcia said. "I—grease splattered on me."

"Grease burns are so painful," Valerie said sympathetically. She moved closer to her husband and drove a dexterous elbow into his ribs. "But we haven't really been very helpful, Miss Bond. Could we take you home?"

"No, Lydia has her car here. But I don't drive and she mustn't, so we'd better find Sally. If you would, Mr. Dundas?"

"Shall I page her?" Michael asked rather sulkily, massaging his ribs. "I should prefer at least to know her last name."

"Sally Rollins. We three live together. Sally is a good deal taller than I am but not as tall as Lydia. She's blonde and wears her hair shoulder-length and she's slim but not too thin and—and wears bright red lipstick—"

"That description would apply to every third woman you meet," Michael objected. "Perhaps if you would come with me and let Valerie look after Miss Courtney—"

"No! I mean, Lydia might— That is, Mrs. Dundas shouldn't be asked to—to exert herself."

Mrs. Dundas blushed. Mr. Dundas did not. He looked his wife over thoughtfully from head to toe.

"You have a remarkable eye for one who is *not* a nurse or a doctor, Miss Bond. I wouldn't know, if I didn't have a tip straight from the feedbox," he said cryptically. "Very well; if you refuse to leave Miss Courtney with strangers, I'll try to find Miss Rollins.

"It should only take an hour or two. And perhaps I won't acquire a black eye during the process of accosting strange females, like the little man who is forever popping up in the comic strip, *Bringing up Father,* saying: 'Pardon me, but you look just like Margie.' Or Sally."

Lydia shivered uncontrollably and turned her face against her shoulder, biting her thin lips. But Marcia was not watching, and she smiled unwillingly.

"Sally wouldn't resent that. But she's sure to be with Jay Stanton and Bill Kemper. Bill is thickset and has a crew haircut, and Jay is thin and taller and a towhead. If you see three people like those together you'll know you have the right three."

"That does give me a sporting chance," Michael admitted. "I'll do my best."

III

He stalked through the halls, the dining room, and the enormous drawing room without seeing any trio that fitted Marcia's specifications. He was on the point of returning to the salon when he remembered the tiled porch outside the dining room.

It overlooked the side garden and was furnished with chairs, tables, and several large umbrellas, though the umbrellas had to struggle hard for existence in San Francisco's blustering winds. After weeks of rain this Friday night in late April was clear and not too cold, though it was cool enough that few people would have cared to sit outside at ten o'clock.

However, the three in possession of the porch appeared entirely comfortable. Michael stayed just inside the dining room, holding the door onto the porch open with his foot. None of the three outside looked his way.

There were lights at either end of the porch, and he could see them clearly enough: a girl stretched out in a reclining chair and two young men doggedly eating at one of the tables. One young man said suddenly:

"This may be Lydia's idea of a good time, but I wish we'd gone bowling."

And this, Michael decided, would be Bill Kemper. He spared a moment to wonder why so many husky young men with crew cuts and fur on their chests turned out to be Bills. As to Jay Stanton, he might, as Marcia had said, be taller than Mr. Kemper, but where Mr. Kemper ran impressively to chest and shoulders and fitted snugly into his clothes, Mr. Stanton rattled about loosely in his garments.

However, he not only had more hair than Mr. Kemper and wore it longer but, as two ominous inlets had already broken through the Kemper hairline, it seemed probable that he would wear it for a longer time. Mr. Kemper's mouth was a slightly sulky Cupid's bow; Jay Stanton's, long and thin. It twitched into a one-sided smile as he said:

"Oh well, you meet a much better class of people. Also, the food is free and good. Though I've eaten too much and can't eat any more, even if it is free."

"Three helpings should be enough even for the Stanton tapeworm," Sally Rollins said. "But the eats are luscious, and if I didn't have to watch my figger you two wouldn't be eating alone."

"The coffee," Mr. Kemper stated, "is hogwash."

"You've gotten particular since you began eating so often at our house, preshie. Though I'll admit you won't find many people who make as good coffee as Marcia does."

"You won't find any," Jay stated positively. "I told her that her coffee's too good to spill, even on herself. Did she use that ointment I gave her for her wrist, Sally?"

"I made her. She mightn't have bothered. You know Marcia. It was nasty-looking goo, but she said it seemed to be pretty good for burns. Did you make it up yourself?"

Jay nodded. "It's a prescription I've filled a lot of times for one of the doctors that throws his business to the pharmacy. And I sent over some phenobarb too."

"Did you? Well, maybe she'll use it tonight. But she—well, I suppose if you don't ever sleep well, it's better not to start depending on things like that. Marcia thinks so, anyway."

"She's probably right. But does she always have trouble sleeping? I didn't—?"

"She has—nightmares," Sally said slowly. "I thought maybe you knew or I wouldn't have mentioned it. Forget it, will you?"

"But—"

"Skip it!" Sally snapped. "In other words, mind your own business, Job. And say, if you think the coffee's bad, you should have tasted the highballs. I took one swallow and I sez to myself: 'Embalming fluid,' I sez."

Jay raised thick pale eyebrows. "When did you fall off the wagon?"

"What made you think I was ever really on it? There's no reason why *I* shouldn't drink."

"Do you mean there's any reason I shouldn't?" Mr. Kemper said truculently. "Steady drinking costs money and puts weight on you. But I can handle the stuff if I want to drink."

"That's what you always say—just before you pick a fight with someone. No, let's don't argue. Nice weather we're having, isn't it?"

Sally regarded her long slim legs approvingly before she sat erect and began combing her shoulder-length, straw-colored hair.

"Well," Jay said, "I can't eat any more, so when you've dealt with that funny arrangement over your forehead—"

"It's a pompadour. And it pomps, which is more than you can say for most of them. I'm one beauty operator that can comb her own hair too," Miss Rollins said complacently. "You were going to say?"

"Haven't we stayed long enough? Let's find Lydia and go home. I'm surprised she hasn't hunted us out a long time ago and re-established diplomatic relations."

"I still don't know what she got sore about," Bill Kemper said. "Was it because I said the party stinks? Not that I care—"

"Come out from behind those barnacles, Bill; we know you," Sally drawled. "You're careful not to make her really mad."

"You can't be thin-skinned *and* happy in our little group," Jay remarked. "So I'm afraid Lydia often isn't happy. But she was posing—"

"Trying to show off how much she knows about art and stuff," Bill said.

"Well, she knows that whenever one of us starts putting on an act it's in the rules that anyone else can pull him up short," Jay said.

"But she thinks she ought to be treated different than the rest of us because she's got a lot of money. So why don't she pick herself friends with money?"

"Because then she wouldn't have any advantage over them," Sally said. "Sometimes I wish I'd never gone to live in that cottage. But I like Marcia, and the joint's a lot nicer than any apartment I could afford to pay even half the rent of. Lydia pays all the rent: everything but two thirds of the food bill."

"Which bill she runs up by insisting on expensive extras," Jay said dryly. "And then she plays Lady Bountiful by insisting on paying more than her third. Not to mention that you and Marcia do all the work around the place."

"Well, I still wish we'd gone bowling or roller-skating," Bill said gloomily. "I've eaten too much. Maybe Lydia was sore because Kirk Vincent didn't come with us. He got us invited, didn't he?"

"In a way," Sally said. "Seeing's how he knows Mrs. Shrader and we don't. Though from the mob that's here, I'd say you could walk in without an invitation. Kirk's probably here by now. Maybe Lydia's with him. She couldn't stand to be alone long. Though I didn't see Kirk last time I looked into the drawing room. Marcia was talking to that pretty girl who came in with that very dark man."

"Which one?"

"Oh, Bill, you know. He had very black hair with a funny white triangle over one eyebrow."

"You mean Michael Dundas," Jay said. "Lydia asked someone who he was."

"Well, who is he?" Bill said.

"He's a *couturier*. Dressmaker to you, Bill. He designed the dress Lydia's wearing tonight. And he's also one of these amateur detectives you read about but seldom see. At least, I've heard he has an in with Inspector Sullivan of the homicide squad."

"Oh, one of these nosy guys?" Bill frowned. "I read something about Sullivan lately."

"Not so lately. A Filipino killed the girl—white—he was living with. Sullivan went to arrest him, unarmed. But the Filipino was full of

marijuana and had delusions of omnipotence.
Sullivan wasn't expected to live after the Filipino
got done working on him with a knife, and he's
still convalescing."

"I remember now. Well, maybe Lydia managed
to meet something she could call a celebrity. Or
what she calls the 'intelligentsia.'" Bill snorted.
"And Kirk Vincent's just as bad."

"No. He knows the correct patter, but he reels
it off with his tongue in his cheek," Jay said. "To
lead Lydia on—and to get a rise out of you, Bill."

"You think I don't know that? And sometime
I'm going to rise—and hang one on his jaw. He's
always had plenty of money, too, so he can say:
'Money can't buy the really worthwhile things in
life.' Nerts!"

"Well, has it—for Lydia?" Sally said. "Just for
instance, you both liked her pretty well when you
first met her. You can still make her happy or coax
her into anything you like if you just turn on the
old charm."

"I showed her apartments and houses for a week
before I rented her that cottage. Then she said
maybe she might decide to buy a home here. Well,
I make my living selling or renting real estate. So
I hung around—and then I met you, Sally."

"Thanks for the compliment, William, but you
still sound like pretty much of a heel," Sally said
dispassionately.

Mr. Kemper turned brick red, scowled at her, and settled into sulky silence. In the drawing room an overtrained soprano voice suddenly attacked the waltz song from *Romeo and Juliet*.

"So now we have music," Jay said. "I feel like singing myself."

He draped one long leg over the arm of his chair and began: "'Her name was Lil, she was a beauty. She lived in a house of ill re-put-ty. Men came far and wide to see Lilian in day-shab-billy.'"

"Jay! Not that song," Sally protested, giggling. "Let's find Marcia and Lydia and go home."

"Suits me." Bill stood up and fastened the top button of his shirt as a concession to formality and tightened the knot of his necktie. "Let's go."

IV

Michael pushed open the dining-room door and stepped out onto the porch.

"Are you by any chance Miss Rollins?" he said to Sally. "Because if you are—"

"I am, but how did you know? I'm just one of the mob. Nobody points me out to people. And I'll be a so-and-so if it hasn't got the *blue*st eyes."

"Come out from behind that fan, Sally; we know you," Jay said. "She talks like that sometimes, Mr. Dundas. She thinks it's cute."

"But you don't? Neither do I. And you were all three described to me by Miss Bond. It's taken me some time to find you. Only the very young or hardy would sit outdoors tonight. Miss Courtney is not well, and Miss Bond wants someone to drive her home."

"Oh, so now she's not well," Bill Kemper said.

"Don't talk like that!" Sally's carefully husky voice went up an octave. She was quickly on her feet, gathering up purse, gloves, and hat. "If Marcia says Lydia should go home and shouldn't drive the car herself— Where are they?"

"In a small sitting room on the other side of the salon where the pictures are hung. Shall I—?"

"I know where it is. You boys wait at the front door."

Sally disappeared into the dining room. Jay got up slowly, staring speculatively at Mr. Dundas.

"I wonder," he said pleasantly, "just how long it really did take you to find us. Well, we aren't really callous, but we know Lydia pretty well and—"

"And so it occurred to you that she only pretended to faint because she wanted to be the center of your attention again," Michael finished as they started through the dining room. "I agree with you that's the sort of thing Miss Courtney might do. But she did faint and she was obviously —not well before she did. But she very definitely did not want any of you to know that."

"Oh. Well, I can see why she might not," Jay said quickly. "Tonight seems to be one of those times when everyone gets on everyone else's nerves and—"

They had reached the drawing room, and he stopped, looking across it.

"Isn't that Kirk over there, Bill? Yes, it is. We'd better go over and speak to him. So we'll say good night now, Mr. Dundas."

"Good night," Michael responded politely.

Mr. Kemper merely grunted, gave him an unfriendly look, and began shouldering his way across the drawing room. Jay grinned deprecatingly and followed him. Neither of them looked back to see Michael trailing them. He stopped before they did glance back and watched Jay tapping a tallish man on the shoulder.

The name Kirk Vincent had seemed familiar and so, when the man turned, were the bright round dark eyes set in a broad, short face. A faint white scar at one corner of Vincent's mouth distorted it slightly so that he seemed always to be on the point of smiling.

He was at least seven or eight years older than Jay Stanton or Bill Kemper—somewhere around thirty-five, Michael decided. Yes, he had certainly seen Mr. Vincent before, probably at another gathering of this kind, possibly in this house.

As Jay went on talking Vincent's eyebrows expressed a nice mixture of concern and reassurance. The three of them, Jay, Bill, and Vincent, turned and made their way toward the hall. Michael hesitated for an instant and then drifted after them.

He was in time to see Lydia go through the front door. "Well guarded," he thought—but apparently pleased to be the center of attention. Her brittle laugh and consciously cultured voice floated back to him as she and her entourage went down the steps to the street.

"So sweet of you to worry about poor Lydia. So silly of me to faint, but I always have if people just so much as look at me unkindly."

"Then you must have looked at her very unkindly, Michael," Valerie said, slipping her arm through his. "And I wouldn't blame you. I've never found anyone more irritating, when I also felt I should be sorry for her. Why did she faint?"

"I'll tell you when we're home, *querida*—if you don't mind."

"I don't mind. And I'm sorry I jabbed you in the ribs. I like Marcia Bond, and you were baiting her."

"And you thought that was not kind. What brought about this sudden change of heart?"

Valerie frowned. "I can't help feeling now that Marcia has been a nurse or at least had a lot of experience with illness. And if she has, why shouldn't she say so?"

"I don't know. Neither do I know why she should say that burn on her wrist is the result of grease splattering on her when what she really did was to spill coffee over her wrist. But go on. That is, you were with them for some time."

"Yes. Well, for a while Lydia just lay there and Marcia watched her."

"Did she try to keep Miss Courtney from talking?"

"N-no. I don't know if Marcia was thinking about Lydia—or just thinking. I've noticed before, in the library, that she often just sits passively. I've known people who can spend hours just sitting and rocking, but they usually aren't very intelligent people. You certainly wouldn't call most of them—vital."

Michael nodded. "I did feel that Marcia Bond may once have had energy and vitality to spare. But now— Well, surely you at least attempted to make polite conversation?"

"It was uphill work. Finally I walked over to the door into the salon to look for you. I suppose Lydia thought I couldn't hear her. She muttered: 'What does this make you think of, Marcia? But of course I know what's going on this time.'"

"Well?" Michael said impatiently.

"I looked around. You wouldn't think Marcia could get any paler, but she did. And she looked at Lydia as if she hated her. Lydia—well, she shrank. But she smiled too. The way one might smile if she'd wanted to hurt someone else and knew she'd succeeded, I thought."

"And then?"

"Oh, I felt I had to say something. So I made some inane remark about Mr. Shrader's paintings, and that was when Lydia sat up and began to talk."

"Did you mention that study of sand dunes?"

"Why—I started to. I said: 'Well, Mr. Shrader has actually turned out one painting I can look at without pain.' Then Lydia began to talk: about how silly she was to faint, how little she eats. 'But then, food is so uninteresting.'"

Valerie sniffed. "Uninteresting! And Junior and I are starving. Well, of course Lydia was only putting on an act, just as she was when she went out just now. She was sickeningly sprightly, and I wanted to slap her face. And—and; I felt like she'd shatter if you touched her. Because—"

Her fingers tightened on his arm. Her hazel eyes, looking up at him, were a shade darker than usual.

"Because she's frightened. I'm not imagining that. I've seen other people who were horribly afraid. And—don't laugh at me, Michael, if I say she isn't just afraid but she's haunted too. And so is Marcia Bond, though I think she's too tired to be afraid."

"I'm not laughing," Michael said quietly.

"You're not, are you? Well, that's why I'm sorry I didn't let you go on heckling Marcia—or both of them. Because Lydia might have fallen to pieces if she hadn't had time to get a grip on herself."

Michael shrugged. "I doubt if I'd have gone much farther—then. I hadn't heard Stanton and Kemper and Miss Rollins talking together then."

"So that's why you were away for so long? Well, Lydia wanted to get up and out of that 'horrid little room' before Sally appeared. She wasn't exactly short with Lydia, just bracing. She looked at Marcia as if she was more worried about her than Lydia. She marched Lydia out, and Marcia said polite things to me. I trailed after them, and three men joined them in the ball and wafted them out. You—you didn't try to speak to Lydia again?"

"No. It wasn't," Michael said slowly, "because I thought I should mind my own business. And I could have fought my way through the mob. But I was afraid to speak to her again. Three of her friends know that I am an amateur detective or, as Mr. Kemper put it, 'one of these nosy guys.' Well, you might as well get your wraps, niña. Don't hurry. I want to speak to our host if I can find him. But I've never met him."

"You will know him when you see him by his red Vandyke. It is a work of art: very dark red and sort of burnished. You might try the butler's pantry. I have heard that's where he retires when the party is several hours old. . . ."

Mark Shrader was sitting on a high stool in the butler's pantry, drinking a very good grade of sherry and eating Roquefort cheese and crackers. He was definitely mellow but perfectly affable: a slim man in capacious striped trousers, silk shirt, velvet jacket, and a flowing tie.

Although he knew Shrader was younger than his wife, Michael was surprised to discover how much younger than Mrs. Shrader he was. He could not be more than forty and he was one of these delicately featured men who appear boyish at fifty. The burnished red Vandyke that Valerie admired merely emphasized Shrader's ageless look.

"Like sherry?" he said. "Give you my word, this is my own private stock. If you've tasted the high-balls tonight you must regard any liquor offered to you in this house with dark suspicion. M'wife buys her supplies for these affairs at closing-out sales. Doesn't drink herself. Her idea—these parties. When I've finished enough canvases to fill the salon respectably she gives a party. No use tellin' her no one wants to look at my work."

"But I wanted to ask you a question or two about that painting of the sand dunes," Michael said.

"Oh—that? M'wife hung it because there was a corner needed fillin'. Like it?"

"Yes. But what sand dunes are those?"

Shrader shrugged. "Dunes are dunes, and sand is sand. They only look different at different times of day: at every different hour of the day."

"Like Monet's haystacks?"

Shrader nodded. "But I dashed that off in my studio from memory. I don't know why. Feelin' old, I suppose. Somethin' I might have done twenty years ago."

He sighed. "Twenty years ago! Those were the days. Lived in a cottage on Russian Hill—on spaghetti and *vino*. Always two months behind on the rent. Place leaked like a sieve when it rained and threatened to blow apart in a high wind. Time didn't exist. Ate when we were hungry, drank when we were dry, went to bed when there was nothing better to do—or when it was obviously the pleasantest thing you could do."

"An idyllic existence," Michael said dryly. "Then you didn't have any particular stretch of sand in mind when you painted that picture?"

"Not that I know of. Memory's a funny thing, y'know. Perhaps I saw sand in those formations once and it stuck in my mind, but if I did I couldn't say when it was or where it was that I saw it."

"I suppose not. Well, I'd like to buy that picture if it's for sale."

"You'd like to—" Mark Shrader hastily revived himself with more sherry. "Well! Another one! M'wife bullies people into buying my work now and then, but people very seldom offer to buy."

He stroked his Vandyke thoughtfully. "M'wife's idea," he explained, catching Michael's eye. "Supposed to make me look like an artist. The clothes too; she buys 'em. Only draw the line at a velvet beret. Don't mind the beard now it's grown. Gives you something to do with your hands."

He eyed Michael thoughtfully. "No portrait painter, but I'd like to see you with a beard like this. Black, of course. Imagine you'd be very much the haughty Spanish grandee: modern Velásquez. Well, you take the sand dunes and see if you can live with them."

He slid off his stool. "If they still don't annoy you after a week or two, then we'll talk price. I'll go along with you and take them down."

"Thank you. By the way," Michael went on as they walked through the dining room, "do you know Kirk Vincent? I feel I should know him."

"Probably saw him here if you've been here before. Or you may have seen his name in the papers in connection with huntin' or fishin' or mountain climbin'."

"No doubt. It's a very interesting—uh—recreation," Michael said, though to him mountains are, above all things, decidedly not something to be climbed.

"Prefer mountains at a distance," Mark Shrader said more candidly. He had stopped, being apparently one who preferred to stand facing and fairly close to the person with whom he was talking.

"However, Kirk's a dabbler. He's always had too much money. Doesn't need to work. Dabbles at photography, dabbles at writin', dabbles at sports. Too much general talent and not enough itch."

"Er—itch?" Michael said.

"Must have an itch that won't let you rest to accomplish anything," Shrader said seriously. "I've been scratching twenty years without getting anywhere. But then, Kirk can laugh at himself. I can't, though I like a man who can. He's a good listener too. See him anywhere around now?"

"I believe he left with Miss Courtney."

"Oh—her. Yes, Kirk spoke to m'wife about asking her and her friends here tonight. Orphan with money, I understand. Well, you haven't thought better of it? Still want the sand dunes?"

"Yes," Michael said, smiling. "And I'd better be collecting them and my wife and starting home."

V

Mr. Dundas jerked awake. He sat up, remarking lucidly: "Walk, don't run, to the nearest exit," discovered that he was in bed and that his wife was speaking.

"Mehitabel wants to be let into the house. Patton said he didn't come home last night."

Michael groaned. He knew and dreaded that wide-awake conversational tone.

"Listen, love. I am prepared to scour the earth to procure strawberries in December if you feel that you must have strawberries in December."

"It isn't very hard any more to get strawberries at any time of the year. And this isn't December," Valerie said reasonably.

"Don't quibble. I'm only too anxious to humor any whims you may develop during the next six months—in the daytime. But, *por Dios,* woman, I thought at the very least it would be fire engines in the neighborhood, and I find you've waked me to tell me that Mehitabel is without and wants within."

"He is a very unsatisfactory cat and he's also very persistent. He's probably cold and he'll hang around yowling until— Yes, there he goes again."

"I don't hear him," Michael said. Mehitabel chose that moment to climb the scale of cat protest from deepest bass to a demisemiquaver.

"Of course you hear him," Valerie said placidly. "I wonder how he knows which is our bedroom window? He's just below it. But he's a very smart cat. Didn't he look the neighborhood over and decide to adopt us?"

"He knew Patton was a pushover for a good-looking cat and that she rules this household. But it's a pity you two misguided females didn't determine his sex before you named him."

"That would have been indelicate," Valerie said primly.

Michael snorted. Mehitabel yowled again—beseechingly. "I wish he would serenade Patton. She'd let him in. I am not going to!"

Valerie merely sighed: a small, plaintive sigh. Michael groaned again and got out of bed.

"I know," he said, groping for his slippers. "You don't really mind lying awake and thinking beautiful thoughts. But you will lie awake until Mehitabel is inside and so will I, fully aware that I am an unfeeling brute."

Valerie giggled. "I didn't say that. And why are you bothering to put on a bathrobe?"

"Because the last time Mehitabel got caught with his paws outside the house I had to follow him over to Florence Street. He turned playful when I opened the door. And that, my dear, was a very cold night." Michael tightened the cord of his dressing gown about his narrow waist and knotted it with unnecessary violence. "And please, if you love me, be asleep when I get back!"

He stalked out of the room, through the quiet house to the front door, flung it open, and whistled. He would not demean himself by calling: "Here, kitty, kitty, kitty!" He did not need to. Mehitabel loped around the corner of the house and approached the front steps, as self-satisfied as only a very handsome cat or a very handsome man can be.

Reaching the bottom step, he leered at Michael, as one man of the world to another, flopped down on his back, and waved his paws in the air. Michael grinned reluctantly.

"I know. *Toujours gai, toujours gai.* You've known some swell dames in your time, dearie. But just come inside before you begin reflecting on your numerous conquests, won't you?"

Mehitabel pranced to his feet and tried to bite the tip of his plumy tail. "The night is young and so are we," he seemed to say.

Michael swore and, against his better judgment, came down the steps to the pavement, hand outstretched invitingly. Mehitabel, being a cat and therefore unpredictable, merely nipped the hand playfully and let it gather him in.

"Because you see that this time I am well prepared for a long chase," Michael said. "If I'd come out in pajama trousers alone— Good God!"

A woman's scream was lopped off by a sound that might have been a car backfiring—and wasn't. Michael dropped Mehitable, turned, and ran as he had not run for years, toward the far end of the block.

Up three short flights of concrete steps separated by stretches of sloping pavement, past thick hedges that shut sleeping houses away from the sidewalk. On to the end of the block where the cobblestone street made a half circle. A waist-high, curved wall closed the block at this, the Taylor Street, end.

The steps that wound down the steep, rocky hill to Taylor began—or ended—on the other side of the street. Lights came on behind an upper window of the house nearest the steps. A masculine voice called out:

"What's wrong down there? Don't you know it's after one? What the hell—? Who is that down there?"

"Michael Dundas. You'd better come down. Someone will have to stay here while I call the police."

"Police! It was a shot then?"

"It was a shot," Michael said.

He dropped to one knee, looking down at Lydia Courtney. She lay in the bright light from a street lamp mounted on a telephone pole, not a hundred feet from the top of the steps. She had been shot neatly through the back on the left side.

One high heel was ripped from her shoe as if she might have tried to run and tripped on the last step before she screamed. But the steps were deserted.

PART TWO

*Why, it stood by her: she has light by her con-
tinually; 'tis her command.*
MACBETH: ACT V, SCENE I

"So, after all, she decided she wanted to take up her conversation with you where she'd left off?" Nicholas Prevost said.

Michael shrugged. "She certainly was coming here. But I don't know exactly why and I imagine that, mentally, she always circled about her objectives."

"Or approached them from the rear? I've noticed," Prevost said, smiling at Valerie, "that women are very good at executing flank movements."

Valerie just did manage to swallow her "Oh, Inspector, how can you say that?" before it was uttered.

"Good heavens," she thought, "if he makes me go all fluttery and coy, what effect does he have on really susceptible females? The youngest inspector on the force, Michael said. How old is he? Forty? N-no."

Nicholas Prevost was nearing forty, but he was still a light heavyweight, as he had been when he was an early Golden Gloves champion. Sooner or later, but usually sooner, new acquaintances assured him that he "looked like the Thin Man. William Powell, that is."

Actually he did not look at all like Mr. Powell, even though he wore a small black mustache and paid up to two hundred dollars for his suits. For one thing, the breadth of his face across the cheekbones was definitely Slavic. And even in his heyday Mr. Powell never had Nick Prevost's shoulders.

"However," he went on in an extraordinarily soft voice that was still completely masculine, "I think I know what Mr. Dundas means: that Miss Courtney wasn't at all straightforward. Everything you've told me about your conversation with her bears that out. If we presume that she went straight home we can guess that she couldn't sleep."

"And, lying awake, turning things over in her mind, she reached the breaking point," Michael said. "At least, she did come to some decision. But did she want to tell me something or did she think that I already knew too much and meant to ask me to forget everything that happened last night?"

Prevost nodded. "She might have meant to do the last. People who have the jitters as badly as she did often don't have sense enough to let well enough alone. However—"

He gestured toward the painted sand dunes propped up on a table in the living room. "If she was going to tell you why that knocked her for a loop and ask your advice—"

"Why ask my advice?" Michael finished. "Well, I did wish that I dared to offer to help her. But I doubt if she decided to come to me because I have a kind face. She knew of my unofficial connection with the police. So do Jay Stanton, Bill Kemper, and Sally Rollins. That was why I hesitated to try to talk to her again at the Shraders'."

"And I imagine Marcia Bond and Kirk Vincent know your reputation too," Valerie said. "It's not very long since we gave evidence in a murder trial."

"Well then, shall we argue that Lydia may have tried to see me because she knew that murder isn't a new story to me and/or I know police procedure and policemen?"

"Doesn't everything point that way?" Prevost said. "Even if she only wanted to make certain that you wouldn't talk. Your reputation would make her particularly afraid of you: afraid you might try to find out what lay behind her reaction to that painting."

Michael smiled wryly. "'One of these nosy guys,'" he murmured.

"And your reputation would be an additional reason why someone was determined Miss Courtney shouldn't talk to you again. Everything points to her being involved in something pretty serious. For one thing—well, I gathered she wasn't normally what you'd call reserved."

"No, her reserve would consist of announcing in a loud voice that she was very reserved. I fancy nothing interested her so much as Lydia Courtney and that she would want to tell everyone about Lydia."

"Then she would have told her friends about any ordinary troubles she had?"

"I'm sure she would have," Valerie said. "She might have held out for a while if what she had to tell didn't reflect any credit on her. But not after she'd reached the state of nerves she was in tonight."

Prevost nodded again. "As I see it, there are three things that would keep her from talking. First, she wanted to save her own skin and she couldn't talk and do that too. Well, since she was killed, someone else knew what she knew. So she couldn't talk without involving this second person. And, three, she hesitated to do that either because she was afraid of him or fond of him—or both."

"And," Michael said, "someone has been watching her, and she knew that."

"From your account, she must have. When she'd gotten hysterical, talking about sand dunes at night, she was afraid someone might have heard her."

"She could have been heard by someone standing in the hall outside the salon door, which was open. And though there was no one in the adjoining sitting room when I opened that door, it has a second door, opening into the hall. Anyone could have left by that door before I looked into the room. Also, Miss Courtney had a high, carrying voice."

"Of course we'll question the Shrader servants and the guests, though the guests will be hard to contact. But if Miss Courtney was afraid she was being watched that narrows it down. If the person who was watching her is the person who killed her, that person would be someone she knew was at the Shraders'."

"And since she'd never met Mrs. Shrader and Vincent was responsible for her and the other four being there, that limits your field of suspects still more," Michael said.

"I have an idea the gang she left with were the only people there that she knew—well enough to count," Prevost agreed. "Well, what was that poetry you quoted to her that made her faint?"

Michael repeated the quotation. "You can do things with that voice of yours, you know," Prevost remarked. "I can see why, when she was already half hysterical, that was the last straw. But— 'And so he dies.'"

"Have you any unsolved murders on hand just now, Inspector?"

"No. Of course," Prevost said somberly, "many a murder slips by as natural or accidental death."

"And a body is an essential item before the police can say that murder has been done."

"Naturally that angle would occur to you." Prevost frowned at the painting on the table. "Those dunes that Shrader said aren't any definite spot he knows of . . . Well, there are other crimes than murder, in spite of her reaction to that quotation. If her secret had to do with murder I'd guess she was only an accomplice, perhaps an unwilling one."

"I agree with you, though there's still the difficulty that she might not have intended to confess anything but only to try to convince me that she had nothing to confess," Michael said. "But even in that case she would have told me more than someone wanted her to."

"Well, when we see where she lived we'll know what sort of cover there is to watch from. You'd looked her up in the telephone book and said you recognized the address."

"It's one of a group of cottages that are really only over a hill and up a hill and down a hill from here," Valerie said. "Those directions would be very confusing to anyone but a San Franciscan, but you know what I mean. Her shortest way here was up the steps from Mason to Taylor at Vallejo."

"They skirt one entrance to Fallon Terrace and end in that small park on Taylor," Michael said. "She then faced the steps from Taylor up to our block here. Probably whoever followed her managed to keep out of sight to Taylor."

"But when she started up those steps he knew for certain she was coming to you," Prevost said. "Well, the old Verdier mansion to one side of the steps is vacant. Everyone was asleep up here. The light was good, and he took the chance. As you suggested, she probably looked down when she started up the final flight of steps, saw she was being followed, started to run, tore the heel off one shoe, and finally screamed. All while he was taking good aim. Then he simply beat it back down to Taylor and disappeared."

"If he'd had to he could have played hide-and-seek with searchers for hours in all the trees and brush and small cottages of Fallon Terrace," Valerie said. "And if we keep on discovering bodies in this neighborhood we're going to be asked to move."

"Well, there was nothing you could call a clue on the scene of the crime," Prevost said. "He took the gun with him. And you heard the shot at about one forty-five?"

"And it's going on four now," Michael said.

"I had to talk to you first. I sent Costello over to break the news to Miss Bond and Miss Rollins. He is soothing and fatherly and he had orders to see that they didn't get a chance to talk together."

Prevost had been sitting in a deep, softly cushioned chair. He seemed merely to uncoil and be on his feet.

"Well, shall we go?" he asked.

"Shall we—? I beg your pardon!" Michael said.

"Why? Oh." Prevost grinned. "It is said at headquarters that Sullivan is the only man on the force who'd put up with you. And he is still convalescing at Palm Springs."

"So we thought we'd get Inspector Hunt who," Valerie said sadly, "knows us and doesn't love us."

"We're shorthanded with Sullivan gone and since Lipmann broke his leg. So they sent me. Hunt wanted none of the case when the news came in that Dundas has found another body."

"So, on the theory that the youngest inspector should take on the most disagreeable jobs, the body and I were handed over to you?" Michael suggested.

"I see why you get under Hunt's skin," Prevost said. "But I— Do you know what they think about me on the force?"

Michael laughed. "You are famous for having donned formal morning clothes to attend a wedding reception in the line of duty, and instead of being immediately spotted for a cop, you were taken for a distinguished guest. And I know your subordinates think you can do no wrong, but I imagine that your fellow inspectors think you've been promoted a little too rapidly."

"I can pull political strings with the best of them," Prevost said coolly. "But they also think I'm too much interested in finding out *why* people do the things they do. But I don't suppose any of this explains why I wanted to be assigned to this case or why I think we can work together.

"There's just one thing though," he added with a sudden glint in his somber black eyes. "I understand you've been known to double-cross Sullivan, and he's put up with it. I won't; that's all."

Valerie braced herself and then relaxed. Michael was merely eying Prevost speculatively, though ordinarily he instantly resented anything that could, under any construction, be called a threat.

However, he particularly disliked being shouted at. He never raised his own voice when he delivered an ultimatum, and it struck Valerie that

Nicholas Prevost had spoken exactly as Michael might have, had their positions been reversed.

Michael wondered, himself, why he didn't resent Prevost's warning. But he was interested in that momentary, very slight rift in the man's suavity. He remembered that Sullivan had said: "Nick can keep his temper longer than anyone I know, but no one wants to be on the receiving end when he does lose it."

Well, Michael thought, Prevost had the thin, strong, almost cruel mouth of a man who has learned early in life that self-control pays more dividends than emotionalism and didn't stop to reflect that the same description applied equally well to himself.

"Double-cross is not the right word," he said. "Sullivan has an exasperating habit of saying: 'Whatever you're going to do, don't do it.' That doesn't lead me to confide in him. Besides, the implication is that I'll still do what I want to. And since I did dress in preparation for this interview, yes, I would like to go with you."

II

Sally sat cross-legged on a large wide couch, wearing a shabby, befrilled blue taffeta house coat and purple mules trimmed with molting feather pompoms. Her eyelids were pink, and she still sniffed occasionally and dabbed at her nose with a wad of Kleenex.

"Well," she said, attempting pertness, "last time I had my fortune told the swami said I'd be meeting up with a tall, dark stranger. And me a pushover for brunettes. And so here's two of you, even if one isn't tall and's married besides, but—"

"Come out from behind that fan, Sally; we know you," Michael drawled.

Sally scowled at him. "You catch on quick, don't you? But that's something I only take from my friends, not strangers."

"He's right, Sally," Marcia said quietly. "Don't try to be bright and amusing."

She moved a red ottoman closer to the fireplace, holding her hands over the coals in its grate. It was cold at four o'clock in the morning, and a fireplace was more an ornament than an efficient heating agent in so large a room.

It was furnished in maple and cretonne. The pictures on the walls owed something—but not enough—to Rivera and Dali. Large windows back of the couch where Sally sat looked out toward the Bay Bridge, and two doors at either side of the fireplace gave glimpses of a square hall and a large kitchen.

Marcia looked about the room as if seeing it for the first time. "These things are all Lydia's," she said, half to herself, and dropped her hands to her lap. "They don't add up to much, do they?"

"I suppose not," Prevost said gently. "You were starting to tell us about Miss Courtney."

"I don't think there are any relatives to notify. There may be some distant cousins in Denver. Her lawyer here, Mr. Dawson, can tell you, I suppose. She was born in Denver, and her parents died before she was three years old. Her father left a good deal of money, and there were trustees to handle it until she was twenty-five."

"And she was certainly pushing thirty very hard," Sally remarked. "So she's been on her own for about five years."

"She was looked after by paid nurses and companions until she was old enough to go from one expensive boarding school to another," Marcia resumed. "When her schooling was done she could go where she wanted and live where she pleased, and after she was twenty-five not even her trustees cared what she did. It's hard to visualize that sort of life when you've been brought up in just an ordinary family."

"It isn't hard for me to visualize, if you subtract the money, governesses, ritzy boarding schools, and trustees," Prevost said. He hesitated and then added, his black eyes on Marcia's bowed head: "I was left on the steps of an orphanage in a cardboard box labeled 'Nicholas, aged five weeks and two days.'"

If he had wanted to make Marcia fully aware of him, for just an instant he succeeded. She looked him over without the least trace of coquetry and finally smiled, as if she understood what lay behind this deliberate injection of the personal into an official inquiry.

Michael, watching them, stifled a groan. "Oh lord," he thought, "has it happened to him that way—too?" And said hastily:

"Then I suppose Miss Courtney spent most of her later life drifting from place to place, trying to make friends, and hoping to marry someone who wasn't merely a fortune hunter?"

"That's not what I'd call chivalry, but it's the truth," Sally said. "She bored men, and that's fatal. I don't know of anybody that actually disliked Lydia. If they weren't indifferent to her she irritated them or bored them. Don't you think so, Marcia?"

"I—well, yes. She could never let well enough alone. She tried too hard. So when she was most to be pitied she was also most exasperating."

"Epitaph for Lydia," Michael said. "Here lies one who never let well enough alone. Did you know Lydia before Miss Rollins did, Miss Bond?"

"Yes. She was living in a Los Angeles hotel, and I had a friend staying there too." Marcia mentioned the name of the hotel and that of a Mrs. Cornish.

"I was visiting her when Lydia asked her to a cocktail party she gave at the hotel. I went with Mrs. Cornish, and she introduced me to Lydia. That was about a year ago. We—went on seeing each other. When I decided to come up here again Lydia happened to be ready for a change of scene. She was at the Palace for a while until she rented this cottage. That's how she—all three of us—met Bill Kemper."

"Bill works for a real-estate firm: Blaise's, on Montgomery Street," Sally contributed. "And Lydia just happened to take a notion one day when she was going along Sutter that she had to have her hair done, but right then. She came into Dmitri's Beauty Salon and she liked me. So she kept coming back and—well—"

She shrugged. "It may sound screwy to you, but Lydia was like that. She'd take a sudden shine to someone and want to see a lot of them. And she made a good first impression sometimes."

"I think she always did," Marcia said.

"Maybe. But if you want to know about Lydia or any other woman listen to me, not Marcia. I see 'em with their hair down. I've been working in beauty shops for four years and, brother, do you learn about women from that!"

Prevost smiled. "I'm sure you do. So Miss Courtney asked you to live here with her and Miss Bond?"

"I was griping about boarding places and saying I didn't like to keep house alone. Marcia'd started coming to the shop, and I liked her a lot. So when Lydia suggested it, about four months ago, I thought: why not? Even," Sally said dryly, "if I did know Lydia thought she was being awfully democratic to ask me. But it made her feel good to patronize me, and sometimes I'd let her get away with it."

Prevost smiled again and turned back to Marcia. If he felt that there were gaps in her story that badly needed repairing he gave no sign of it.

"You said you decided to come up here 'again.' Have you lived here before?"

"I was born in Berkeley. None of my immediate family is living. But you can—can check on me. You—you will, won't you?"

"Yes, we'll check on all of you."

"Well, everyone out around Mission Dolores knows the Rollinses," Sally said. "I have a brother and sister living out there still. I stayed with Mom till she died, and I've been on my own since I was twenty: four years now. Okay?"

"Thank you. Now, coming up to date: what time did you arrive at the Shraders'?"

"Oh, I don't know. Around nine, I guess."

"And how long did your party remain together?"

"We stood and watched the monkeys for a while. Then Lydia got started on art and litrachoor and the drahma. And passing out information about people she thought she recognized like she'd gotten it firsthand. Well, Jay pulled her up short, the way we would when she started putting on an act.

"The way Mr. Dundas did me just now," Sally explained. "Only to Lydia we'd say: 'Come out from behind that testimonial, Lydia Pinkham; we know you.' It always made her mad. And she said: 'Oh, you're all quite impossible tonight' and flounced off."

"Then there was no definite quarrel?"

"Oh gosh, no. It's happened before, Inspector. Though, as Bill would say, she certainly had the screaming-weemies last night and she'd—"

"We'll take that up later, please," Prevost said. "You four went into the dining room then?"

"Yes. We stood around eating."

"And then I left them," Marcia said.

"Why?" Prevost asked.

"I wasn't hungry, and the dining room was crowded. So was the drawing room. I looked about for Lydia."

"What time was that?"

"Oh, past nine-thirty, I suppose."

"What does it matter what time it was?" Sally demanded.

"Because it was about nine forty-five when Miss Courtney and Mr. Dundas went into the salon to look at Shrader's paintings. They had a rather interesting conversation that ended when Miss Courtney fainted."

Sally looked at Michael unfavorably. "A blue-eyed wolf?"

Prevost's lips twitched, but he continued gravely: "And apparently she believed that she was being watched and was very anxious that no one should have overheard what she had said to Mr. Dundas. Go on, Miss Bond."

"What? Oh—I didn't see Lydia. So I stood and watched people for a while until Mrs. Dundas spoke to me. In a few minutes we went into the salon and—I suppose Mr. Dundas has told you about that."

"Yes. Were you and Mr. Kemper and Mr. Stanton together all the rest of the time until Mr. Dundas found you, Miss Rollins?"

"Well—no. When I finished eating I went looking for the powder room. Jay and Bill kept right on eating—I guess. When I came back they'd discovered that porch and we went out there, but I don't know how long we were out there or what time it was."

"I see. And the five of you, including Mr. Vincent, were the only people there who knew Miss Courtney well?"

"I s'pose. Anyway, you'll find out we're the people who knew Lydia best—in San Francisco."

"You said that Miss Courtney was unusually nervous last night. Were you also going to say that she hadn't been herself for some time?"

"We all noticed it, only it wasn't for some time. Just from last Wednesday on," Sally said. "She looked like she'd been dragged through a knothole Wednesday."

"Then what had she been doing Tuesday night?" Prevost asked.

Sally shook her head. "Tuesday's a night when we hardly ever do anything."

"Why?"

"You do love that word, don't you? I work Tuesday and Thursday nights and I have to catch up on my sleep sometimes. The rest of the week the gang drops in and we get to talking and singing, and somehow it gets to be one o'clock in the morning. So I went to bed at nine on Tuesday, and when I hit the bed I'm asleep in two minutes."

She nodded toward the kitchen door. "There's what was meant to be a big sun porch or breakfast room on the other side of the kitchen. I put curtains over the windows and got a couch to sleep on. I often get up earlier than Marcia and Lydia or come home later when Bill and I go places. Sometimes not the last if Lydia got a restless streak."

"I open the library at eleven and seldom get home before eight," Marcia said. "Sally is gone all day, and what other acquaintances Lydia had would be working too. She hated to be alone here, so she'd kill time downtown—shopping and 'just looking.'"

"Time didn't mean anything to her. I mean," Sally said, "her day never divided itself into working hours and after work. If she got hungry downtown she'd eat or make at stab at it to kill time. Or she'd go to a movie. She loved movies, though she wouldn't admit it because she thought that wasn't high-brow enough.

"But she'd get a crush on some actor and see one picture three or four times. I was asleep though when she went to bed Tuesday night, and she didn't wake me up. I suppose she did you, Marcia? Especially if— Was that the night she started it?"

"Yes. Sally means that Tuesday was the first night Lydia kept her bedside lamp lighted all night."

"Oh. You mean that ever since then she's been afraid to be in the dark?"

Marcia and Sally looked at each other. Then: "I guess she was scared," Sally said thoughtfully. "I didn't think of that—then. I've known people who burn a light all night."

"But Lydia had never done that," Marcia said. "She came in very quietly Tuesday. I thought she was trying not to wake me, but I'd been awake for a little while. She got into bed and then in a few minutes she sat up and put the light on."

"Did she say anything?" Prevost asked.

"No. I was lying with my back turned to her bed so I suppose she thought I wasn't awake, and the light isn't strong and it's shaded."

"What time was that?"

"There's no clock in the bedroom. I keep my watch under my pillow, but I didn't look at it that night. I had an idea it was around midnight, not unusually late for Lydia. She said the next morning that she'd seen a double bill at the Paramount, and that would take more than three hours. But Wednesday night she asked me if she could leave the light on when we went to bed."

"And what did she do Wednesday?"

"While I was at the library I don't know. Jay and Bill and Kirk were here in the evening."

"And one minute she'd be laughing too loud and the next snapping at us and clenching her hands," Sally recalled. "Thursday I went bowling with Bill at the Polk-Van Ness Bowl after work and he stayed awhile after he brought me home, but not late. Lydia didn't have much to say that night. Hadn't you two been to a show, Marcia?"

"Yes, she came over to the library, and we went to the Royal on Polk Street from there. But we weren't there long. Lydia said the picture bored her, and we left in the middle of it. And of course you know what happened tonight—Friday night, that is."

"And during all this time she never said anything that would give you any idea what was worrying her?" Prevost asked.

"Not a thing. She talked a lot about being nervous because she wasn't well. I thought it wouldn't be long before she took her hair down," Sally said. "Because she usually told you a lot more about herself than you wished she would."

"And tonight she didn't tell you why she had fainted?"

"Just her silly nerves, she said, and because she hadn't eaten all day. I drove home, and we came up here and left Bill to put her car in the garage she used on Taylor. We went right to bed, only I insisted on sleeping in the bedroom with her."

"Why?"

"I said to look after her, but really so Marcia would get her sleep. That light burning all night wouldn't bother me. It didn't," Sally said grimly.

"I slept like a log while she slipped out. We didn't know she was gone until your policeman woke us up and told us what had happened."

"So Costello said. And you didn't hear her either, Miss Bond?"

"I don't sleep well," Marcia admitted. "But I—I wanted to sleep last night so I took a stiff dose of phenobarbital. I thought Lydia did too. She said—she said: 'If I don't sleep I'll go mad.' So I gave her some tablets."

"But I found them on the bureau," Sally said. "So she must have changed her mind about sleeping."

"Evidently. Well," Prevost said, "I think Mr. Dundas might like to ask some questions. You don't have to answer them, but it will save time if he doesn't have to relay them through me."

"You mean we'll answer them one way or another? Oh well, we won't stand on our constitutional rights then," Sally said virtuously. "Go right ahead. What's on your mind?"

III

"I'd like to know why you remarked, when you had spoken of sampling the highballs at the Shraders', 'There's no reason why *I* shouldn't drink,'" Michael said.

"Why—why, *you!* You stood in that dining room and listened to us talking."

"Yes," Michael agreed, "for some time. Well, Miss Rollins?"

"I think you're a heel!"

"Me and Mr. Kemper both?" Michael said pleasantly.

"Oh, so you heard that too? Well," Sally said sulkily, "I've changed my mind about cooperating."

"I've no idea why Sally called Bill a heel," Marcia broke in. "Not that he isn't, rather."

"He is not! You just don't understand him."

"I understand that he doesn't mind who pays the bills so long as he doesn't," Marcia retorted with unexpected sharpness.

"He's no worse than Jay is. He's just more honest about it, that's all."

"I'm not defending either of them. But I'll answer your question, Mr. Dundas. Lydia couldn't drink—decently. If she had more than one cocktail or highball she—well—"

"She got coy and said things she thought were daring and was generally nauseating," Sally said bluntly. "She talked too much and got to feeling very reckless and—and—and silly," she finished lamely.

"What form did this recklessness take?" Michael said.

"Oh, I don't know." Sally looked furtively toward Marcia and went on too quickly: "Like wanting to go out and take in all the dives in town. And if she did have something on her mind she didn't want anyone to know; that's why she didn't do any drinking these last few days. Jittery as she was, you'd think she might have, but I guess she was afraid she'd talk too much if she did."

"It wasn't just on Lydia's account that we decided not to do any drinking here," Marcia said. "You might not think so, but usually we're a very congenial group and never at a loss for conversation. We found that a glass in one hand didn't add anything to our talk. And liquor runs into money. Also, it makes Bill very truculent. I'm sorry, Sally."

Sally's full red mouth set in sulky lines. "At least it don't make him sick all next day like it does Jay," she muttered. Marcia ignored her.

"Lydia didn't really like to drink," she went on. "At least, she didn't oppose our decision not to drink at home. What anyone did away from here was no one's business but his own."

"I was wondering," Michael said, "if it's possible that when Miss Courtney would come home and tell you that she'd been to a movie she might have been spending her time elsewhere."

"The night spots, you mean? Without an escort?"

"No, not without an escort."

"Oh." Marcia frowned. "She has wanted all of us to go night clubbing together, but we couldn't afford to go where she wanted to. We wouldn't let her pay the bills."

"One of you might have let her pay them without telling the others about it. If some night she and Mr. Kemper or Mr. Stanton went the rounds together she wouldn't have minded keeping that a secret, would she?"

"Oh, you make me sick!" Sally said. "Bill wouldn't—"

"Well, Miss Rollins, I somehow got the impression that Mr. Kemper might have danced attendance on Miss Courtney for a while. Until he met you and until he realized he wasn't going to sell her a home here."

"People who listen in hear a lot of things," Sally said childishly. "Maybe Lydia would have thought it was smart to coax him to take her places on one of my working nights. But she'd have thought it was just as cute to run around with Jay behind Marcia's back."

"The point is, Sally, that we can't swear Lydia wasn't with Jay or Bill on Tuesday night," Marcia said. "It seems now that something must have happened that night that led to her death. And you and I can't alibi each other after nine o'clock. We each know the other went to bed. But after that—"

"You mean, if Lydia had come back and— Oh, I get it!"

"That's more than we do, Miss Rollins," Michael said.

"What do you want for your money? You're so smart: figure it out for yourself. But don't leave Kirk out of this. He could've been out with Lydia Tuesday night or any night. And he can pay the bills himself."

"That's true, though Kirk hates night clubs," Marcia said. "But they might have been together. Only if Lydia did any drinking Tuesday night she was well over the effects before she came home. And if Kirk and Lydia were in the habit of going about together there was simply no reason why they shouldn't say so."

"N-no," Sally admitted. "No one has any strings on Kirk. But the thing is, if youse guys are determined Lydia wasn't alone Tuesday night—"

"You agree she'd had a very severe shock Tuesday night?" Prevost said. "And that she was afraid to confide in anyone? Well, if she had killed herself we would suppose something happened Tuesday that concerned her alone. But since she felt she was being watched and since she was murdered before she could reach Mr. Dundas . . . But you were going to say?"

"That Lydia could've picked someone up Tuesday night."

"Someone who just happened to be at the Shraders', watching her, last night?"

"Oh. But someone could've been and us not know it."

"Let's not, at this early hour, go out of our way to make things difficult," Michael said. "We can get along nicely, thank you, without a mysterious unknown. Miss Bond, why did you say that your wrist was burned when grease splattered on it?"

"Why, Marcia!" Sally said. "I was gone before you two got up Thursday morning, but that night you told me Lydia had jostled against you so you spilled coffee over your wrist."

"Did something startle her?" Michael said.

"N-no. That is, she was very nervous. Her—her movements were jerky, and when she started to get up from the table she did knock against me just as I started to pour coffee. Well, she—she felt very badly about it, so—"

"So when she was lying there in that sitting room off the salon you didn't want to distress her further by explaining to me what had really happened when I noticed how neatly your wrist was bandaged," Michael said smoothly.

Marcia flushed but: "Yes, that was it," she agreed. "And, Mr. Dundas, why, before you carried Lydia into that sitting room, was she talking about something being meek and still and not wise but foolish?"

"She was repeating something I'd quoted to her, though the word 'foolish' was her own. Also, you may remember that she said: 'The wind shall blow. . . . And many shall—shall make— I've forgotten'?"

"I didn't, not having a flypaper memory."

"Well, that part of her mumblings had nothing to do with the lines I had quoted to her. Do they touch any chord in your memory?"

"I'm afraid not. Another quotation, you mean? No."

"Nor do they in mine—yet. I've gathered your little group has the usual collection of catch phrases that mean something to you if to no one else." Marcia nodded. "Is 'Pardon me, but you look just like Margie' one of them?"

"Jay says that. Yes, and Lydia simply took his head off about that last night," Sally recalled. "She said it was a stupid, silly expression. Why?"

"I used it myself last night, and it seemed to disturb Miss Courtney considerably then too. I don't believe Miss Bond was watching her when I used it."

"I wasn't and I can't imagine why it disturbed her." Marcia appeared genuinely bewildered. "Jay does run phrases like that into the ground, but—

I never heard Lydia mention anyone named Margie, did you, Sally?"

"No. But it's a common name." Sally moved restively. "Does this go on much longer? I'd like a cup of coffee and to lie down awhile. I've got a job to keep, you know."

She got to her feet and fumbled for the wad of Kleenex she had thrust into a pocket of her house coat. She pulled it out—and something else that glinted as it struck the floor.

She dived for it, but Nicholas Prevost moved too quickly. He held up a flat, thin key and read out the numbers engraved on it.

"Seventeen-eleven. This is the key to a safe-deposit box."

"Why, Sally! That's Lyd—" Marcia began and stopped.

"Exactly," Prevost said. "The key to Miss Courtney's safe-deposit box. And what is it doing in your pocket, Miss Rollins?"

IV

Sally scowled at Prevost defiantly, looked from him to Michael and everywhere but at Marcia.

"It was in the bureau. Lydia kept it there. I just stuck it in my pocket, that's all. And I'm not going to answer any more questions. Try to make me!"

"We won't try—now," Prevost said politely. "But I'll leave Costello here, and I wouldn't advise you to try to do anything about that."

"He means," Michael said helpfully, "that if you don't like that arrangement he can take you to headquarters for questioning."

"Oh!" Sally turned and slammed out of the room, through the kitchen. Prevost's soft voice followed her.

"You may go to work as usual, Miss Rollins." He turned to Marcia. "And you may open your library at the usual hour, if you wish."

"Thank you," Marcia said dully. She sat very still on the ottoman, staring at the dying fire, her thin shoulders sagging. "I suppose I will go over to put a sign on the door saying I won't be there today."

She got to her feet. "I'd—I'll make some coffee. Will Mr. Costello share it with us?"

"If you ask him to. By the way, can you put your hand to a photograph of Miss Courtney?"

"A—a photograph?" Marcia said.

"Yes. I want Miss Courtney's picture in the newspapers. Someone may have seen her Tuesday night and remember. What did you say?"

"N-nothing. Only that I supposed they'd manage to—to get a picture sooner or later. Just a minute."

Marcia went into the bedroom and returned at once with a framed photograph of Lydia.

"Thank you." Prevost took the picture from its frame. "Where do Kemper and Stanton live?"

"In the same rooming house."

"Do they share a room?"

"No, their rooms are on different floors. The place is on Pine." Marcia gave the street and telephone number. "Kirk Vincent is in the telephone book. He lives on a hill too: Broadway Hill, I think it's called. I suppose you'll go there—"

"Yes. We won't drag Stanton and Kemper out of bed this early since they're workingmen. Mr. Dundas understood that Stanton is a pharmacist."

"Yes. He works for his uncle in a prescription pharmacy near Dante Hospital."

"I see. Well, just one more question, Miss Bond. What becomes of Miss Courtney's property?"

"If she made the will she talked of making it comes to Sally and me." Marcia's voice was perfectly expressionless. "Though if she did make a will to that effect she might have changed it. She'd made a good many wills since she was twenty-five. Is—is that all?"

"Yes, that's all," Prevost said. "Good-by, Miss Bond. Coming, Dundas?"

They stepped out onto a narrow front porch overhanging the hill that dropped steeply away toward the street. A short flight of wooden steps with a narrow handrail led from the end of the porch to a small wooden landing. In turn other flights of steps, broken by other small landings, climbed the hill to the other cottages perched on its various levels.

Prevost sighed. "Six or eight cottages above this one but none below," he observed. "And doesn't anyone connected with this case live on level ground?"

"San Francisco is a hilly city, and there is a strain of mountain goat in its inhabitants that apparently causes them to go out of their way to hang homes on hillsides. Here's Costello, Inspector."

Costello panted up the stairway to the cottage's porch. "I looked over the hill and the street below, like you said to. It's all old apartment houses across the street but plenty of cover in doorways for some-one to keep an eye on the street entrance to these here cottages. However, no one left any signs he stood watchin'. Like cigarette butts, I mean."

He stopped to take breath. "But there's good cover closer than that."

He pointed across the central system of steps to the cottage opposite the one on whose porch they stood. It nestled into the hill instead of merely hanging on it, and one side of the house was half concealed by a heavy growth of shrubbery.

"That house is vacant," Costello said. "And of course there ain't anyone stirrin' in the other cottages farther up the hill, and you said not to wake anybody up yet."

"People aren't apt to be cooperative when you rouse them from a sound sleep this early," Prevost said. "We'll get around to them later. You stay here, Costello. See that Miss Bond and Miss Rollins have no chance to talk to each other alone. And that they don't use the telephone. It's in the living room. Miss Rollins may go to work—at nine, I imagine. And Miss Bond opens her library at eleven."

"Would I follow 'em then—and which one?"

"Neither one. I want you to go through Miss Courtney's belongings in the bedroom. And you'd better get in there before Miss Rollins decides to make a dash for that telephone."

They went gingerly down the cottage's private stairway, then down another flight of steps to a landing, and finally, after making a right-angled turn, descended a third flight. This ended at a wooden door set in the stone wall that ran along the street.

Having gotten into his car, Prevost did not start it. He sat still, frowning at the steering wheel.

"That girl knows a lot she isn't telling," he said finally. "And she's got to be made to talk!"

"Marcia Bond?"

"Yes. Oh, Miss Rollins too. But—"

"I'm not certain how we did it, but we did manage to drive a wedge into what had been an united front. We left them distrusting each other," Michael said. "Of course the first rift occurred when Marcia spoke in uncomplimentary terms of Bill Kemper."

"Yes. And she may have been trying to cast suspicion on Kemper."

"Perhaps. She was unusually wide awake just then. Then later, when she remarked that Lydia could have come back to the cottage after nine o'clock Tuesday but before midnight—"

"And that didn't make sense," Prevost said. "She's the one that says Miss Courtney came home about midnight. Miss Rollins says she never woke up after she went to bed. So why not just leave it that Miss Courtney came in at midnight? Though it was Sally who seemed to think Marcia was suggesting Lydia might have returned to the cottage more than once."

"And she not only steered Marcia off that subject but refused to explain."

"Well, I agree with you that by now those two don't understand each other so well. I think each one of them wonders what's in the other's mind, especially since Sally pulled that key out of her pocket. Hell, what did she think she could do with that? Of course we'll get into Miss Courtney's safe-deposit box as soon as we can, but that sort of thing takes time. Meanwhile—well," Prevost said slowly, "you handled Marcia Bond with gloves—too."

Michael shrugged. "There were questions I might have asked her and didn't. But you had first chance at her, and I was guided by you."

Prevost grinned. "I wish Jim Sullivan could hear you say that. Well, I know Marcia's story of how she met Lydia and about the progress of their friendship was as full of holes as Swiss cheese. She didn't say what she's been doing all her life or what kind of job she had, if any, before she came up here."

"And since you didn't ask her that, neither did I ask her again if she hasn't been a nurse. Or why she lies awake nights and has nightmares and has lost a good deal of weight sometime during the last three years. That robe she had on was well cut, of very good material, but it wasn't new and it was too large for her."

Prevost grinned again. "Nothing like that slips by you, does it?"

"It's automatic. I owe my reputation as a *couturier* to the fact that I can take one look at a woman and tell her what she should be wearing.

But," Michael added, his eyes on Prevost's superb-
ly tailored shoulders, "my wife chooses my clothes
and my tailor makes my suits and delivers them
without my seeing them until I take them out of
the box."

Prevost flushed. "I wore orphanage clothes till
I was fourteen and what odd garments I could
scrape together for a long time after that. My living
expenses run around sixty dollars a month and—
Well, I rose to that bait, didn't I? But we agreed,
coming over here, not to mention Shrader's painting of the sand dunes. You did agree with me?"

"Certainly. If someone did overhear Miss
Courtney's conversation with me in the salon we
might catch him out on that. I think we shouldn't
mention that conversation or the painting to anyone. And I'm not criticizing your handling of Miss
Bond, Inspector."

"Well, I'll give her a little time to think things
over and have a few nightmares in the daytime.
And by noon or earlier I may know something
about her. Though that was funny too."

"That she seemed almost to invite you to inves-
tigate her past life? I couldn't decide whether she
was apprehensive, just didn't care, or knows that
you won't get far, quickly, with your inquiry."

"I hope it won't turn out to be the last. I'm not
forgetting Mrs. Dundas says that Marcia seemed

quite anxious to locate Lydia last night. Or that she didn't want to give her liquor after she fainted. She just skipped that angle when Sally had told us that liquor made Lydia too talkative.

"And," Prevost said, "another thing I mean to hammer away at is what Lydia meant when she said: 'What does this make you think of, Marcia? But of course I know what's going on this time.' Is that right?"

Michael nodded. "And Valerie got the impression that Marcia looked at Lydia as if she hated her and that Lydia was both frightened and triumphant."

"I'm not forgetting." Prevost started the car, drove toward Pacific, and turned into it, a narrow and dingy street in this neighborhood. "Or that while I can't see why it should matter that Lydia spilled coffee on Miss Bond, she's holding out on us about that too. And I don't think Miss Rollins knows why. Also, it's funny, but the last part of what you called Lydia's mumblings tantalizes me."

"I know. 'The wind shall blow. . . . And many shall—shall make—' Damn it! Do you read much poetry, Inspector?"

Prevost turned into Jones and followed it to Broadway. "The older poets. Don't tell Inspector Hunt. You think she had a poem in mind too? Well, maybe she did."

He stopped the car at a sidewalk bounded by a concrete wall. On the other side lay a very steep hill paved with cobblestones, overgrown with weeds and grass. They had been forced to approach this section of Broadway by a roundabout route because some years ago the hill had been pronounced dangerous for automobiles and closed between Jones and Taylor.

The inevitable and necessary steps for pedestrians ran down either side of the hill. Prevost paused halfway down before a flat-faced wooden house painted pale green.

"This is Vincent's," he said, putting his forefinger on the doorbell. "And it's still only five-thirty. Well, if the doorbell doesn't wake him we can always shout. . . ."

PART THREE

Yet, when we can entreat an hour to serve,
We would spend it in some words upon that
*   business,*
If you would grant the time.
MACBETH: ACT II, SCENE I

"Oh, your account makes everything damnably clear, Inspector," Kirk Vincent said. "I knew Lydia had been in a fine state of nerves since Wednesday night. But frankly, I never have known a more pronounced neurotic, so—"

He shrugged. His hair was rumpled and he yawned frequently, but his dark eyes were bright and alert. The coffee he had insisted on making in an electric coffee maker boiled up just then, and he reached over and turned off the electricity.

One whole side of the room in which they sat was windows that opened onto a narrow balcony with potted ivy hanging on its railing. The furniture was colorful early California. There were a few odd bits of statuary scattered about the room but no pictures except on one back wall.

That was covered with mounted photographs which Prevost was already eying speculatively. But he did not comment on them now. He asked, instead:

"So you didn't think she was frightened?"

Kirk loosened the top bowl of the coffee maker, laid it on a newspaper, and poured coffee.

"Help yourselves, gentlemen. You must need it. No, it didn't occur to me that Lydia was frightened. She was a lonely, frustrated woman and she was as restless and given to nerves as that type always is."

"How did you meet her?"

"Through Jay Stanton. I've known Jay for years and I know his uncle. His name, incidentally, is Job. But for years he's signed himself J. Stanton."

"And who would blame him?" Michael said.

"No one except this uncle for whom he was named. Jay's parents died before he'd been in college very long. Stanton took charge of his education and meant him to be a doctor. But Jay didn't really want to be a doctor so he flunked out of medicine, and his uncle never lets him forget that. He is one of these estimable men who doesn't allow you to forget you're under obligation to him."

"So Jay is not only working for his uncle now but still paying for his education?"

"That's it. I've seen quite a bit of Jay, off and on, for the last five years. I know his faults, but it does seem a pity he isn't doing some work that really interests him."

"What would interest him?" Michael asked.

"Well"—Kirk smiled deprecatingly—"writing, he thinks, or music. But he insists he can never accomplish anything along such lines so long as he is forced to be a 'wage slave.'"

"And does Mr. Kemper have any—? I'm sorry, Inspector," Michael said. "One thing seems to lead to another. You've questions to ask."

"I'd like to hear yours answered," Prevost said. "What were you going to ask about Kemper?"

"Does he have any frustrated ambitions?"

"I think Bill's only ambition is to make money quickly," Kirk said. "He has a mother partially dependent on him. She lives in Marysville, and I know she had to have a major operation several months ago. Bill and Sally are intelligent enough. At least they are shrewd, and Sally is very adaptable and quick to pick things up. But frankly, Bill often seems out of place in our little group."

"I thought he might be, though Miss Bond said that, on the whole, you're all very congenial."

"That's true. We all like to talk, and if Marcia and I sometimes do as much listening as talking, that works out very well. We did have to ban the war as a topic of conversation."

"Why?" Prevost said.

"Well, Marcia and I are all-outers."

"You're what?"

"All-out aid to Britain. The others sometimes call us the lease-lenders. Bill," Mr. Vincent said, grinning, "is a pacifist."

"You mean he doesn't want to engage in any but personal battles?" Michael said. "In other words, he doesn't want to be drafted. And where does Sally stand?"

"She doesn't say. But she is rather a primitive person, and simple patriotism is a primitive emotion. She'd be proud of Bill in uniform and bury him under badly knitted garments. Jay says he is a communist."

"Isn't he?"

"No. He's just a have-not who envies all haves. But if he's drafted he'll go quietly—and be the kind of soldier that exhausts even a top sergeant's vocabulary, though in actual battle it's often his kind that wins the medals. Bill would be quite at home in the army. He's used to camping out, hunting, and fishing."

"I suppose he's a good shot and Stanton can't handle a gun at all," Prevost said.

"I suppose Bill's a good shot, and you would guess that Jay wouldn't know anything about firearms," Kirk said uncomfortably. "But his father was a crack pistol shot, and he coached Jay until he was a better one. But Jay doesn't like to kill things. And you don't want to take what I said about Kemper too seriously. We don't like each other."

"So I gathered from something Mr. Kemper said. Did you, by any chance, think that he treated Miss Courtney badly?" Michael said.

"Oh." Kirk hesitated. "When we first met he was rather—attentive. Then he transferred his affections to Sally. I imagine that was something that had happened often to Lydia. She should have avoided competition. And Jay seemed rather attracted to her at first, but now he fancies he's in love with Marcia. I hope it's only a fancy because he hasn't a ghost of a chance with her."

"No, one hasn't much chance when he falls in love with a ghost."

"You feel that about her too? Of course that appeals to Jay's romantic nature. I'm very fond of

Marcia." Kirk reddened slightly. "I hope no one realizes that."

"Hasn't she ever told you what she's done all her life?" Prevost asked. "She's twenty-five or -six —maybe older. I'd suppose she's had to earn her own living—"

"Since she hasn't told you, I wouldn't answer that if I could—but I can't. For all she's ever said, her life might have begun when she came to San Francisco four or five months ago."

"Well, even if she hasn't confided in you, or anyone, was Miss Courtney equally discreet?" Michael said.

Kirk grimaced. "Oh lord, is it beginning to be so plain that I'm one of these middle-aged bachelors women tell their troubles to? But the fact that Lydia and I didn't have to scramble after a living sometimes set us two apart. So perhaps that's one reason she would criticize the others to me when they'd hurt her feelings."

"Did she come here to do it?" Prevost said.

"To this house? She was welcome to drop in, as anyone is, during the day and early evening. I have a Negro woman who looks after me when I'm living here and after the house when I'm away."

Kirk's tanned catface curved into a grin. "Her name is Astoria and she has a husband, a very superior colored gen'leman, named Leroy. She comes at seven-thirty in the morning and goes home soon after eight in the evening if I have dinner here. Well, I had to discourage Lydia from 'just dropping by' after eight o'clock. It wasn't my reputation or hers that I was thinking of, but, dammit, she could ruin an entire evening for me."

"I can easily understand that," Michael said. "And I imagine she always made the error of trying to push a slight intimacy too far."

"I'm afraid so. I know that. But she wasn't here Tuesday night, Inspector. That's Astoria's day off, and I had dinner at Omar Khayyám's and got home about eight. And neither was Lydia here even in the daytime Wednesday, Thursday, or Friday. I did talk to her over the telephone yesterday morning to tell her I wouldn't be able to go with her and the others to the Shraders' last night."

"Why couldn't you?" Prevost said.

"Because I had dinner with the Preedys. They live on Chestnut, and it must have been nine-thirty before we left their house. You can check with them. It would take us about ten minutes to reach the Shrader house. I looked for Marcia and the others and had to stop to talk to other friends. That was what I was doing when Jay and Bill found me."

"From nine forty-five until after ten?"

"Probably. I wasn't watching clocks, Inspector."

"And did Miss Courtney know anyone at the Shraders' except you and the party she came with?"

"I doubt it. It was the first time I'd gotten her invited there. And if she had known anyone she thought might be there, she probably would have mentioned their names—frequently."

"Do you have any mutual acquaintance named Margie?" Michael asked.

"Not mutual—that I know of. I've known a lot of Margies in my time, as who hasn't? Er—I suppose you wouldn't like to explain?"

"Oh, it's only that a silly phrase: 'Pardon me, but you look just like Margie,' seemed to disturb Miss Courtney."

"I can understand its irritating her," Kirk said. "Jay runs catch phrases into the ground. Once it was: 'Ain't it a shame about Mame?' He listens to Bob Hope's radio program religiously and mimics Jerry Colonna rather well. It was 'We learn something new every day, don't we?' until we began giving him the Bronx cheer every time he said it. More coffee?"

"Not for me," Prevost said. "Have you any guns?"

"Isn't it rather a waste of time to ask that? No one would use a gun he's known to have."

"It's a waste of time when we don't have the gun that was used," Prevost agreed. "But we go through the motions anyway."

"Well, I have a small arsenal: two automatics, two revolvers, several rifles, a shotgun. The rifles are upstairs and the smaller weapons in a cabinet in the dining room across the hall. Locked," Kirk said, "and none of them missing and all of them in need of cleaning. Do you want to take a look?"

"You wouldn't make a statement like that unless it was true," Prevost said. "I think that's about all."

"Mr. Vincent, who are your heirs?" Michael said abruptly.

"My heirs? What has that to do with—? Oh, good lord!" Kirk struck his forehead with the flat of his hand. "Did Lydia make that will?"

"Miss Bond said she intended to make one, leaving everything to her and Miss Rollins."

"With myself as executor. Well, I hope she did make it, though even if she didn't I suppose the library is in Marcia's name and—"

"In Marcia's name?" Prevost repeated. "You mean Miss Courtney owned the library?"

"I'm sorry I mentioned it. I supposed Marcia would have. Well, I'm sure it was understood that she does own the business. But," Kirk said uneasily, "Lydia bought it outright from the last owner. There's no reason why she shouldn't have done that, is there?"

II

"No," Prevost said finally. "No reason at all, especial-ly if she—thought she owed Miss Bond something. May I look at those photographs before we go?"

"Never ask an amateur photographer that if you're not prepared to be shown everything he has on hand." Kirk got up and led the way to the back of the room. "These are my best efforts."

"You seem to like sand dunes," Prevost said.

"H-mm? Yes, I do." Kirk stared at Prevost specu-latively. "Why? Or why not? Don't you?"

"Very much. This is a good one."

Prevost pointed to a photograph of craggy dunes, half in light and half in shadow. Kirk looked at it more closely and smiled.

"That is Mark Shrader's favorite, but those aren't really sand dunes," he said. "Though the place—in New Mexico—is called White Sands, I believe it's a vast area of powdered gypsum. I drove through there last summer with Jay when he had his vacation. Several more of these pictures were taken there, but the other sand shots were taken around Carmel.

"I didn't answer your question as to who my heirs are, Mr. Dundas," Kirk added abruptly. "Perhaps you didn't expect me to, but I've been thinking. . . . For years three cousins in Oakland have been my residuary legatees. But none of them needs money, and my will is remarkable for its codicils. It's hard for me to say, offhand, how many people would cut themselves at least a small slice of the melon."

"But Jay Stanton and perhaps Marcia Bond would get a slice?"

"They're down for fairly substantial sums and Sally for two thousand dollars."

"And are you going to make a new will now?" Michael asked.

"Why should I? I don't believe Lydia was killed by one of her heirs if she did make the will we've been talking of. From what you told me of the events leading to her death—"

"But her disposition of her property might have been an additional motive," Prevost pointed out. "And Stanton and Kemper might hope to gain from her death, through Miss Bond and Miss Rollins Also, I imagine there was always the danger that Miss Courtney would suffer a sudden change of heart and make still another will."

"That's true," Kirk admitted.

"And there's a question I haven't asked. You've said you weren't with Miss Courtney on Tuesday night. But did you two ever go around together— alone?"

"Good lord, why should we?" Kirk said irritably. "If I want to go places I can—well—"

"Find more attractive companions than Lydia?" Michael suggested.

"Yes, though I prefer to have you say that. Oh, I don't mean that if I happened to run into her downtown I wouldn't see her home if I was alone. And we might have something to eat or drink first. Naturally, that wouldn't happen often. Also, I tried not to drink with her when I'd learned what effect liquor had on her. Do you happen to know if Marcia is going to continue running that library?"

"She won't need to, will she, if she inherits part of Miss Courtney's property?" Prevost said. "Why do you ask?"

"I hoped she'd give it up or at least find better quarters if she really likes that kind of work and wants to go on with it. Have you ever been in her library?"

"No. It's on Sacramento, near Grace Cathedral, isn't it? There are libraries nearer us," Michael said. "But my wife goes there because she wants to walk, and that gives her a definite destination."

"Well, like so many small libraries, it's one of these little basement apartments. That is, there is just one small front window practically level with the street. It's a dismal cloister for Marcia to spend most of her daylight hours in."

"I know the sort of cubbyhole you mean. Small libraries, giftie, tailor, radio- and shoe-repair shops move into them, fail, and disappear."

Michael looked questioningly at Prevost, but the inspector, after a final glance at the photographs on the wall, turned and started toward the front door. Mr. Vincent followed, his eyes on Prevost's straight back.

"Has anyone mentioned to you," he said abruptly, "that Lydia liked to—well, she rather liked to play Lady Bountiful?"

"Well, if she bought that library for Miss Bond—"

"Oh—that. I wasn't thinking of that."

"Then what were you thinking of?"

"Oh, just that Lydia was generous—and she wasn't," Kirk said unsatisfactorily. "She expected to be repaid, if not necessarily in money. But what woman doesn't? May I get in touch with Marcia later?"

"Whenever you like," Prevost said. "But one of my men is with them now."

Kirk grinned. "It's kind of you to warn me. But I've nothing to say that a third party can't hear. I suppose I'll be seeing you again. . . ."

"You didn't warn him not to call Kemper or Stanton," Michael remarked as they went back up the steps toward the car.

"I don't think he'll try to, and we'll be with them in ten minutes. Would you mind driving? I want to make some notes."

"On the interview just concluded?" Michael said, starting the car.

"No. I'm like you: I carry that sort of thing in my head. Just reminders," Prevost said, scribbling in a small loose-leaf notebook. "I have to start men ringing doorbells, you know."

"You agree with Sullivan that most cases are solved by cops ringing doorbells and asking questions?"

"Most of them. Let's see. . . . The Shraders, their servants, eventually their guests. The people Vincent had dinner with. Then we have to cover the houses near the scene of the crime more thoroughly, this neighborhood where Vincent lives, the other cottages and that street, Stanton's and Kemper's rooming house. Which will all take more men than I have. I'll try to look into this business of Miss Courtney's safe-deposit box myself and see her lawyer. I hope he isn't the stuffy kind."

"He won't be an old family retainer," Michael said encouragingly. "What do you think of Vincent?"

"He's a cool customer. He wouldn't want his life disarranged. I imagine it's been an easy, pleasant one."

"Yes. Though I have never been able to decide which is most apt to undermine character: being handed everything you want on a silver platter or never being able to get quite what you want by your own efforts. I've no patience with those who counsel patience; who say that everything comes to him who waits. It's when you're young that you really want things badly."

He stopped, smiling apologetically. "Pardon this digression."

"This business of not wanting your life upset is apt to bear on this case," Prevost said. "When you're young you don't want anything to interfere with your plans for the future. Say that Lydia did know something that would do that—"

Michael nodded. He had passed up Jones with its nearly perpendicular hill between Bush and Pine in favor of Leavenworth. They were skimming along that street in a fashion that drew no protest from Prevost but several from drivers of early-morning trucks.

"When you are young forty seems extreme old age," Michael said. "You don't want to give up any of the years before extreme decrepitude assails you at forty. And when you are nearing thirty-five you think: 'What, is it gone and I have nothing?'"

Prevost smiled. "Yes, when you're nearing forty you think that you've just begun to live and that you have a hell of a lot to get done before fifty. That would apply to Vincent. But I'm glad we talked to him first."

"Yes." Michael turned into Pine. "He does seem to view himself and others with a certain detachment, though we don't know how much of that was genuine today. But I'd still pay more attention to what Vincent says about Bill Kemper, for instance, than I ever would to anything Kemper might say about Vincent."

He stopped the car in front of a melancholy building, red brick to its lower windows, bilious yellow paint above them. Several signs made it quite clear that desirable rooms were available. One was framed in very elaborate and very dingy lace window curtains. Another, a chaste, enameled product, was above the doorbell.

Prevost rang and almost immediately was told to "Come in. The door's open." They stepped into a dark hall which seemed to have sucked down the smell of all the coffee and toast lodgers were supposed not to make in their rooms.

A broad-hipped woman in a large, violently flowered kimono was standing at the foot of the stairway. She took so deep a breath that her thin pigtail of hair vibrated agitatedly.

"Mr. Kemper!" she bellowed then. "If you're doing them culture exercises again I'll thank you to stop before you shake the house down. Well, will you listen to that now!"

There was a sound from above that suggested someone had suddenly leaped feet first onto a bed and broken all its slats. This was only a prelude to the sort of noises that might be achieved by some-one falling down an uncarpeted flight of stairs with an armful of milk bottles.

"Police," Prevost said briefly to the landlady and leaped up the stairway.

III

Milk had been spilled and blood had been shed. It had been Mr. Kemper's milk, but it was Mr. Stan-ton's blood. He reclined on the threadbare carpet in the middle of the small room. He had apparent-ly fallen in whirlwind, taken a table with him, and left a lonesome place beside the bed.

His nose was bleeding and his eyes slightly glazed. But one hand groped for the milk bot-tle lying on the floor along with ashes, cigarette stubs, a rancid-looking piece of Danish pastry, matches, and a battered alarm clock. He hurled the bottle accurately at Mr. Kemper's shins.

Mr. Kemper howled, hopped one-legged about the room, and swore. He used only four words— counting compound words as one—but he used them over and over and fervently.

"He lacks imagination, don't you think?" Michael said to Prevost. Prevost grinned.

"Not much vocabulary," he said critically. "Now, boys. What's this all about?"

". . . to hell!" Mr. Kemper concluded and turned. "How did you get in? Oh, it's the nosy dressmaker."

"Something tells me this is the beginning of a beautiful friendship," Michael remarked. "Why, the door was not locked, Mr. Kemper. And though I take it you are addicted to physical-culture exercises—*¡Si por cierto!* The latest issue of *Physical Culture* in a room otherwise devoid of literature. But does the manual recommend the use of a human punching bag in these little workouts? Oh yes: this is Inspector Nicholas Prevost of the homicide detail."

"Hom—homicide?" Bill stammered.

Jay had gotten himself, by installments, to his feet. He sat down on the rumpled bed.

"Homicide?" he echoed. "Great fallen Lucifer!"

"Lydia Courtney was shot and killed around one forty-five this morning," Prevost said. "We have already seen Miss Rollins, Miss Bond, and Mr. Vincent. I suppose it hasn't escaped your attention that for the last three days Miss Courtney was worried and afraid."

"She had the screaming-weemies," Bill said. "But I didn't know she was scared. Sure, she snapped our heads off Wednesday night. And Jay was under the weather, too, so we didn't have much fun."

"Were you, Mr. Stanton?" Prevost said solicitously. "Why?"

Jay flushed. "I eat like a fool and I have one of these wacky digestive systems which I don't discuss. If you want to be popular always say you feel fine. Only," he added, scowling at Bill, "don't carry it to extremes and thump your chest and make muscles to show you're in the pink. That's tiresome too."

"Well," Prevost said before Bill could speak, "Miss Courtney was out late Tuesday night, and we have evidence that suggests the events leading to her death date from that night. Were either of you with her then? No? Well, did either of you go about with her often—alone?"

"Hell, no! That is," Bill added as Jay smiled unpleasantly, "not for a long time. I did go round with her some when we first met. Afterward—after I met Sally—she wouldn't have liked me to go around with Lydia, even if I could have afforded to."

"Ah, 'would that they could fall into our arms without remaining on our hands!' If you will take the advice of a man older than yourself, Mr.

Kemper, you will try, even though you know you are irresistible to women, to conceal the fact," Michael said nastily.

Jay lay back on the bed and laughed. "We learn something new every day, don't we? No, Inspector. Lydia and I never went around together. We weren't together Tuesday night. I had dinner at Barney's on Van Ness and ate too much. Then I went over to the Alhambra, saw a double bill and got home about ten-thirty and went to bed."

"And I did practically the same thing, except I ate at Compton's on Powell and went in to see an old picture at that little Powell theater. And I was home by ten."

"I hope," Prevost said mildly, "that neither of you will be inconvenienced by our turning up evidence that you were with Miss Courtney Tuesday night. Now: were you two together all evening at the Shraders'?"

"But nothing happened there," Bill objected. "And I don't see what business this is of Dundas'."

"That is for the inspector, not you, to decide," Mr. Dundas said gently. "I talked to Miss Courtney last night just before she fainted. And I resent the fact that she was killed practically on my doorstep."

"Oh. You mean she was— Oh. Well, we were together, weren't we, Jay?"

"Is this the sixty-four-dollar question? No, pal. We weren't. After Sally went looking for the powder room I decided to locate whatever similar facilities were available for males. When I got back to the dining room Bill said he had located that nice breezy porch."

"Is that right, Kemper?" Prevost asked.

"I'd forgotten that. But anyway, after we left the girls at the cottage last night we put Lydia's car in the garage and walked straight back here and went to bed and—"

"We can't prove that we stayed in bed," Jar said indifferently. "Inspector, do blackmailers ever kill the goose that lays the golden egg?"

"Now and then. Not often. Why?"

"Because an odd thing happened Thursday. I took money over to the bank—American Trust at Polk and California—about noon. And after I got in line I saw Lydia about two people ahead of me.

"I stuck my neck out and I heard the teller say: 'All in twenties, Miss Courtney?' Well, I watched. All of us did while he shelled out at least fifty twenty-dollar bills—maybe more. And she just stuck them in her purse and walked away."

"And you didn't speak to her?" Prevost said.

"No. I'd meant to, but it seemed odd. She wasn't one of these people who carry a lot of cash around."

"That's right," Bill agreed. "She was a charger and a check drawer. She'd write checks to cash for just five or ten dollars if she was caught short."

"We'll check with the bank," Prevost said. "A few more questions. Do either of you own a gun?"

"A shotgun," Bill said. "It's in the closet. I get a little hunting sometimes when I go to see my mother at Marysville. Do you want to see it?"

"We aren't interested in shotguns. Mr. Stanton?"

"I haven't any guns."

"What became of your father's?"

"My—oh. Oh, Dad did have some pistols. But after he died and I had to dispose of his things I stored what I kept in the basement of my uncle's home. My room downstairs isn't any larger than this, and I haven't room for keepsakes."

"I suppose not. What college did you attend, Mr. Stanton?" Prevost said.

"Oh, I went to Cal."

"I know it is a very large university, but did you happen to know Miss Bond there? I'd say you two are about of an age. Or did she simply go into training as soon as she was out of high school?"

"Training?" Jay said. "What do you mean? That Marcia was a nurse? I didn't know that."

"We know a lot less about Marcia than about Lydia," Bill said. "Lydia did talk about what she'd done and where she'd been, only you got confused; she'd been so many places. But not Marcia! She don't give out. She don't even mention her family— Sa-ay!"

"Yes?" Prevost said encouragingly.

"Marcia did mention a brother once. Hell, what had we been talking about?"

"I don't remember," Jay said flatly.

"She'd been sitting by the fire, the way she does, looking like she was listening, only you wonder if she really is. And she said: 'My brother used to—' and then she stopped. And she looked at Lydia."

"You're making this up," Jay said coldly.

"I am not! She did look at Lydia like she was afraid of what Lydia might say. But Lydia," Bill admitted regretfully, "didn't say anything. Hell, what had we been talking about? Well, maybe I'll remember or Sally will. And I'll bet Marcia was a nurse. Look how she took charge of Lydia last night."

Prevost waited, but Jay said nothing. He sat on the bed and stared at the floor, shirtless, as Bill was, his hair uncombed.

"And what," Prevost said finally, "were you two fighting about?"

"Oh, we weren't fighting," Bill said quickly.

"Just an overabundance of boyish high spirits," Michael suggested. "Good, clean fun?"

"Yes," Jay said blandly. "Bill doesn't really mean to play rough. He just doesn't know his own strength. I'm out of razor blades so I came up to get one from him."

"And I was using my last one," Bill broke in eagerly. "So Jay said maybe he could make do with it when I was through."

"Because I shave once a day whether I need to or not, and Bill shaves twice a day whether he wants to or not. Shaving makes him cross. So when I snapped his suspenders—"

Jay reached out quickly, pulled Bill's suspenders back perhaps a foot, and released them. Bill yelped with all the fervor of a man who has just sat on a needle. Michael leaned back against the doorway and laughed.

"That's when he bopped me one. I don't know that I blame him," Jay said sweetly. "After thinking it over, that is. Just good, clean fun."

Prevost smiled briefly. "I should have asked why you were fighting before I told you that Lydia Courtney had been killed."

"But you had no right to ask questions before we knew that. And that's what happened, isn't it, Bill?"

"Yes," Mr. Kemper said unenthusiastically, trying to rub the small of his back. "Can I finish dressing? I've got a job to keep."

"We're going," Prevost said. "I'll try not to embarrass you at your places of business."

"Good. My uncle Job wouldn't like to have me embarrassed—during business hours," Jay said.

Mr. Kemper was buttoning himself into a clean shirt and studying Prevost. He progressed slowly from hat crown to hand-sewn shoes. Then:

"I don't see," he said rashly, "how an honest cop can afford to dress like that."

Nicholas Prevost stiffened. Michael watched him hopefully, but after an instant Prevost began to whistle softly through his teeth. The tune was that of an old song called "The Durant Jail." Michael smiled thoughtfully as he supplied words for two lines: "'It's both of my feet bound in the cell, My hands tied behind, God damn him to hell!'" And, still smiling, turned to Bill Kemper.

"I hope your mother has recovered from her operation," he said sympathetically.

"My—operation?"

"I suppose, if she lives in Marysville, she was either at the Woodland Hospital or in Sacramento? Well, perhaps their prices aren't so high as they are in this city, but hospitalization costs a great deal, doesn't it? And hospitals won't wait to be paid."

"You mind your own goddamed business!" Mr. Kemper bellowed. "You leave my mother out of this!"

He advanced threateningly. Michael turned to Prevost. "You will bear witness that he attacked me first?"

"Not only that, but that he attacked you entirely without provocation," Prevost said in his silky voice. Mr. Kemper halted. "You've thought better of it? Well then, good morning, gentlemen."

IV

The landlady could give them no information regarding Jay's or Bill's whereabouts on Tuesday night and hadn't heard them come in last night. She hadn't time, she added crossly, to care what her roomers did as long as they were quiet and paid their rent. And she was going up to talk to Mr. Kemper right now. . . .

Prevost got into the car and drove a block down Pine before he said abruptly: "Thanks."

"For what? Didn't you bring me along to say the things your official position keeps you from saying?"

"Maybe. Sullivan was right when he said you have a knack for stirring up witnesses."

"And some day someone is going to tell me to mind my own business instead of merely suggesting I do so. Or change the shape of my nose and separate me from a few teeth."

"Don't you think Kemper could?"

Michael grinned. "Not with you there. And he bluffs easily. Even if Mr. Kemper was a nice boy, I wouldn't like him. He breathes through his mouth."

"He isn't a nice boy. But young Stanton is—like Vincent—twice as slippery. Well, I should have thought of that last question, though Kemper may just have gotten sore because you brought his mother into it."

"Mother's Day isn't until May," Michael said cynically. "And he may have reacted as he did because Lydia loaned him money when he needed it. And Jay Stanton may have— But we have passed the stage of needing to explain our various questions to each other. I know you have a tremendous amount to do that I can't help you with."

"Even when I see Marcia Bond again?"

Michael frowned. "I hope you won't mind my saying that you'd do better to see her alone. Then you won't be conscious that I'm there and bend over backward in an effort to be severely official. And you won't have to make an effort not to resent any questions I would ask her—or my manner of asking them."

"Damn you," Prevost said pleasantly. "I might have known you wouldn't miss anything. And nothing anyone has said, even those who like her, suggests any simple, innocent answers to the questions I'm asking myself about Marcia Bond. Well, shall I take you home?"

"Yes. You can get me at the shop until around five. Will you have breakfast with us?"

"Thanks. But I'd better save time by getting a bite at some lunch counter. . . ."

And, having done so, Prevost went on to his office where he talked to all available reporters, told them frankly that he was interested in Lydia Courtney's movements on Tuesday night, and handed over her photograph. After that he sent men out to ring doorbells in the neighborhoods he'd mentioned to Michael. Presently a redheaded police surgeon strolled in, cleaning his fingernails.

"Well, I did a rush job for you, Nick. Nothing much to add to what you already know since you already knew almost to the minute when she was killed. She was around twenty-nine or thirty."

"Had she ever been married?" Prevost said.

"How nicely you put it, Nick. But she had preserved her virginity. She had a scar on her left upper arm: not very old and pretty deep. That is, the arm was gashed pretty badly and deeply sometime. Also, a very small scar on the back of her head. About the same date as the one on her arm."

"Oh. What kind of injury would make that scar?"

"On her head? Oh, a blow from something heavy but smallish and with a sharp edge."

"She'd probably be unconscious for a while?"

"Probably. Anyway, if she got that gash on her arm at the same time, unless she had medical attention immediately, she'd lose a lot of blood. Why?"

"Oh—I wondered."

Prevost, remembering that Lydia had said to Marcia: "What does this make you think of, Marcia? But I know what's going on this time," moved restlessly. "And the bullet?" he said.

"They have it in the lab, but they won't make much of it. You can't tell what bullets will do if they hit a bone, and this one isn't in good condition. Well, I'll be seeing you."

Prevost disposed of what other routine jobs there were, waiting for nine-thirty when he could hope to find Lydia's lawyer in his office. The man he had sent to question the Shraders' servants telephoned in before then.

"I haven't had much luck, Inspector. They're willing to help, but there were too many people there last night for them to remember any four or five of them. One maid thought she remembered seeing a thin girl in a purple dress talkin' to Mr. Shrader early in the evening."

"What does Shrader say?" Prevost asked.

"He says he remembers the dress. He kind of shrugged and said the girl tried to talk art to him and seemed to think he knew her. I took it from what he *didn't* say that he's used to having women he don't remember or's never met do that. He went off to the butler's pantry to drink some good liquor by himself when he got away from her, he says."

"He did go off to the butler's pantry sometime during the evening. Well, anything else?"

"None of the maids were anywhere around that room they call the salon about nine forty-five to ten. So they didn't see anyone hanging around there like they were listening. Shrader gave me a long list of names of people that were there, but he says that's not half of them and there were probably a lot there he and his wife wasn't ever introduced to. And I got the name of the caterers and an agency where they got an extra maid. Should I work on them?"

"I suppose so," Prevost said. "The caterer's men in the dining room might remember something about Kemper and Stanton. Check with them and the couple Vincent had dinner with. You'd better report back before you tackle that list of guests."

He put down the telephone and went off to see Mr. Dawson in the De Young Building. Dawson was also willing to be helpful but, as he said:

"I hardly knew Miss Courtney. Her property didn't take any looking after. Her father had salted his money away in gilt-edged stocks and securities. I don't mind telling you the terms of her will. She left everything to Marcia Bond and Sally Rollins."

"Share and share alike?"

"No. Miss Rollins gets the car and certain stock that should bring her in two or three thousand a year. Miss Bond takes the rest: what should amount to an income of at least five thousand a year. Miss Courtney had two distant cousins in Denver that are down for small legacies. I advised that."

"Did you advise her against making a will leaving everything to two girls she didn't know very well?"

Dawson shrugged. "She had no close relatives. And I gathered this wasn't by any means the first will she'd made. She knew too much about the laws of inheritance. Also, I thought this wouldn't be the last will she'd make. I drew it up about three months ago. She didn't show me any of her previous wills. Kirk Vincent is named executor in this one."

"Then I suppose it's up to you two to open her safe-deposit box," Prevost said. "If you'll get in touch with him and speed up the formalities as much as possible? I want to be there when the box is opened. Thank you, Mr. Dawson. . . ."

It was now just after ten o'clock, and he could go on to the branch bank Jay Stanton had spoken of. Prevost parked his car in a "No Parking" space, went into an Owl drugstore and dialed Lydia's number.

"Everything all right there?" he asked when Costello answered.

"All okay. Miss Bond gave me breakfast. Miss Rollins drunk some coffee, but she acted sulky. Neither of 'em tried to use the phone and didn't seem to want to talk to each other. They got dressed in separate rooms. I searched Miss Courtney's, but I didn't turn up anything interesting like letters or papers. Nor any guns."

"Miss Rollins isn't there now?"

"She left about quarter of nine. A Kirk Vincent and Jay Stanton called up, just offerin' to do anything they could for Miss Bond and sayin' they'd see her later on."

"I'd like to talk to Miss Bond. . . . Do you still intend to go to your library, Miss Bond?"

"Yes," Marcia said. "To put a sign on the door and get some books for myself. I won't stay there. It's—it's a rather dismal place. Will it be all right if I go over there in fifteen minutes or so?"

"Any time you wish," Prevost said. "But I want to talk to you and I wish you'd wait at the library until I come. I should be there by ten-thirty. May

I talk to Costello again? . . . Costello, Henson is working the street below."

"I seen him. He's a smart youngster, but I was hopin'," Costello said wistfully, "that maybe you'd want me to cover these here other cottages."

"I do. When Henson comes up to them you two can work together. If you turn up anything you think is really important I'll be at the Polk-California branch of the American Trust Company for a while and then I'm going to Miss Bond's library."

Prevost left the telephone booth and walked across the street to the bank. It took time to discover who had cashed Lydia's check Thursday morning. But when the man was located his evidence was definite and unhesitating. He had, at about noon on Thursday, handed out fifteen hundred dollars in twenty-dollar bills to Lydia Courtney.

"Naturally I remember it," he said. "I had to verify her signature since I didn't know her by sight. She seemed so nervous when she came up to the window that when she handed in a check of that size, drawn to cash, I wondered if it was all right.

"But the signature was okay, and her checking account was a large one. Then she said: 'Twenties, please.' I said: 'All in twenties?' She nodded, so I gave it to her that way, without copying down the serial numbers."

"She probably thought you wouldn't, with twenties," Prevost said. "Do you remember Jay Stanton being in here that day or seeing him talking to Miss Courtney?"

"I know young Stanton well. He made a deposit for the Stanton Prescription Pharmacy, as he often does twice a day. But I couldn't say if he talked to Miss Courtney. I waited on several people before he came up to the window."

Prevost hesitated, glanced at the clock, and decided he had time for other inquiries. He wanted to know if Lydia Courtney had had her safe-deposit box out of the vaults recently.

But there was no record of Lydia's having signed a slip requesting admission to her box since she had first rented it four months ago. Those who generally admitted box holders to the vaults did not remember her even after Prevost's painstaking description.

He was just stepping out of the door onto Polk Street when one of the bank employees caught up with him.

"There's a Mr. Costello who wants to talk to you, Inspector. He asked me to call you back."

"Oh—all right." Prevost walked back through the bank and was escorted to a telephone. "What is it, Costello? It's after ten-thirty and—"

"Yeah, I know. I tried first to get you at the girl's lib'ary. She don't answer."

"She doesn't answer! When did she leave home?"

"Oh, about twenty minutes ago, but she said she would walk and it's quite a little walk, and she may've had something to do on the way. You told me not to tail her. And look, Inspector: I hit pay dirt first try. An old maid in the cottage above Miss Courtney's. And I think you'd ought to talk to her yourself."

"I can't talk to her now! I've got to get over to that library."

"You're the boss. Only I think," Costello said mildly, "you had oughta talk to this dame, and I'd rather you done it before I tell you—"

"I haven't time to listen to you now anyway. Hang around Miss Courtney's cottage until I get there."

Prevost dropped the telephone and hurried out to his car. He went down California with the throttle wide open, cable cars notwithstanding, swerved into Jones, and parked before the great grayish bulk and stained-glass windows of Grace Cathedral.

Marcia's library, if he remembered his street numbers, was just around the corner on Sacramento, in the middle of the block. There were no

houses on one side of that block, only a neglec-
ted tennis court that was part of the cathedral
grounds.

In an instant he saw the library's sign, a large
painted sunflower rocking slightly in the morning
wind. As Vincent had said, the sill of the one window was only a few feet from the pavement, with
half a dozen jackets of new books propped against
its pane.

A short flight of brick steps led down to the
library's front door. The words "Sunflower Library—Hours: 11 to 7:30" were painted on the
door, but there was no sign pinned to it stating
that the library would be closed until further
notice.

Prevost pushed the door open and stepped into
a small dark room lined with bookshelves. A large
flat desk faced the door. There were more books
in a row across the front of the desk and a chair
behind it whose back was only a few feet from
another door.

Prevost cleared his throat uneasily. "Miss
Bond!" he said. "Miss Bond!"

There was no answer. Prevost strode across the
uncarpeted room, around the desk, and kicked
open the door behind it. It opened on a kitchenette, barely large enough for a gas plate, sink, and
a few shelves.

The upper half of its back door had been clouded glass. The glass was shattered now. A few jagged fragments remained in the doorframe. The rest of it lay on the floor; a few fine slivers were caught in the loosened hair that fanned across Marcia's face.

Nicholas Prevost did not speak again. But in all his thirty-nine checkered years he had never known so black a wave of depression as swept over him when he knelt down beside Marcia's body.

PART FOUR

She has spoke what she should not, I am sure
of that: Heaven knows what she has known.
MACBETH: ACT V, SCENE I

Mr. Joseph Tingley unwound himself from his dubious bedclothes at ten-thirty, slouched down the hall to the bathroom, and washed sparingly. Returning to his small, stuffy room, he passed a comb gently over his oily hair and smoked a cigarette.

He opened a bundle of laundry, selected a pair of socks, and stared morosely at the holes in them. It was hell what these laundries did to your clothes, Mr. Tingley reflected. A man got so he didn't take no pride in his appearance, living alone in a crummy hotel with no one to look after him.

What a man needed was a wife to be waiting for him when he got home after a hard night tending bar. And if Babe wasn't so unreasonable . . .

Mr. Tingley sighed, put on the socks, frayed shorts, a soiled t-shirt, and a pair of unpressed green slacks. Before he went to work he would shave, use bay rum and hair pomade generously, don a clean shirt and a more respectable pair of trousers. But now he was only going out to get his breakfast.

He left his down-at-the-heels, self-effacing little hotel and walked the half block to the lunch counter on Fillmore where he always ate breakfast. The early editions of the afternoon papers were already on the streets. Mr. Tingley bought his favorite and propped it against the sugar bowl on the lunch counter.

There was a picture of a woman on the front page. Mr. Tingley glanced at it briefly and started to turn to the sports section. Then he muttered: "Sa-ay!" spread the paper out, and studied the photograph closely.

He was reading the story beneath it when the counterman slid a stack of wheats striped with bacon over to him. Mr. Tingley buttered the wheat cakes mechanically and went on reading. The police would be interested to learn what the murdered woman, Miss Courtney, had done on the Tuesday previous and who her companion or companions had been. . . .

"Well, what d'you know?" Joe Tingley muttered.

He ate the wheat cakes without realizing he hadn't, as usual, drowned them in what passed for maple syrup at the lunch counter. Mr. Tingley was thinking, and though he drank the black liquid in the thick white coffee cup he forgot to ask to have it refilled.

He got up abruptly, found a nickel, and walked over to the telephone on the wall opposite the counter. He dialed the number of the restaurant where Babe was cashier, crooked an elbow over the telephone, and waited.

"Hi," he said when he heard her voice. "Look: how's about us going up to Reno next week and saying 'I do'?"

Babe laughed. She was a great girl to laugh, but you soon found out that didn't mean a thing when it came to changing her mind once she'd made it up.

"Now, Joe. We've been over all this before—"

"And you won't get married till I've got two hundred and fifty to match your two-fifty. Well, I've got fifty and I think I can lay my hands on the other two hundred by Monday or Tuesday."

"What long shot are you putting the fifty on this time?" Babe said.

"Honey, you got me all wrong. I just think I know where I can get two hundred smackers, that's all."

"Oh," Babe said. Joe Tingley could see her: plump, naturally blonde, pink and white and clean-looking behind her cash register. "Well—you're not going to do something you hadn't ought to, Joe?"

"Me?" Mr. Tingley was all injured innocence. "You know me better than that, Babe. I'm just going to do somebody a favor."

"A pretty big favor to be worth two hundred bucks, seems to me like."

"It might be worth more, but I'm no hog," Mr. Tingley said virtuously. "And there's that old saying about not killing the goose that lays the golden egg. What I mean: no sense in asking for more than you can get. Almost anybody can raise two hundred bucks if they got to."

"U-mm," Babe said dubiously. "Yes, I guess most anybody could borrow that much if they have to. But don't you know if this person you're going to do a favor for has got that much money?"

"Well—no. I got to find out. Maybe I'll have to settle for less or maybe I'll find out I can raise the ante. I don't know."

"I wish you'd tell me more about it. I don't want you doing anything reckless, Joey."

"I can't explain over this phone," Tingley said. "I'm at Ted's place. I got to scout around and find out the best way to get in touch with this party. I don't even know if I can do it by phone. But the drugstore up the street's got a city directory.

Don't you worry. You don't know anything about this if anyone should ask. But we'll get that nest egg, so we're all set. And next week we'll borrow a car and start for Reno. . . ."

II

Michael had just announced virtuously that he would skip lunch in order to catch up with his work. But as his manageress, Fanchon Weiss, pointed out:

"You're just trying to look busy and thinking about your latest murder. And I don't remember anything about Miss Courtney that would help you. I remember her getting four models and giving a check for them. I tried to talk her out of that Parma violet you say she had on last night. I thought: 'Purple by any other name, very few women can wear it, and you aren't one of 'em.' But she would have the color because it was 'new.'"

"I know. 'A person and face of strong, natural, sterling insignificance, though adorned in the first style of fashion.' A fitting epitaph for Lydia Courtney. And you don't remember Marcia Bond?"

"How could I, if she just bought the one dress three years ago. Well, I'll beat it and let you work."

"I will. Unless," Michael said honestly, reaching for the telephone, "this should be Prevost."

It was Sally Rollins. "Mr. Dundas, where's Marcia?"

"Why, at her library, I supposed, or at home."

"She isn't. And I don't know how to get hold of that inspector. Do you suppose she's with him or he's—taken her someplace?"

"I don't know," Michael said truthfully. "He might have held her for questioning, but in that case she is quite safe. And she would be allowed to notify her friends if she felt she needed a lawyer."

"Oh. Well, Kirk don't—doesn't know where she is. And I called Jay at the pharmacy, but he wasn't there. I just finished talking to him at his rooming house. He said he took a notion he wouldn't go to work after all today, but he don't know where Marcia is."

"Why are you so anxious to get in touch with her?"

"Oh, I just—just want to know where she is," Sally said and hung up.

Michael shrugged, tried to concentrate on the sketches that littered his desk, and wondered if perhaps he had better not eat lunch after all. But it was still only eleven-thirty.

He yawned and fingered a number of samples Fanchon had submitted for his consideration. The telephone jerked him from this state of suspended animation.

"Dundas?" Nicholas Prevost said. "Things aren't going quite as we'd planned. Someone tried to kill

Marcia at her library this morning. They didn't quite succeed. Well, she isn't really so badly hurt, but she's still unconscious."

"Where are you?" Michael asked.

"St. Francis Hospital. I—I didn't want to take her to Emergency. I bundled her into my car and took her to the nearest place, and to hell with red tape!"

"Amen. When did this happen?"

"If she walked straight to the library and was attacked as soon as she got there, about ten-ten. Not later than a quarter of eleven, when I got there. The library's in one of these little basement apartments. Someone came in by the service' entrance, broke the glass in her kitchen door, reached in, and unbolted it.

"The library didn't look like it had been searched, but I suppose it had. And I'm wondering now what she wanted to get from it when she insisted on going there this morning. I'd guess she went straight into the kitchen. And someone grabbed her from behind by the throat: someone hiding in the kitchen.

"He didn't choke her too much," Prevost said grimly. "But somehow or other she hit her head on the corner of the gas plate. The doctor says she's too frail to stand any kind of shock. So I'm waiting."

"Sally Rollins just called," Michael said. "She seems anxious to locate Marcia. And she told me that Jay Stanton didn't go to work today."

"I found that out when I called the pharmacy. I sent a man to question him, but I suppose he'll say he was in his room. What time did Sally talk to him?"

"Just before she talked to me, which would be a little before eleven-thirty."

"Well, we're trying to locate Kemper, too, but they say at his office he is out trying to contact several prospects. I telephoned Vincent right away. He was home then, but that doesn't mean anything. I told him to stay there until the man I sent over has talked to him and that Negro servant of his. After that he can come here if he wants to.

"I suppose Miss Rollins has an alibi," Prevost added. "So if she wants to come here she can. You tell her what's happened and see what she wants to do, and then I'll tell you what else is on my mind."

"I'll call you back," Michael promised, reached for the telephone directory, and looked up the number of the beauty salon where Sally worked. A lilting voice, at once obsequious and condescending, inquired what it might do for him.

"You may call Miss Rollins to the telephone."

"Miss Rollins," the voice regretted, "is not with us any more."

"As of what hour?"

"I *beg* your poddon?"

"I," Michael said severely, "am a member of the San Francisco police force: the homicide detail. I want to know why Miss Rollins threw up her job and when. If you'd prefer that I come over to your shop—"

"Oh no! Our clientele." The receptionist lowered her voice, and Michael could see her glancing apprehensively at rows of pink-faced women sitting under bell-shaped driers. "Miss Rollins left here a little before ten. She was impertinent to her nine-thirty appointment and—"

"Deliberately?"

"Poddon? Oh." The voice became humanly speculative. "It did seem like she almost went out of her way to be fired. The customer had read in the papers about Miss Courtney being killed and she asked Sally about it, and Sally—well, she just blew up. So the boss had to fire her, and she just walked out.

"Mr. Dmitri would have been willing for Sally to finish the day out, what with it being Saturday and her booked up solid. He's not in just now, but he isn't going to like—"

"I won't tell him you gave me any information," Michael said. "We'll get the story from him."

After some delay he spoke to Prevost again.

"Miss Rollins has no alibi for this morning after all," he said and told Prevost why. "I don't know where she was when she called me."

"Well, we'll have to try to find her. But I'd like to stick around here for a while. They can't say when Marcia may regain consciousness. I want to be here when she does, and she might say something even before she's conscious that would give us a lead."

"What is it you want me to do?"

"Go over and meet Costello at the cottage. I'll telephone him you're coming. There's a woman there whose story I want you to hear. Costello doesn't have to explain who you are. You know him pretty well and get along all right, don't you?"

"We always have. Besides, he won't question your orders. I'll go gladly. I can't concentrate on women's clothes today."

III

"This Miss Wendell is the kind of dame I'd hate to live near," Costello said. "But they sure are useful times like this. I don't know what Nick and you will make of it." He produced a battered notebook. "But I know shorthand and I'm going to take down what she says this time."

They were climbing the steps up to the cottage just above Lydia's. There was space enough between them so that the upper cottage's occupant also had an unobstructed view of the Bay Bridge, though there was nothing to prevent her from looking down on the back of Lydia's cottage if she preferred that view.

Miss Wendell opened her front door as soon as they set feet on her small side porch. She was not one of your lean, sour-faced gossips. She was plump, round, and gray, with a broad face that looked as if it was frequently scoured with strong soap.

She had frogeyes and a soft, syrupy voice. Michael took one look at her and hauled out the deferential manner he reserved for a few very difficult but extremely lucrative customers and managed to give the impression that he'd been waiting all his life to meet a witness of Miss Wendell's charm and perspicacity.

"You remember I said the inspector would want to hear what you told me," Costello said misleadingly.

"And," Michael said truthfully, "I put everything aside and came over here as quickly as I could."

Miss Wendell purred. She asked them to sit down in a room furnished mainly in fumed oak, settled herself in a comfortable rocking chair, and began:

"Now I do hope you aren't going to think I'm just terribly curious, Inspector. But I'm an awfully friendly person. Mamma always said: 'Adeline can make friends with anyone.' And I'm just naturally interested in people, that's all."

For an instant Michael wished he had remained at Gisele's. Not only did Miss Wendell's tongue and her rocker wag in unison, but she was one of these rockers who cover great distances in an hour.

It was disconcerting to find that she and her chair had traveled the space between you and were practically touching your knees. But Miss Wendell merely slid the chair back to the middle of the room and began all over again.

"Only it's so hard to make friends in a city, and I was unhappy in apartment houses. I was so glad to find this sweet little nest and I thought all of us in this little hilltop haven would be so chummy. But most of the people who live up here work and are busy. Of course Miss Courtney didn't—"

"But she wasn't home a great deal," Michael said.

"My goodness, no! It seems she always had her things on to go out every time I'd run down for a little visit. I never saw anyone so restless. And that Sally, when I've talked to her, was just plain fresh. And those three men there so often, so late—"

"Did they annoy you when they kept late hours?"

"When they're in the living room you can't hear them," Miss Wendell said regretfully. "But you can hear people coming up the steps outside if you have your own windows or door open, and I'm a regular fresh-air fiend."

Michael was unable to produce any suitable answer to this declaration. Costello plugged the gap by observing that a little fresh air never hurt anyone.

"Of course not." Miss Wendell shivered slightly and buttoned her heavy sweater up to her throat. "But I've hardly talked to those girls this last month. After all, when people are rude and abrupt—"

"So you haven't seen any of them since Tuesday through yesterday?" Michael said.

"I wouldn't say I'd *seen* them. Mr. Costello asked me about that. But if you'll look out my front windows—"

She and her chair had again traveled to within six inches of Michael's. She slid deftly back across the faded floral carpet so that he was able to escape to the windows.

"Such a lovely view," she said perfunctorily. "But if you look down—"

"I see what I suppose is a bathroom window, since it is clouded glass. And several windows covered with dark curtains."

"Those are the sun porch off the kitchen: the one Miss Rollins fixed to sleep in. The windows of the real bedroom are on the side of the house. Well, on Tuesday night I was still up at ten o'clock. I happened to look down and saw a light in the room where Miss Rollins sleeps. She opens a window after she is in bed, and then if the light's on you can see it. And you'd be surprised at the way sound travels up the hill from that room. I often hear her talking to the others on Sundays when she's cleaning her room.

"Well, Tuesday she'd gone to bed about nine, I thought. And Miss Courtney had left the cottage in the middle of the afternoon, and while I can't see their front door, I didn't think she was home yet."

"Then you think she came back at ten o'clock?"

"It must have been her in Miss Rollins' room. Because with the sun-porch window open and my windows just happening to be open and it being so still—"

"You could hear them talking?" Michael said, repressing a violent desire to take Miss Wendell by the shoulders and shake her story out of her.

"Well, Miss Rollins' voice was loud, the way people talk sometimes when they've just been waked up. Usually her voice is husky, but I think that's just an affectation and not natural at all.

She said: 'I could kill you!' Naturally that caught my attention.

"Then I could hear Miss Courtney giggling and I caught something about 'Wouldn't you like to know, Sally?' But I guess she was whispering because if she'd spoken in her ordinary voice it would have been easier to hear her than Miss Rollins, you know. I think Miss Rollins was still provoked because I heard her say: 'No, I won't. One of us had better not be a damned fool.' And then something about 'Sometime it might turn out to be just too bad.'

"Miss Courtney laughed again, and I thought she said something like 'Don't be that way' and then 'losing your nerve.' And then Miss Rollins said quite angrily: 'No! And take my word for it, this isn't going to get you anywhere.'"

"And then?" Michael said.

"Oh, in a minute the light went out. But in a few minutes more I thought I heard their front door close and someone going down the steps to the street. Miss Courtney, I supposed. And that she did come home again. But I went to bed at eleven."

"I see. Well, thank you very much and—"

"But that's not nearly all. This other happened Thursday. It was around six-thirty in the evening. That was a cloudy day, so it was already pretty dark, though I hadn't seen any lights in Miss

Courtney's cottage. I opened these windows to air out because I'd been cooking cabbage. And all of a sudden I heard Miss Courtney. . . . I suppose she was in the sun porch."

"She must have been," Michael agreed, allowing Miss Wendell to lengthen her pause for effect.

"And maybe for once she was getting her own dinner, and then when someone came they stepped out of the kitchen into the sun porch. Or with the sun-porch windows open you might hear what they said standing in the kitchen. At least, I could. A number of doctors have told me my hearing is quite phenomenal."

"And one will get you ten you very nearly dislocated your neck leaning out of your own window to listen," Michael thought. Aloud he merely remarked that he had always envied people whose hearing was unusually acute.

"Well, I couldn't mistake Miss Courtney's voice. She said: 'I know—I know! I'd go mad in a month. It would be so much worse for me than you. You do seem to understand.'"

Miss Wendell stopped, frowning. "It was the way she said that that made me keep on listening closely. I really felt sorry for her. She sounded like she was at the breaking point."

"I'm afraid she was," Michael said. "You didn't hear the voice of the person she was talking to?"

"Not even to say if it was a man or woman—if it was a husky woman's voice. Whoever it was must have spoke to her for quite a while, every now and then. I thought he couldn't be so close to the sun-porch windows as Miss Courtney. Besides, her voice was like she kept walking around and never standing still for long.

"And it would keep dropping and then getting high and hysterical-like again. The next thing she said was: 'I never have told anyone here. Only you. I had to tell you that night, Mark, when you—'"

"What!" Michael said. He stared at Miss Wendell. In an instant she looked away, rocking more violently than usual.

"Are you quite certain that she was addressing someone named Mark? If you say yes, are you prepared to swear to that in court and maintain it in the face of cross-examination?"

"Well, no. Because she did drop her voice. And I really didn't catch a couple of words between 'night' and 'Mark.' I wouldn't want to make trouble for an innocent person, and it didn't really sound like she was speaking to anyone by name. Mark, that is."

"Are you sure that she didn't, just for instance, say Kirk instead of Mark?"

"Kirk—Mark. They sound a little alike, but I'm sure she said Mark," Miss Wendell said stubbornly.

"But not like she was addressing him. More like she just mentioned someone named Mark. And she may have been starting a new sentence when she said, 'When you,' because that wasn't all of it. Only she mumbled so I couldn't get the rest."

"I see. Was that all?"

"Not nearly." Miss Wendell recovered her glibness. "She said: 'But I can't sleep. The walls press in on me if I don't have a light on. And I keep seeing her and—and sometimes I even wonder if—if—'

"Well, it was maddening not to hear what this person with her said. Then she said: 'And no one could do anything for her, either?' And then she laughed—hysterically. She said, after someone had answered her: 'I do try but I can't. Oh, I know we're tied together too—with a rope of sand that won't break.'"

"You're sure she said that?" Michael asked sharply.

"Oh yes. Because it was so strange. There's that phrase about giving a person enough rope and they'll hang themselves. But a rope of sand! Though when I was a girl I used to recite a poem called *Lord Randall*. This young man's sweetheart poisoned him, you know. And he tells his mother he leaves his sweetheart a 'rope of my hair to hang her.'"

Michael nodded. "It's a rather gruesome thing."

"And this was gruesome too. I think the person with Miss Courtney cut in when she said that last. I couldn't get the next thing she said, but there was something in it about 'burial.' And, as nearly as I could make out, that some old poem ran in her mind all the time. Something about 'many a one for—'"

"Oh. Oh!" Michael said in dawning comprehension. "That poem? Why didn't I—? Go on, please."

"Then she laughed again and said 'it' or maybe 'she' was morbid, as morbid as some of those awful stories of Poe's. Stories about people that—and I couldn't hear the rest. I think she was interrupted again. Then she said: 'No! No, I can't do that. Though if we had—'

"And then, after another pause: 'I suppose he would remember. No, it's too late now.' And after that she said she was glad this person had come over because the afternoons were so long and she couldn't bring herself to go out. But she said rather bitterly she knew this person was watching her.

"And after he'd said something she laughed and said: 'We shouldn't, should we? But how do I know you won't?' And after that she said that there was one thing that had had to be done the 'next morning.' She dropped her voice then, but I thought she said something about 'washing.'

"When she spoke again," Miss Wendell continued, "she sounded quite angry. She said: 'I couldn't
do it myself. And the man won't tell if he does
remember.' And when she spoke again she sounded just sulky. She said: 'You can't blame me for
thinking that after what you said. And it's done
now.' She went right on, but she sounded more
pleasant. She said: 'I know you can't stay now but
you'll be back.'"

"Well, I should have run to the door right then,"
Miss Wendell said shamelessly. "But I waited too
long. And I never did see who was with her. I've
been thinking maybe he heard my front door open
and dodged back into the doorway of the vacant
cottage across from Miss Courtney's."

"One could do that very easily," Michael agreed.
"Well, Miss Wendell, we do thank you. But—this
happened Thursday. You didn't know Miss Courtney
would be killed, so how can you be so certain that
you remember even one side of a long conversation?"

"You'll remember it," Costello remarked, closing his notebook. "Word for word."

"I know that it is important," Michael said impatiently. "Oh, I'm sure you do have a remarkable
memory, Miss Wendell. But I may have to convince others that your memory can be trusted."

"It's just a matter of training," Miss Wendell
said, mollified. "Though I'm sure you'd never

guess it, when I was a girl I loved amateur theatricals. I always knew my lines before anyone else did, and before we were nearly done rehearsing I'd know the whole play. Then dear Mamma was bed-ridden for ten years before she died. And she used to say it was as good as a play to hear me repeat conversations.

"Not just what our friends said, but even what I'd hear strangers on streetcars, and so on, say. I told you I've always been interested in people and I got in the habit of listening and remembering anything I thought might amuse poor Mamma.

"Not," Miss Wendell said severely, "that I ever exaggerated. Mamma didn't approve of that. As she always said: 'Adeline, the truth itself is stranger than fiction and doesn't need to be embroidered.'

"And you must admit that when you hear a girl who's always struck you as a sort of morbid, unhappy person saying she'd go mad in a month and can't sleep and then talking about ropes of sand, you're going to listen carefully to every word she says and go over it in your mind afterward, trying to think of some explanation."

Michael raised his hands. "I do admit that. You've convinced me, Miss Wendell. Thank you again."

"Do you think what she told us is important?" Costello asked when they were a safe distance down the steps from Miss Wendell's cottage.

"I think it is very important. But I doubt if she would ever be allowed to tell that story on the witness stand. What a witness claims he heard one person say to another person is seldom admissible evidence."

"Not unless it's words spoken on the scene of the crime within a few minutes of the crime," Costello agreed. "Look, what was that pome you thought you recognized?"

"Another old ballad. I think you'd better come to the hospital with me, Costello. I imagine Prevost can find something more for you to do now."

IV

He was right. After hearing their story Prevost sent Costello off to try to find out where Jay Stanton, Bill Kemper, Kirk Vincent, and Sally Rollins had been from about six-fifteen to a quarter of seven on Thursday.

"Miss Courtney was talking to whoever killed her," Prevost said, walking restlessly up and down the corridor outside the private room where Marcia Bond lay. "So it's important. Sally works nights on Thursdays. So when you're checking with them about that night, Costello, also get the beauty-shop proprietor's version of her row with him this morning. We haven't located her yet.

"Vincent's Negro cook should be able to tell you if Vincent was at home Thursday evening—but I don't depend on it. She swears Vincent was in the house all this morning, but when you take her story to pieces she can't swear he wasn't out of the house long enough to get over to Marcia's library and back.

"Some of his neighbors may have seen him if he went out of the house, but I don't depend on that either. See what you can get on Kemper and Stanton at their rooming house for Thursday. It's a long job but keep at it. And, Costello, don't mention Miss Wendell to anyone when you're working on the Thursday angle. We don't want anyone to know—yet—that she overheard so much."

"Have you any line on the others for the time when Marcia was attacked?" Michael asked when Costello had gone.

"Kemper says he spent the morning trying to contact some people who are in the market for income property. But two of 'em weren't home, and that covers the period between ten-ten and ten forty-five. Young Stanton says he had breakfast and then went back to his room and stayed there when he'd taken a sudden notion not to go to work. But the landlady had cleaned his room by that time, so no one looked in on him.

"I found out Stanton told the truth about Lydia drawing a wad of cash out of the bank Thursday. But apparently she hadn't been into her safe-deposit box since she rented it. So I wonder more than ever—especially since she's disappeared— why Sally wanted that safe-deposit-box key. If we could find— Well!"

Kirk Vincent and Jay Stanton stepped out of the elevator and came toward them.

"We couldn't learn anything at the desk except where Marcia was," Jay said. "So we sneaked upstairs when the receptionist's back was turned."

"You could have come openly," Prevost told him. "I told Mr. Vincent that Miss Bond's friends may inquire after her."

"So long as they inquire of you?" Kirk said, smiling. "Well, how is she?"

"Just the same. There's a nurse with her: one I know and can trust."

"It isn't fair to set someone watching her, taking down anything she might happen to mutter when she's unconscious," Jay said hotly.

"No? Well, if it will ease your mind, I doubt if she saw the person who attacked her."

"She wasn't killed," Kirk said thoughtfully. "Was there any reason why she shouldn't have been?"

"I doubt it," Prevost said. "I don't think I interrupted anyone before he could finish the job."

"Then it looks as if what someone mainly wanted was something from the library."

"There are plenty of good hiding places there," Jay said. "And even if Lydia didn't go there very often she could have hidden something there. That is, she would walk over to get there at closing time and come home with Marcia. So do I, sometimes."

"You didn't do that Thursday night. No; Miss Courtney and Miss Bond went to a movie after the library was closed."

"I went bowling with Bill and Sally."

"Did you?" Prevost said. "Where did you meet— and what time?"

"Eight o'clock at the bowling alley. Sally was a little late."

"Why?"

"I don't know," Jay said impatiently. "She often is nights that she has to work. Does it matter?"

"It does. Where were you at six-thirty?"

"Thursday? I suppose I was in my room changing clothes. I get off work at six. Then I had dinner on Polk Street about seven. And, no, Bill wasn't with me. I'll answer the thirty-two-dollar question now before you ask it. I don't know where he was before he turned up at the bowling alley."

"And you didn't go back to the cottage with him and Miss Rollins when you'd finished bowling?"

"No. Bill can't stand to have anyone beat him, and I licked the pants off him that night," Jay recalled with a grin. "I had my pet hook working just right, and he was so damned surly that I went straight home from the bowling alley."

Kirk sighed. "I see where this is leading. I had dinner Thursday night with some people named Dunlap. But we didn't dine until seven-thirty, so I was home at six-thirty."

"But Astoria would have gone home early since you were going out?" Michael suggested.

"Yes. Oh lord!" Kirk rapped his forehead with his knuckles. "Must you question Astoria again? Then there goes dinner too. Astoria is a genius in the kitchen and, like most geniuses, she is temperamental. The soufflé this noon resembled a pancake, and Astoria was as depressed as it was."

"Speaking of food, when Miss Rollins works at night does she get time off for dinner?" Prevost said.

"Not more than a sandwich," Jay said. "But why isn't she here? She called me to ask if I knew where Marcia was. So why—?"

"She threw up her job at the beauty shop, and we can't locate her."

"Sally did! Well, from what Lydia's lawyer told Kirk it looks like Sally won't need to work unless— But where could she have gone to?"

"Mr. Vincent," Michael said abruptly, "why didn't you tell us that Lydia knew Mark Shrader?"

"Knew— Oh, good lord!" Again Kirk rapped his forehead with his knuckles. "Poor old Mark. I told him you'd turn that up. But it would be an act of kindness if you didn't tell his wife."

"Was it because of his wife that he didn't admit to knowing Miss Courtney even before she was killed? He didn't deny he knew her: he simply gave me to understand you'd mentioned her to Mrs. Shrader and asked if you might invite her and her friends to Mrs. Shrader's little gathering last night."

"And while he admitted this morning that he talked to her last night, he implied he might have met her but didn't quite remember if he had," Prevost said. "I will have to talk to Mr. Shrader."

"Well, I wish you'd try to talk to him alone, because this is mostly my fault," Kirk said. "Mark isn't much older than I am, and I've known him for years. Since Lucy Shrader married him he has no financial worries, so naturally he sometimes pines for the days when he had no money but could call his soul his own."

"Does he rebel now and then?" Michael asked.

"When Lucy goes to meetings of women's clubs and can't take him—or when he's supposed to be painting at night. Lucy thinks painting under artificial light is one of the things that makes her genius different from other geniuses, and she seldom disturbs him in his studio. Well, one night about a month or six weeks ago, I took Mark over to the cottage."

"He had a swell time. I never saw anyone eat so much spaghetti—after he helped cook it," Jay said. "And he added greatly to our stock of peculiar songs and stories."

"He did enjoy himself," Kirk agreed. "He wanted to go back when he could elude Lucy again. I don't know if he saw any of us again—but me. He certainly wasn't attracted to Lydia."

"He liked Sally. But Sally wouldn't—"

"Don't sell Mark short, Jay. He has always been very attractive to women. But I imagine Lydia made it a point to see him again or telephone him. Because he told me several days ago that Lydia wanted to be invited to one of Lucy's blowouts."

"And he asked you to speak to her instead of doing it himself?" Michael said.

"Yes. Mark said he'd like Lydia's friends to come, but if he invited three girls Lucy would ask questions. She's a stupid woman, but she has a better idea who is present at those parties than you'd think she could have. But if I got permission from her to ask some friends she'd never bother to learn whether they showed up—and it wouldn't matter if she did.

"I said one of the girls I wanted an invitation for was a pretty young blonde," Kirk added. "Lucy just said: 'Oh, you terrible man!' and forgot it. If it had been Mark she wouldn't have stopped until she had Sally's, Marcia's, and Lydia's life histories. And it smacked of polite blackmail on Lydia's part, if you ask me. I made the relations between Mark and his wife quite clear to everyone after he'd been at the cottage."

"And I'll bet Marcia and Sally were gents and didn't mention him," Jay said.

"They didn't. And it didn't occur to me, then, to ask if they knew Mr. Shrader," Prevost said.

Michael broke in with another abrupt and apparently irrelevant question.

"Did Miss Courtney acquire a family physician or dentist after she came here to live?"

"Great fallen Lucifer!" Jay said. "What have dentists to do with this?"

"Answer his question," Prevost said.

"She had to go to a dentist once. She wouldn't go to Kirk's."

"Why?" Michael asked.

"I don't know," Kirk said. "Perhaps dentistry was one of her pet economies and she thought Dr. Glover would charge too much. He does. His office is in the four-fifty Sutter Building on the twenty-second floor."

"Which means you help pay his office rent," Jay remarked. "My dentist works in his home, and you pay him only for what he does to your teeth. Lydia went to him. But look here: there's—there's no question of—of identification, is there? I mean—"

"I was able to identify Miss Courtney," Michael said. "It isn't a question of identification."

"Well then, what—?" Jay looked from Michael to Nicholas Prevost and shook his head. "No, those stony faces don't encourage questions. Is there anything at all we can do for Marcia?"

"You might find Sally Rollins," Prevost said briefly.

"Dismissed," Kirk said. "Come on, Jay."

Prevost waited until they were gone. Then: "What was behind those questions about a dentist?" he asked.

"A very fantastic theory. But I'd rather think it over, if you don't mind."

"All right. Well, what Miss Wendell heard Miss Courtney say could apply to any of them but Marcia Bond. I mean, her saying: 'I know you can't stay now but you'll be back.' And that could apply to Marcia except that she'd stuck alone in that library until seven-thirty. And Sally was probably working too."

"But she might have rushed over to the cottage for a few minutes to be sure Lydia wasn't weakening," Michael said. "She'd have to get back to work while Bill and Jay had engagements to keep, so they couldn't stay."

"And if she was talking to Vincent she might not have known he had an engagement when she spoke and thought he'd drop in again that night. That seems to let Shrader out, because it's doubtful that he would be able to come back. I'll have to talk to him. But—"

He opened the door of Marcia's room very quietly and stepped inside. The square-faced, competent-looking woman sitting by the side of the hospital bed looked up and shook her head.

"A while ago she muttered something about 'sand.' I was going to call you, but then she was perfectly quiet again and hasn't said anything more."

"All right." Prevost closed the door behind him but stood with his hand on the doorknob. "By the way, Michael, you haven't told me what poem it was that ran in Lydia Courtney's head."

"I'd guess it was an old Scotch ballad. 'Mony a ane for him mak's mane.'"

"I imagine that's very good Scotch," Prevost said, smiling. "But give it to me in English if you—"

He stopped. Two nurses were passing along the hall. The two men could hear the swish of their starched skirts and one clear feminine voice saying:

"Yes, Marcia Bondurant. She seems to be calling herself Bond now but—"

The other nurse said something they couldn't hear, but the first speaker's voice floated back to them again.

"Oh yes, Mildred Bondurant. That's the way her name was in the newspapers. But I trained with her at Lake Merritt in Oakland, and her friends always called her Marcia. I hardly knew her; she's so much thinner. She used to have trouble keeping under the maximum weight. One twenty-five, isn't it?"

Michael and Nicholas Prevost stared at each other. At last Prevost began:

"Mildred Bondurant! Isn't that the girl—?"

"Yes," Michael said. "Good God! No wonder she sees ghosts. . . ."

                                    V

Valerie had settled herself for the afternoon on a chaise longue in the bedroom with two books, a box of candy, and Mehitabel. Mehitabel was now a drowsy house cat, and when he slept he slept all over.

Merely watching him, Valerie felt her eyelids grow heavy. She had just tossed her book to the floor and was trying to draw down the window shade without getting up when Patton entered.

"I'd hoped you'd be sleeping now to make up for last night," the maid said. "Because that person is here. That—that character."

A number of their acquaintances were "persons" to Patton, but only one was "that character."

"You mean Squiffy Bain?" Valerie said.

"Yes. Since Mr. Dundas isn't home and he hasn't too much time, he wants to talk to you. He insists," Patton said reluctantly, "that it is important."

"I'd love to talk to Squiffy," Valerie said, getting up. "Squiffy fascinates me."

"Then shall I say you will be with him presently?"

"Presently? Oh." Valerie caught Patton eying her lounging pajamas and grinned. "For your sake and propriety's I'll put on a house coat. Tell Squiffy I'll be out in a minute."

"Yes, madam," Patton said resignedly.

And looked sympathetically at Patton in the mirror as she withdrew. After nearly a year and a half her employers still mystified her at times. This baby, for instance. Mrs. Dundas was positively lighthearted, and some of her remarks on the subject were not even ladylike.

While Mr. Dundas was distressingly matter-of-fact. Only this morning he had said: "I'm very sorry Valerie lost her sleep last night but I haven't had any sleep either, and we expectant fathers need our rest. I don't care how much you pamper Valerie, but she's a strong, healthy girl and she even looks her breakfast in the eye without flinching. Which is more than I have managed to do very often for a good many years."

Well, that was just Mr. Dundas' way of talking, but still. . . . Patton went into the living room and informed Squiffy Bain that Madam would be out presently. Squiffy moved forward another three inches and balanced uneasily on the extreme edge of his chair while Patton dusted two perfectly clean ash trays and checked on all the small, easily movable objects in the room.

Because Mr. Dundas admitted that Mr. Bain was by nature a pickpocket. He even added that it was "rather a pity so much God-given talent should be wasted." Patton gathered that as a pickpocket Mr. Bain could not long exist in San Francisco, yet he could not happily exist anywhere else.

He was a leftover from what she thought of as "our" last murder case. As he could not safely pick pockets, Mr. Bain drove taxis and private cars. He had been employed as a chauffeur last August by one Bernard Gould. Certain information he had given Mr. Dundas about Mr. Gould had led to his discharge.

Patton never consciously eavesdropped, but she absorbed information through her pores. So she also know that Mr. Dundas had helped Mr. Bain to acquire a small garage in the Mission district. And probably, Patton thought, Mr. Bain wanted money now.

Valerie came in, and Squiffy's licorice-drop eyes lost their hunted look. But he did not dare sit comfortably back in his chair until Patton had left the room.

"Jeez, dat dame gives me the creeps," he breathed then. He spoke pure south-of-Market, which is often at least first cousin to Brooklynese. "Say, you look swell, Mrs. Dundas."

"Don't I?" Valerie said complacently. "We're having a baby in October, and so far it's very becoming to me. I'm sorry Michael isn't here, Squiffy."

"Is him and Nick Prevost woikin' on this moider case together?"

"Is that what you've come about? But, Squiffy, how could you know anything about that?"

"It's a small woild," Mr. Bain remarked sagely. "Well, look. You got no idea when he'll be home?"

Valerie shook her head. "Nor any idea where he is now. Wouldn't it be easier to locate Inspector Prevost? You spoke as if you might know him."

"Sure, I know Nick. I knew him when he was just a sprout. I'm goin' on fifty. Nick's aces with me, but I'll tell you somet'ing about him. If he hadn't been a copper he'd of been a—well—"

"A crook?" Valerie suggested.

"We-ell. He'd of been a big shot too. I was just t'inkin' him and your husband would've made a team. Maybe they still will, in a different line of woik. But Nick missed refoim school by the skin of his teeth. If it hadn't been for old Judge Prevost—I guess you never heard of him."

"No. Did the inspector take his name?"

"Um-hum. The judge didn't have no fam'ly. And Nick don't know what his last name oughta be. Probably some hunky name ending in 'ski,' he says. They clapped some handle on him at the orph'nage: I forget what. But when he was twenty-one he took the old judge's name. I guess because the judge give him the right steer. What the coppers pulled Nick in for was just kid stuff, but some of the guys he was runnin' wit' then is in San Quentin now—and one of 'em on the Rock."

"Is Mr. Prevost an honest copper, Squiffy?"

"The way he dresses he probably don't get credit for bein', but he is. He says to me once: 'A crooked copper's a lot more dangerous than a guy ever'body knows is a crook and watches out for.'"

"Well," Valerie said, smiling, "how much do you want for your information, Squiffy?"

Squiffy looked grieved. "I ain't goin' to hold out on Nick or your husband, Mrs. Dundas. I just kinda t'ought if I come to your husband foist— well, the garage ain't doin' so good, and if he could give me the loan of a coupla hunnert—"

"You know Michael never lends money, and even to spare your delicate sensibilities he won't call a gift a loan. But I'll lend you the money, and you needn't mention it to Michael."

"I can't take no money from no dame," Squiffy protested feebly.

"Pooh! I'll send you cash tomorrow after I've been to the bank. I'm consumed with curiosity and I haven't the slightest idea what those two men may have been doing since eight-thirty this morning. It will be nice to have something to tell them. Go on."

"Well." Squiffy pulled a folded newspaper from his pocket. He pointed to a large picture of Lydia Courtney. "This wasn't in the morning papers, and the dame's name didn't mean nothin' to me."

"But the picture does? It's a very good likeness, though her hair was dark brown where it looks fairly light in the picture, and she was thinner."

"It's the dame," Squiffy said positively. "You know that garage of mine is off Mission several blocks and pretty far out. I been thinkin' she went lookin' for some place like that. Anyway, round noon this Wednesday she drives up in this classy convoitible, top down.

"The bus ain't really dirty, but she wants it washed right then. The kid 'at does that work ain't in, an' I wants her to bring it back. But, no: I gotta do it right then or not at all. She says she's in a hurry and she'll pay me double. Well, I t'ink, in that case—"

"So you did wash the car?" Valerie said eagerly. "Did she stay to watch you?"

"There wasn't nowheres for her to set, and I don't fink she could've stood still. She said somethin' about getting cigarettes and walked off. Well, I was playin' dumb, so maybe she t'ought I was safe."

"Was the car in—in good condition?"

"I t'ought about that myself. It didn't have no new dents or scratches. No; it was the inside that got me to t'inkin' after I read this paper. I cleaned the inside too. And I smelled it right away."

"Smelled what?"

"Booze," Squiffy said. "Somebody had smashed a bottle in the car. I found a few pieces of glass. And they'd tracked a lot of sand in."

"Sand?" Valerie repeated. "No, I can't explain, Squiffy. Go on."

'Well, I did the best I could and washed the floor boards too. She come back and drove the car off. I didn't say anyt'ing, and she didn't neither."

"But Michael and the inspector will be glad you've said something now. I'll try to locate them."

"I washed the floor boards," Squiffy said again. "But I didn't try to do anyt'ing to the cushion."

"The cushion? What was wrong with it?"

"It was on the right-hand side," Squiffy said uneasily. "Way over to the side, and she'd tried to wash it out. But if it hadn't been a smear of blood then my name ain't Algernon."

VI

"Well," Michael said, "more than one reporter is going to be very unhappy because he hasn't remembered yet that Lydia's name has been in the newspapers before. Of course it happened a year ago, and the local papers didn't play it up as much as they would have if it had happened near here."

"And I can't claim I had even an uneasy feeling that I'd heard Lydia's name before," Prevost said. "The details are only coining back to me now. Mildred Bondurant was an airline hostess."

"And her brother James was copilot on the same plane. They were flying out of Los Angeles and they crashed somewhere short of Albuquerque. They had a full load, and everyone was killed but

Marcia, Lydia, and some old lady. I can't remember her name, but the miracle was that those three lived. Marcia had a broken leg and some broken ribs, but she crawled out of the wreckage."

Michael stopped. "I just remembered that they identified the pilot easily enough. That's how they guessed the man beside him must be Marcia's brother."

"I remember," Prevost said. "And Lydia was unconscious. That's how she got those scars on her arm and head, I suppose. Because they said Marcia kept her from bleeding to death."

"It was Marcia the newspapers played up. And she did all she could for the old lady, but she was seriously injured. Didn't she die before help came?"

"Yes. That was all that happened for quite a few hours. Lydia was unconscious; Marcia wasn't. The old lady died, and help finally arrived."

"And Miss Bondurant was a heroine for a week," Michael said. "Knowing who she is explains a good many things that have been bothering us, and a good many of them have nothing to do with Lydia's death."

"But Marcia still didn't tell us a lot that she should have. She might have told us who she is."

"If Lydia's death was a shock to her I can understand why the effort of discussing that plane crash

might be more than she could face this morning.
She knew you'd find out what her real name is,"
Michael said. "But if she feels that way about that
incident in her life I don't see why she put up with
a living reminder of it in the shape of Lydia."

"Lydia was probably grateful—and should have
been," Prevost said. "And probably she wanted—
Yes?"

The nurse had come to the door of Marcia's
room. "I think you'd better— There, she's said it
again."

"Sand in your shoes?" Marcia muttered. "But
where have you been? . . . Of course it doesn't
matter. We'll sweep it up."

She lay straight and still, but her fingers
plucked at the sheet and finally at the narrow bandage about her wrist.

"Don't throw it away," she said fretfully. "Tell
someone."

"Yes, dear?" the nurse prompted, putting a soothing hand over one of Marcia's. The girl clutched it
eagerly and then pushed it away, frowning.

"Tell someone—coffee—"

"I'm afraid it doesn't make sense," the nurse
murmured.

"Yes, it does." Prevost took Marcia's thin hands
between his own broad, hard palms. "Tell someone what, Marcia?"

"Not to throw the newspaper away."

"We won't throw it away. Which newspaper is it?"

"The one Lydia spilled coffee on," Marcia said reasonably. "Don't let them throw it away."

"Where did you put the newspaper? Is it in the cottage? Does Sally know where it is?"

"Yes—no—I don't know."

"I'm afraid you're asking her too many questions, Inspector," the nurse said uneasily. "I wouldn't—"

"Sally knows—where I put them." Marcia moved her head restlessly, but her hands clung to Prevost's. "No, I don't mind the light. . . . But, Lydia, you don't want to send that new coat to the Salvation Army."

Prevost hesitated. Before he could frame his question Marcia spoke again in a changed voice:

"Jimmy! Oh, Jimmy! Jimmy—"

"I will not be responsible if you insist on going on with this," a professional voice announced. A white-jacketed doctor pushed Prevost aside. "I understand this girl isn't under arrest. I didn't approve of this arrangement to begin with. But I'm willing for Miss Abbott to remain here. I want you to get out, away from the hospital. When the girl is conscious and wants to talk and is, in my judgment, able to talk—"

"He's right." Michael took Prevost's arm and shoved him toward the door. "Come on, Nick. *Que siembre.*"

"Meaning?" Prevost said ungraciously.

"Oh, let things work themselves out. This isn't doing you any good. A drink will do you more. And I want one badly myself. Shall we pick up one, or even two, on our way to the cottage?"

Prevost had Lydia's keys to the cottage, turned over to him by Costello, who had locked the place.

"It would be odd," Michael said as they climbed the steps for what he complained was at least the tenth time that day, "if we found Sally here."

But the cottage was still locked, and inside there was no sign that Sally had even come back to it and managed to slip away again without being seen.

"Well, we'll locate her before long—I hope. We're keeping an eye on Kemper in case she gets in touch with him," Prevost said. "And if she'd left town by train we'd know that by now. I'll put a man here after we leave though, in case she comes back or telephones. But now we want a newspaper: Thursday morning's, I suppose. That was the morning Lydia upset coffee over Marcia's wrist."

"But Marcia didn't say whether she put that newspaper away. She only said, 'Don't throw it away.' Oh well: 'They sought it with thimbles, they sought it with care; They pursued it with forks and hope.' I suppose we'd better try the large bedroom first.

"And it is large," Michael added thoughtfully, stopping in its doorway. "Very nearly as large as the living room and with as many windows."

"Yes," Prevost said impatiently. "You take the chest of drawers, and I'll take this bureau. Though if she stuck the newspaper away in here I don't think Costello would have overlooked it."

"This would be Lydia's lingerie," Michael said, making hay of it. "Nothing under ten dollars. And— Well! This is interesting, and Costello slipped up on it."

"What? Oh." Prevost stared at the framed painting Michael held up. He closed one eye, frowned, closed the other eye, and then blinked protestingly. "It looks like a plate of spaghetti to me."

"It's Mark Shrader's impression of War—1941," Michael said. "This was under Lydia's lingerie. I imagine Mrs. Shrader doesn't hand over much cash to her little white hyacinth, so I also fancy this sale was strictly between Lydia and Mark Shrader."

"I've got to talk to Shrader—but God knows when. This is more important right now. I haven't turned up any newspapers in this bureau. See here: if Marcia had hidden the newspaper in a safe place why should she say, 'Don't throw it away'?"

"Well, what becomes of newspapers in well-reg-ulated households? You wrap garbage in them and—"

"Build fires with them," Prevost finished, start-ing toward the bedroom door. "They must keep wood and coal somewhere besides in that iron basket by the fireplace."

"Which," Michael said, "only leaves the kitchen."

An enclosed section beneath the drainboard in-tended for pots and pans provided storage space for fuel. There was a bundle of kindling, half a sack of coal, and a thick stack of newspapers which Prevost threw on the kitchen table. Michael eyed them pessimistically.

"I would expect that Thursday's paper went to make Friday's fire," he said.

"But these papers on top are old ones. Two Sun-day papers: April sixth. I wonder . . ."

Prevost turned the bundle of papers complete-ly over. "Let's begin at the bottom instead and—Yes, she did, God bless her!"

"Put the latest newspapers at the bottom of the stack? What a remarkable woman! I've never yet particularly wanted to consult yesterday's newspa-per that it wasn't wrapped about potato peelings in the garbage can. Well?"

"Here it is. Thursday morning—and stained with coffee. Second news section, and that's a break. It must be this first page. There wouldn't be anything in the women's, theatrical, or sports pages or want ads that would have given Lydia a shock. Well . . ."

It was any first page of a second news section in a day when world and national affairs crowd all but sensational local news out of the first news section. A retired civil-service employee had leaped to his death from a downtown hotel. May Day would be celebrated as usual by San Francisco children in Golden Gate Park.

A widow who had supposed she was a wealthy woman was demanding an accounting from the executor of her husband's estate. Two young girls in Oakland had been jailed on a charge of burglary. An ocelot cub, three months old, would be at home from now on in Fleishhacker Zoo.

And Mrs. Thomas Cason was concerned because her daughter Margaret, fourteen, had not returned home on Tuesday night and was still missing. The girl had left home at about half-past ten on Tuesday night, following a slight disagreement with her father.

When Mrs. Cason discovered that her daughter had not spent the night with any of her friends and had not attended school on Wednesday she had notified the Bureau of Missing Persons.

"Margie," Mrs. Cason said, "never did anything like this before. She didn't have any boy friends."

"'Pardon me, but you look just like Margie,'" Michael said softly. "There's a picture too. . . ."

The picture was obviously a reproduction of an indifferent snapshot. It showed a slim youngster with long hair blowing about her shoulders, her features blurred in a dazzle of sunlight.

"I never did repeat the verse from that poem that ran in Lydia's mind, did I?" Michael said. "Well, minus the Scotch dialect: 'Many a one for him makes moan, But none shall know where he is gone; Over his white bones when they are bare The wind shall blow forevermore.'"

PART FIVE

Thunder. Second Apparition, a bloody child.
MACBETH: ACT IV, SCENE I

Prevost struck the newspaper with the flat of his hand. "It fits! These Casons live—where's that address? Yes, that would be out in Sunset, near Fleishhacker and the beach. Wait a minute. . . ."

He went into the living room to the telephone. Michael remained in the kitchen, brooding over the vague features of Margie Cason, aged fourteen. When last seen she had been wearing a brown skirt and sweater, an old brown coat, no hat. She was five feet tall and weighed one hundred pounds.

"In Missing Persons' opinion, something stinks," Prevost reported. "But they can't do anything about it. This Thomas Cason is a tough customer. He hires out with a truck which wasn't paid for."

"'Wasn't?' It is now?"

"He came in Friday morning and told them that he and Mrs. Cason knew where Margie was and that everything was all right. She's visiting friends, but he prefers not to say where. If he'd had his way the mother never would have reported the girl missing, and he'll thank the police to mind their own business and let him look after his family. And then on Friday he finished paying for his truck, including back payments overdue."

"And along with everything else we know, there's the fact that Lydia went to the bank to draw out a large amount in cash the same day she read this newspaper and— Would that be the hospital so soon?"

Prevost was already halfway back to the telephone. "I left this number there, but I don't suppose— Oh, Mrs. Dundas. Yes, he's here."

"Michael, I've just been talking to Squiffy Bain," Valerie said. "He saw Lydia and her car Wednesday morning. As he says, it's a small woild."

"Come here and listen to this, Prevost. . . . Go on."

When Valerie had finished her story Prevost turned and walked over to the windows and stood staring out of them.

"And how much money did you give Squiffy, my love?" Michael inquired.

"I haven't given him a cent."

"Then don't. Though it's your own money, and who am I to say what you should do with it? You'd better take a nice long nap. Don't count on me for dinner."

"I won't. But—Squiffy thought it was only co-incidence that Lydia brought her car to his garage. Maybe she did just go looking for a garage a long way from where she lived. But I wonder. However, Squiffy didn't recognize the names of any of the people involved when I mentioned them."

"Squiffy hires a woman to keep books for him," Michael said. "And he doesn't keep what I'd call a vigilant eye on the business or he might not be running too close to the red."

"I know. I asked him if his garage had a reputation for any special sort of service. He assured me that his business is strictly on the up-and-up. But he said that while he's only a fair mechanic, one man who works for him is an unusually good one."

"Yes. I coaxed the fellow away from a garage farther downtown myself. Is Squiffy going to make inquiries?"

"Yes. He'll get in touch with you later. Come home sometime tonight, please. . . ."

"I suppose," Michael said to Prevost, "that you want to use the telephone now?"

"Yes." Prevost called headquarters, spent some time listening to negative reports, and then ordered a man to the garage where Lydia had kept her car.

"Ask them what time she brought it in Tuesday night and if the garage attendant noticed what condition it was in. And find out when she first took it out on Tuesday. And any other items you might gather about her from the garage-man.

"I slipped up on that," he told Michael. "I should have been interested in that car of hers. But she was supposed to have been downtown Tuesday afternoon, and most people don't use their cars when they're going shopping or to a show on Market Street when they live as close downtown as this."

"Not with the parking problem what it is in our fair city," Michael agreed. "Well, Squiffy thinks there had been a smear of blood on the car seat. And Marcia muttered: 'But, Lydia, you don't want to send that new coat to the Salvation Army.'"

"That would be the coat she was wearing Tuesday night. And Squiffy smelled liquor in the car and found broken glass—and sand. If Lydia was in that car and drinking—"

Prevost broke off and pounced on the telephone as it rang again.

"Yes—speaking. . .. So soon? . . . She does? . . . Well, what does the doctor say? . . . Oh. Well, in that case I'll be over as soon as possible."

He put down the telephone and looked at Michael. "Marcia's conscious and wants to talk, and the doctor says she can try since it distresses her not to. But—"

"But you also want to hear what Mrs. Cason has to say about Margie—and to see just where the Casons live. You aren't telling me not to go out there, are you?"

"No," Prevost said, smiling briefly. "I'm not warning you not to go, though of course I'm not telling you to go. But if you did, of course I'd have to listen to what you had to tell me when you got back."

"We understand each other perfectly," Michael said. "You can go back to the hospital and hear what Marcia has to say, and then we'll both be happy. I'll drop you off at the hospital. . . ."

He left Prevost at the corner of Hyde and Bush, said: *"Hasta la vista,"* and drove away. Prevost hurried into the hospital and up to Marcia's room. She lay looking toward the door and smiled when she saw him.

"I hoped you'd come soon."

"But do you feel like talking?" Prevost said.

"Yes. I want to talk to you—alone. Would you mind, Miss Abbott?"

"I'll call you the minute I think she shouldn't talk any more," Prevost promised as the nurse

hesitated. She looked from him to Marcia, shrugged, and left the room.

"I've caused you a lot of trouble, haven't I?"
Marcia said. "But Miss Abbott says you know my
real name now and all about me."

"You don't have to talk about that," Nicholas
Prevost said almost angrily.

"But I want to—though it's strange I should.
I've gone out of my way for so long to keep from
talking about it. After the—the crack-up, while I
was still in the hospital and afterward, while people still remembered my name, they'd ask questions. All some of them really wanted was the—
the details.

"I finally thought: 'I'll never speak of this again.'
I decided to arrange things so I wouldn't have to.
That meant cutting loose from my old friends.
They were all other airline hostesses or Jimmy's—
my brother's—friends. So I changed my name and
simply dropped out of sight in Los Angeles.

"I was a miserable coward. Worse things than
happened to me are happening to people every day
all over the world now. To just ordinary civilians."

"Even seasoned fighters get shell-shocked,"
Prevost said gently.

"I suppose it was a kind of shell shock. But
I was an experienced nurse and—well, there was
no excuse for my trying to forget I'd ever been a

nurse and carrying it to such extremes that I'd shy away from admitting it to Mr. Dundas last night. But I always had a foolish idea if I said I'd been one people might recognize me and—

"Well, I wouldn't have been any good as a nurse for a long time after the—crack-up. I took anything I could get: worked in stores and as a maid and looked after children. But it didn't do any good because—well, Lydia—"

"She was too grateful to let you work things out for yourself," Prevost said.

"Yes. I did meet her at a cocktail party she gave in that hotel in Los Angeles, just as I said. I think it was talking to me that made her decide to go somewhere by plane."

"Hadn't she ever, as much as she'd traveled?"

"She'd always been afraid to fly and she wanted to leave the plane when it was too late. I had to watch her and talk to her constantly to keep her from being half hysterical up to the very minute we crashed. Well, I was in the hospital much longer than she was. She paid my bills and saw that I had everything. She visited me every day and—and—"

"Basked in reflected glory," Prevost said grimly.

"Perhaps. She'd never been conscious, you see. There was just an instant when she knew we were going to crash and then she came to in a hospital bed. So the whole thing was just something exciting that had happened to her. Well, I told you I tried to go my own way. But she hunted me out and insisted it was ridiculous that I should be drudging away at poorly paid work when she had so much and wouldn't be alive to enjoy it if it wasn't for me.

"And I was tired to death and barely making ends meet and wanted to get out of Los Angeles. And Lydia was always looking for friends, thinking she'd found some, and then seeing them drift away from her. She felt that what had happened to us was a bond. It was. You can't save a person's life and not feel a little responsible for her afterward. And she felt at least a financial responsibility toward me.

"I shouldn't have done it. Seeing her constantly kept me from forgetting, though on the other hand, as she knew all about me, I didn't have to make an effort when I was alone with her. But that was bad for me too. Still I agreed to come up here with her and let her buy me some sort of business."

"She certainly owed you that much," Prevost said.

"I let myself think that because I was tired of arguing. And I made it a condition that she should never mention the—the crack-up. Well, she bought that library for me and she kept her word. She even put me down in her will as Marcia Bond, didn't she? She said she would, though perhaps that's not legal."

"She broke her word at the Shraders' last night," Prevost reminded her. "Why do you think she did?"

"Oh, I think that was just the instinct all of us have to hit out at someone else when things aren't going right for us. It helped her to know she had the power to hurt me."

"There are a lot of nasty kinks in the human mind. I suppose that was one of hers. Well—you didn't know that she came home around ten o'clock on Tuesday?"

"Did she? I didn't know. I'd rearranged the books in the library that day and I was very tired. When I am I often go to sleep at once and sleep very soundly for several hours. Then I wake and—well, I was awake when Lydia came home for what you say was the second time. You're sure she did come back to the cottage earlier?"

"Sure enough. And she woke Sally, and they had a short conversation."

"Oh." Marcia closed her eyes. "I'd better tell you that the reason I'm willing to tell you everything I do know is—well, because of this." She touched her bandaged throat.

"You can't be sure it wasn't Miss Rollins who attacked you in the library this morning?"

"No. If you'd ever had Sally shampoo your hair you'd know she has very strong fingers. I'd rather it was anyone but Sally. But it could have been anyone."

"What time did you get to the library?"

"It was about a quarter after ten."

"Then since I didn't get there until a quarter of eleven, there was nothing to keep someone from killing you. So I think you simply surprised him while he was searching the library. What did you want to get from there?"

"An envelope—just a plain, large envelope—that Lydia gave me about a month ago and asked me to keep for her in one of the desk drawers."

"I see. And we didn't turn up anything like that when we searched the library. Was the envelope bulky? And why did she want you to keep it in the library?"

"I thought the envelope had very little in it. And Lydia said it was something she didn't want to bother to put in her safe-deposit box."

"Why? Why not keep it in the cottage then?"

"I've gotten out of the habit of asking questions," Marcia said apologetically. "But Lydia explained too much in spite of that. She said the envelope wasn't important enough to put in her safe-deposit box. I thought she meant it was something she wouldn't want whoever opens safe-deposit boxes in case of death to see. Then she said she didn't want to keep it in the cottage; that she'd rather leave it where I'd be certain to get it first if 'anything happened to me.' Of course a month ago she said that very lightly, not expecting anything would happen to her."

"But what did you think?" Prevost persisted.

"I thought she wanted me to ask her why she didn't want to keep the envelope in the cottage," Marcia said wearily. "And that then she would say that Sally was too curious and hadn't any regard for others' belongings."

"Is that true?"

"Sally isn't unusually curious and she doesn't search bureau drawers. She's been used to borrowing clothes all her life; from her sister and other girls who've lived in the same boardinghouses with her. There's nothing unusual about that."

"No. But didn't you think that Sally wanted Lydia's safe-deposit-box key to get something from the box—something that Lydia hadn't put in it but had given to you instead?"

"I was afraid Sally wanted that envelope," Marcia admitted. "And I didn't think she knew it was in the library. And Sally would be quite capable of taking that key to the bank and trying to pass herself off as Lydia."

"And since Lydia wasn't well known at her bank, she might have pulled it off. Well, did you think that whatever was in that envelope concerned Sally directly—or only as it concerned Bill Kemper?"

"Bill—or Jay. Sally's more than half in love with Jay. He appeals to her maternal instinct. I like Jay and Kirk and I don't like Bill, but there's really not much to choose between the three. They are all selfish and self-centered."

"And what do you think Lydia's feelings were toward them?"

"Lydia would have loved anyone she thought really loved her. They were rude to her sometimes, but when Bill or Jay took the trouble to be nice to her they could make her, as Sally says, 'eat out of their hands.' I suppose Kirk could too. He didn't bother and he wasn't often definitely rude to her. Just—flippant or a little satirical, you know."

"Well, Miss Bondurant, I can see why you'd think that envelope only concerned Sally indirectly—unless it occurred to you that while it's not likely Lydia would ever have omitted your name from her will, she might have decided to strike out Sally's name almost any time. Had you thought of that?"

II

"I've been thinking it," Marcia confessed. "Because there was getting to be more and more friction between her and Sally. And Lydia could have written a holograph will. If she did she might have mentioned the fact to Sally without telling her where the will was. But I thought you believed it was something that happened to Lydia Tuesday night that led to her being killed."

"That is almost a certainty. But that doesn't mean her money mightn't have been an added incentive to someone who'd decided she must be killed anyway. And— Are you sure you aren't too tired to go on?"

"No, I'm not too tired."

"Well, I didn't let you finish telling me what happened at the library this morning."

"I walked into it, intending to get that envelope, and—I was going to read whatever was in it." Marcia looked very guilty and very much younger. "But the faucet in the kitchen leaks, and I could hear water dripping. So I went straight in there instead.

"You noticed the kitchen door's behind my desk? I put the desk there to get as much space for bookshelves as I could. Well, I kicked the swinging door open, and then there were hands around my throat. I kicked and fought, and things began getting black and I lost my footing. I was falling, and something sharp hit my head—and that's all."

"Then let's go back to the fact that Lydia did come back to the cottage twice on Tuesday night. When you mentioned the possibility that she might have—or hinted at it this morning—it seemed to me that Sally warned you off the subject. And you didn't go on. Why?"

"Because Lydia liked to drive at night at about seventy miles an hour. And if she'd been drinking—well, that was one thing Sally meant when she started to say that one or two drinks made Lydia reckless. She usually wanted to get the car out and drive."

"And Sally has no objections to speed?"

"No. She and Bill love cars and fast driving. And one night when Lydia and Sally were still getting along pretty well Lydia came home, and she and Sally slipped out while I was sleeping heavily early in the night. They went riding and very nearly ran into another car. I said they were terribly foolish and I believed Sally agreed with me. But if— Why don't you ask Sally about this?"

"She isn't available at present," Prevost said.

"You don't know where she is? Oh. Well then, I thought that if Lydia had come back Tuesday night and wanted Sally to go out in the car with her they'd have been very quiet since they knew I wouldn't approve. I gave Sally her chance to tell you if Lydia had. When she didn't take it I hoped she had nothing to tell."

"She had something to tell, and it's still a question whether or not she went out with Lydia. I understand drinking makes Kemper quarrelsome. What does it do to Stanton and Vincent?"

"Jay is very amusing and—yes, a little reckless. Then he takes bicarbonate of soda all the next day. I guess Kirk would carry his liquor very well, but I've never seen him drinking anything but beer."

"Well, if Sally did go out with Lydia at ten and return with her around midnight, you didn't know it?"

"No," Marcia said. "And if she had been with Lydia when something happened that had such a devastating effect on Lydia it would have affected Sally, too, wouldn't it? And I did tell you everything that happened that night after Lydia came in to bed."

"What didn't you tell me then?"

"That when I got up Wednesday morning I noticed there was sand on the floor and in her shoes. Just a little. When I spoke of it she looked so frightened and angry that I didn't mention it again. Then later on I came into the bedroom and found her bundling up a new light coat she hadn't worn more than twice. She said she was sending it to the Salvation Army."

"And you naturally protested against that?"

"Yes. And she acted just as she had when I'd spoken of the sand. The coat wasn't in the closet this morning, so she must have taken it away after I left the cottage Wednesday. Well, this morning the coat and the sand and her car were all vaguely connected in my mind. And the car made me think of Sally, so I thought I wouldn't speak too soon."

"I didn't ask you to tell me what Lydia was wearing Tuesday because I didn't suppose you'd know. But she must have been wearing that coat."

"I'm afraid that won't help," Marcia said. "It was like a thousand others: a light, furred, casual coat. Almost as light as cream with a little darker fur collar. They're 'the thing' this spring."

"You wouldn't have to tell Michael Dundas that, but I didn't know," Prevost said, smiling. "Well, did anything else happen Wednesday you haven't mentioned?"

"No. Sally was gone before we two had break-fast either Wednesday or Thursday. It was Thursday that Lydia was sitting at the table, just drinking coffee, not eating. She took the second section of the morning paper, spread it out on the table, and looked at it for a minute. Then she started up just as I'd leaned over to fill her coffee cup.

"The coffee went partly over my left wrist and onto the paper. Lydia sat down again. She was shaking so she couldn't stand. The coffee had been boiling, and my wrist hurt. I went to bandage it."

"And what did Lydia do?" Prevost asked.

"Oh, she kept saying she was sorry and that she was so nervous. But she didn't admit it was something she'd read in the newspaper that startled her. It was all tied up together in my mind though. That's why I lied so foolishly when Mr. Dundas asked about my wrist last night."

"You didn't need to tell him why Lydia had spilled coffee on you," Prevost said reasonably.

"I know that now. But he frightened me. First, out of a clear sky, he took for granted I'd been a nurse and—well, that way he has of asking unexpected questions is demoralizing. You can't guess what he'll say next, and he makes you feel he knows more than he does. Lydia felt the same way, I know. My bandaged wrist must have made her think of that newspaper. So I said the first foolish thing that came into my mind."

"But even if you didn't ask questions Thursday morning, hadn't you read the newspaper afterward?"

"Yes. But that morning I didn't think there was anything in the paper that explained Lydia's reaction. However, there was one item, just a few lines at the bottom of the page in one corner, that said police were still looking for a hit-and-run driver who struck an elderly man Tuesday night around ten o'clock. He was only shaken up."

"We missed that one," Prevost muttered. "But we'd already found what we wanted."

"Did you? Well, this morning when you began asking what might have happened to Lydia Tuesday night I thought it was at least possible she and Sally had slipped out and gone riding together. I wanted to talk to Sally before I mentioned that item in the newspaper to you."

"You didn't discuss what happened Thursday morning at the breakfast table with Sally?"

"No. She didn't ask to see the paper that day. But she knows where I put them, with the latest papers at the bottom of the pile in case someone should want to refer to them."

"And when did you begin to distrust Sally?"

"It was that safe-deposit-box key that really disturbed me. And you saw to it that we couldn't talk together, but I don't think she wanted to talk to me. And I didn't dare hunt out that newspaper with Mr. Costello in the cottage."

"You're tired," Prevost decided, standing up. "I don't think there's anything else I need to ask."

"But you did find the newspaper? Then that's all right. I talked before I was conscious, didn't I? I seem to remember trying to tell someone something important and wanting someone to hold to."

Marcia put out her hand and touched his. She smiled sleepily. "And then someone did pull me up out of the whirlpool. It was you, wasn't it?"

III

Michael had always found the Sunset district depressing. It did provide a much-needed section of moderately priced homes for families with moderate incomes. But he often thought the houses must be bought in lots of a thousand each from some large mail-order firm.

Almost always they were wooden buildings with false fronts of stucco, one large front window with garage doors beneath, front door at the end of a short flight of steps on one side of the house. This monotony of architecture, with entire blocks of homes that differed only in the numbers over their doors, depressed him more than the fog that often hangs over Richmond and Sunset even when the sun is shining on the other side of the avenues.

The Casons' house had a false stucco front; it had a pocket handkerchief of lawn; it had a large front window with garage beneath. Michael was glad to see that the garage doors were open and that no truck was parked in front of the house. He was prepared, if necessary, to deal with the tough Mr. Cason, but he was weary enough to feel this would be more an effort than a pleasure.

He climbed the steps to the front door. The dumpy little woman who finally opened it had been crying. Her eyelids were pink, and her rabbit nose twitched while she apologized for "keeping you waiting so long. I guess I didn't hear the doorbell. Was it my husband you'd want to see? He's out on a job and won't be in till late."

"Good," Michael said. He walked past her into a rigidly neat living room and sat down in a chair so overstuffed that it pouted. "I want to talk to you about your daughter Margie, Mrs. Cason."

"Margie? Have you found?—I mean, my husband said you was to stop looking for her."

"When you've once asked us to find someone who is missing we aren't going to stop searching until we're certain that person has been found, Mrs. Cason. Especially when a girl as young as Margie is missing. And you don't really know where she is, do you?"

Mrs. Cason began to cry again. "No! No, I don't know where she is! I don't care what Tom says; I've got to know! I'm a-scared of him, but I'll leave him, that's what! If Margie's done something bad I'm her mother and I got a right to know. And we hadn't ever ought to've taken that money."

"The fifteen hundred dollars in twenty-dollar bills?" Michael said.

"You know about that!" Mrs. Cason wriggled as far as possible back into her chair and dried her eyes on the sleeve of her faded percale house dress. "You find out everything. I told Tom you would."

"But we don't know if there was any letter with the money, Mrs. Cason."

"Oh. But you couldn't know that. I kept it. Tom says not to, but I did. I got it right here if—if you'll just turn your head. . . . There!" Mrs. Cason said finally. "It was safest to keep it on me. Here."

She held out a half sheet of cheap white paper. On it was typewritten: "Your daughter is all right. This money is for you if you don't ask questions."

"An old typewriter," Michael said, purely for effect. "You didn't keep the envelope?"

"Tom threw it away, but I seen it was post-marked here in the city. You see," Mrs. Cason faltered, "Tom ain't Margie's pa, though she took his name when I married him. That's why he's so willing to think bad of her. He says she's run off with some man and there isn't no use hunting her now. She'll come home—in trouble, he says. So we'd better take the hush money while we can get it."

"So doubting Thomas doesn't doubt that earth hath no sorrow that a handful of folding money can't heal."

"Beg pardon?"

"Never mind. The money arrived Friday morning, didn't it? Well then, tell me what really happened here Tuesday night."

"Oh, sir, if I'd just been here it wouldn't happened. But I was down the street setting up with a sick lady. Margie should've been in bed, but Tom got to nagging her about that. He won't tell me all that was said, but I know how it would be. Him saying mean things and Margie sassing him back because she has a temper and don't get scared like me. But I've always been here to hold her back when she says she's going to leave the house and Tom says: 'Go on, get out and see who cares.'"

"So Tuesday night she did leave the house?"

"Rushed right out with no hat and not a cent in her pocket. I know she didn't even have carfare."

"Oh. What time did she leave the house?"

"It was later than it said in the paper. Tom says it wouldn't look well if we said he let Margie go out alone so late. It must've been at least eleven o'clock. I just barely missed her."

"What did you do?" Michael asked. "That is, where did you think she had gone?"

"I hoped she'd just walk around and cool off and come home. But when she didn't come and didn't come I called one of her girl friends that lives right near here. Margie wasn't there, but that wasn't her very special girl friend."

"Who was her very special girl friend?"

"A girl named Betty that don't have any phone. So I couldn't call her, and Tom wouldn't let me go over there that night, but the next morning I did walk over."

"Then Betty lives within walking distance of here?" Michael said.

"Yes sir, though it's a pretty long walk. I don't walk as fast as Margie but I walked fast's I could, and it took me a good half-hour. Even though I did hope Margie had stayed all night with Betty it worried me to think of her walking over there late at night."

"Some of the streets aren't too well lighted?"

"Not that so much as that she'd have to go by quite a few vacant lots. Just sand dunes, they are, and awful lonely at night. I guess she'd go out Ortega until she hit Forty-sixth or Forty-seventh. And then turn over toward Fleishhacker because Betty lives just off Wawona, almost at the beach, you might say."

"I see." Michael stood up. "If I were you I wouldn't mention our little talk to Mr. Cason."

"Oh, I won't! I mean, if there was someone like you here to keep Tom from being mad at me—"

"I don't believe he will dare be angry with you when the police talk to him about Margie again," Michael said. And added hastily because he shirked even hinting to Mrs. Cason what news the police might finally bring of her daughter: "You'd better give me Betty's last name and address."

He wrote these down in his pocket notebook, left Mrs. Cason standing on the steps smiling after him hopefully, and went looking for a drugstore. When he found it and a telephone he was lucky enough to catch Prevost just as he returned to his office.

Michael told Mrs. Cason's story. Prevost interrupted only once to ask: "Mrs. Cason is sure the girl didn't have carfare?" When Michael finished he groaned softly.

"I know," Michael said. "It's going to be a hellish job and take a great many men."

"I've kept a small army busy all day, and all our doorbell ringing hasn't gotten us anywhere. Well, this will have to be done."

"You'll probably find any number of small boys eager and willing to help, besides some curious and interested citizens."

"Those curious citizens are one of the problems. Did you drive out that way when you left Mrs. Cason?"

"I decided it would be wasting time. But I would think you could concentrate on Forty-sixth and Forty-seventh, between Ortega and Wawona. That's about sixteen blocks if you cover both avenues. I'd begin at Wawona and work backward. Lydia said, 'Sand dunes at midnight.' It probably wasn't quite midnight, but by eleven-thirty Margie must have been fairly close to Betty's home."

"It sounds easy, the way you put it. Well, I'll start things going. Wait a minute. Yes, here it is. Lydia took her car out of the garage around two on Tuesday afternoon. She never did bring it back until late Wednesday afternoon, after she'd had Squiffy Bain wash and clean it. She'd never kept it out all night before, though she often brought it in after eleven or close to midnight. Alone, lately. When she first began keeping it there, about four months ago, Kemper used to be with her fairly often. And once or twice Sally was with her."

"And Sally is still missing?"

"Yes, dammit! But she was alive at four-ten. At least the guy I posted in the cottage says a woman with a young voice called in, asked if Marcia was there, and hung up when he tried to stall. We couldn't trace the call. And I haven't time to talk any more. Suppose we meet in as near half an hour as we can make it at—"

"At Foster's: Geary at Kearney," Michael said. "Their coffee is passable, and I'll drink several cups while I wait for you."

IV

But he had not finished drinking even one cup of coffee when Prevost entered the restaurant and came quickly over to him.

"The man on Kemper called in to say he's at that bowling alley on Broadway," Prevost announced. "Sally has had opportunities to call him today and arrange a meeting place. The bowling alley might be it. So let's get going. I'm double-parked."

"Isn't the right to double-park, even downtown, one of your special privileges? Oh, very well." Michael hastily swallowed the rest of his coffee and scalded his tongue. "I put my car in a garage on Post," he said, following Prevost out to the street. "I'll drive yours."

"Don't you like my driving?" Prevost said, grinning.

"Not so well as I do my own, and that goes for everyone's driving." Michael started the car. "What has Kemper been doing?"

"He didn't work after one. He had a shave and a haircut and lunch and went back to his room. But Jay Stanton evidently decided he'd better go to work after all. He went over to the pharmacy about two-thirty, after he and Vincent were at the hospital. But I have a question or two to ask Kemper anyway."

"Yes?"

"Oh, I've talked to Costello." Prevost stiffened slightly as Michael suddenly inched by the string of Geary streetcars that had been delaying them. "And Sally went out Thursday to get something to eat when she was between appointments. The beauty-shop proprietor remembered that because she kept her six forty-five appointment waiting. The proprietor's version of her row with him this morning is the same as you gave me.

"But we still don't know where Kemper was on Thursday after he left the real-estate office at six until he turned up at the bowling alley. As for Jay, his landlady 'thinks' maybe she did see him going up to his room sometime after six Thursday evening, as he claimed he did. But she isn't certain, and Costello had no chance to talk to any other roomers since it's Saturday afternoon and everyone on the first floor where Stanton's room is has been out."

Michael turned into Larkin, covered the distance between Geary and Broadway in less than five minutes, and parked in front of the bowling alley, a large building next to a public playground that took up the rest of the block on that side of the street.

"And Vincent certainly did dine out, as he said he did, on Thursday," Prevost added, getting out of the car. "But whether or not he was home at six-thirty or over at the cottage talking to Lydia, only Vincent knows. By the way, let's have that message that was with the money she sent to the Casons."

Though it was nearing the average family's dinner hour, as it was a Saturday, every alley downstairs was taken. No teams had appeared yet, but the attendants were already clipping cards lettered with the names of various organizations onto wires above the alleys. The bowlers were mostly couples and beginners, with a few solitary caglers like Mr. Kemper, who had the last left-hand alley to himself.

Mr. Kemper's shadow was sitting in one of the red-and-cream leather-and-chromium seats provided for spectators.

"Nothing stirring," he told Prevost. "Of course he spotted me when I tailed him here. He wanted me to come down and throw a few."

"We'll throw a few with him. And look after him for a while," Prevost said. "You can run along. . . ."

Bill was scowling at a seven-ten split. He threw, missed both pins, and transferred his scowl to Michael and Nicholas Prevost,

"What's the big idea, tailing me?" he demanded. "If you think I'll lead you to Sally you're nuts."

"Then you know we can't locate her?" Prevost said.

"Jay came back home and told me that before he decided he'd better go to work after all so his uncle wouldn't be too sore. And I'm worried about Sally," Bill said grudgingly. "I stayed cooped up in my room most of the afternoon, hoping she'd call. I finally got fed up and decided I needed exercise. And I'd better give that pin boy something to do."

He threw a strike and grinned complacently. The couple at the next alley had been eying them furtively, and their minds had plainly not been on bowling for some time. But now they bundled up their belongings, took their score sheet, and left.

Michael sat down in the curved booth behind the alley and looked at Bill thoughtfully. The room was warm and foggy with cigarette smoke, and Bill was sweating. Yet he wore not only a polo shirt but a heavy long-sleeved sweater. Michael closed his eyes and saw Mr. Kemper sitting on the porch outside the Shraders' dining room at ten o'clock at night with his shirt unbuttoned at the throat.

"I wonder," he said, rose, approached Bill unobtrusively, and suddenly grasped his right forearm. Bill yelped.

"Sh-h!" Michael said. "Inspector, was the glass neatly removed from that back door or were there a few jagged pieces sticking up from the frame that someone reaching in to unlock the door might scrape his arm on?"

"What back door? Oh, the one at Marcia's library?" Prevost stared at Bill, who was shaking his arm gingerly. "Would you like to step into the men's room and talk to me, Kemper? Or would you prefer to go to headquarters?"

"Neither one. You haven't any right to—"

"There's a little matter of fingerprints in the library, on the desk, to be considered, Mr. Kemper," Michael said helpfully.

"Fingerprints? I couldn't have left any. I mean, I've never been in Marcia's library!"

"Will you," Prevost said softly, "come where we can talk privately? Or shall I drag you out of here by the heels and down to headquarters?"

"I'll talk here," Bill decided hastily.

He stumped up the steps between the spectators' boxes and on toward the men's room. Prevost followed, whistling between his teeth: "It's both of my feet bound in the cell, My hands tied behind, God damn him to hell!" Michael, bringing up the rear, grinned expectantly.

"Five," he thought, "will get you ten that this time that safety-valve doesn't work."

Prevost kicked the door shut and turned to face Bill. "So Marcia surprised you in the library," he said. "And when you'd choked her enough and she was out cold you just went off and left her lying there. Someone might happen to come in and find her or she might come to and maybe be able to drag herself to the telephone. Why, you—"

Michael leaned back against the green wall and gave Prevost his earnest and admiring attention. Prevost not only had a remarkably extensive vocabulary of terms not used in polite society but he showed great discrimination in his application of them to Mr. Kemper. He did not raise his voice, but it became increasingly evident that in his youth there had been nothing to choose between his accent and Squiffy Bain's.

Bill's complexion changed slowly from red brown to brick red and finally took on a purplish tinge. "If you think you can talk to me like that," he bellowed and hung one on Prevost's jaw.

Prevost took the punch going away. He sank his right up to the wrist in Bill's stomach and, before he doubled up, caught him with a left to the chin that knocked him all the way across the green linoleum floor. Bill came to rest with his head and shoulders against a large trash can and decided not to get up.

"I'll—sue you!" he gasped painfully.

"On what grounds," Michael said blandly. "I am a witness, Inspector, that Mr. Kemper attacked you entirely without provocation. Resisting an officer, I'd call it, if not assault with intention to do bodily harm."

"T'anks," Nicholas Prevost said. He straightened his tie—unnecessarily. "You heard what Dundas said? Am I going to take you in and book you on suspicion of murder"—he did not quite say "moider" and, as he went on, slowly reverted to his usual way of speaking—"and hand out the news to all the newspapers? Or are you going to talk?"

"You don't know—"

"I can find out."

Prevost yanked Bill to his feet and removed him from his sweater. He pointed to a long fresh scratch on Bill's forearm.

"How're you going to explain that? Just where you'd scrape yourself on the glass left in that doorframe when you reached over to unlock it from the inside after you broke the glass."

"Probably he left some of his life's blood on the glass," Michael suggested. "There will probably be a report to that effect from the men who examined the library."

"They wouldn't miss anything like that. There was blood on the kitchen floor, and it looks like it wasn't all from the cut on Marcia's head. We can have it analyzed and maybe—"

"All right!" Bill said. "But get this straight—I didn't kill Lydia! And I was sorry about Marcia, but I lost my head. I mean, I didn't expect her to come to the library so early. When she came straight into the kitchen I grabbed her and—well, after that what could I do? It was accident she hit her head on the stove, and after that you wouldn't expect me to run to the police and tell 'em that I—"

"Never mind," Michael said hastily as Prevost began whistling again. "What was in that envelope you wanted from the library?"

"You seemed to have guessed this morning that Lydia loaned me money. That's what started Jay's and my row. Either he guessed or Lydia told him about the—the loan. Anyway, he did come up to borrow a razor blade, but just as I finished shaving he piped up: 'What's the emergency this time, and are you taking it all in twenties?'"

"He thought Lydia had drawn that fifteen hundred from the bank for you?"

"Evidently. I said: 'What do you mean?' and he said: 'Aren't you taking money from Lydia again?' And then I hit him."

"And how much, to put it vulgarly, did you get into her for?"

V

"Two thousand. Well—hell! Do you know how much operations like my mother's cost? Hospital bills and special nurses? A guy can't let his own mother die when she needs an operation, can he? Or let her go in the charity ward if he can manage anything else. And there was Lydia all sweet and sympathetic, and the money was just nothing to her and I must take it and not to worry about paying her back. But if I insisted on being businesslike of course I could sign an I.O.U."

"You poor little woolly lamb!" Mr. Dundas said witheringly. "To owe another man money is not pleasant, but to be in debt to a woman—*¡ni lo permita Dios!*"

"If that means anything like God help you, that's right," Bill said gloomily. "Think she'd ever let me forget it? Always getting in dirty little digs about it or hinting, so I was afraid Sally and the others would catch on. And, by gosh, I started to pay her back. I cleaned up in a poker game and I backed some long shots at Bay Meadows. I gave her a couple of hundred, but do you think she'd let me have that I.O.U.? Or even make some arrangement about me paying her back regularly so it'd be on a strictly business basis? Not on your life! She'd get kittenish and say: 'What's a little thing like that between friends?'"

"But she did tell you where the I.O.U. was?"

"Yes. That was when I said: 'Just suppose something happened to you when you're in your car, just for instance? It's going to look nice when they find that I.O.U. in your safe-deposit box.' And she laughed and said that was why she hadn't put it in her box and then she told me where it was."

"So you decided this morning that you were going to get the envelope before anyone else did, even if you had to break into the library," Michael said. "Though Lydia's heirs are not apt to press you for payment."

"Jay says Kirk's her executor."

"But you didn't know that when you broke into the library," Prevost pointed out. "Or if you did it wasn't Stanton who told you so that early."

"Well, Lydia made no secret who she'd left her money to. She wanted people to be grateful to her beforehand. And Kirk don't like me, and neither does Marcia. Marcia would've found that I.O.U. and showed it to Sally and then to the police. And you'd say that gave me a motive for killing Lydia. And I'm telling you this so you can't frame me for something worse. But you can't prove anything: even that there was an I.O.U."

"Naturally you'd burn it," Prevost said. Mr. Kemper smiled complacently. "And anything else that was with it. We know enough about Lydia now to realize she might have changed her will at any time without employing a lawyer and for the purpose of cutting Sally out of the new will. And you'd hate to see that happen to Sally, wouldn't you? What were you doing from about six-fifteen to six forty-five Thursday?"

"In the evening? Why? Oh well, let's see. Oh, that was the night I met Jay and Sally here. After I got through work I had dinner and then had time to kill before Sally could get here. So I went in to the Telenews. On Market, you know, across from Hale's. Their show only runs an hour, so that filled in the time."

"It filled it in very neatly," Prevost remarked. "Have you a typewriter?"

"Hell, no. What would I want one for? Jay says sometimes he's going to buy one, when he thinks maybe he'll try to write."

"Did Miss Courtney have one? Or Miss Rollins? There was none in the library, and I can't remember seeing one in the cottage."

"There isn't, that I know of. Anyway, Lydia said once she thought she'd get one, so she couldn't have had one. But why?"

"All right. If you've had enough exercise"—Prevost grinned briefly—"we'll take you home. It's on our way. Come along. . . ."

"And," he added when they reached the rooming house on Pine and Bill was out of the car, "if you find out where Miss Rollins is—"

"I'll let you know," Bill said ungraciously. "I don't feel like being helpful, but Sally's such a crazy kid. Yes, that from me—"

"Mr. Kemper, did you ever take Lydia to the Sky Room in the Empire Hotel or to the Top of the Mark?" Michael asked abruptly.

"Why, no. We just went where she wanted to. Almost as soon as we'd get settled one place she'd want to move on to another," Bill complained. "If a movie didn't happen to interest her she couldn't sit still and insisted on leaving. I don't care much about movies, but when I've paid my money I'm going to see what I paid to see.

"But when we first went around together I guess Lydia wanted to see everything because she hadn't been in San Francisco for a good many years. Is that all? Well, when you—when you see Marcia, tell her—well, say I'm sorry," he finished, turned, bolted up the steps into the rooming house.

"Say I'm sorry!" Prevost snorted. "Just like that! If I wasn't a cop and he didn't have that cut on his arm I'd— Well, let's get over to Vincent's while we can. That note Lydia sent to the Casons with that money—"

"And wasn't that a peculiarly Lydian stunt?" Michael said, heading back toward Broadway again.

"Hmm? Oh, I've noticed women often can't leave well enough alone. They have to be doing something. But that often goes for murderers of either sex. And Lydia's stunt worked."

"Yes, though she couldn't have known that it was going to be so easy to buy Cason off. That story in Thursday's paper frightened her. She recognized Margie's description and picture and learned her name. Then she turned to the only weapon she'd ever used very successfully: money. But what were you going to say about the note she sent with the money?"

"Oh, it was written on an old typewriter."

"Was it really? I told Mrs. Cason it was, but only to impress her."

"Well, it will be easy enough to identify the machine. And Vincent should be home."

But the door was finally opened by a very tall, very thin Negress wearing the latest thing in spring prints. Mr. Vincent, she informed them haughtily, would not be home for dinner, and she was just leaving.

Mr. Vincent had gone out to apologize to some of his friends he was afraid had been bothered by the police asking questions about him. And he had called back to say the Preedys wanted him to stay to dinner.

"We'll only keep you a minute," Prevost promised, stepping into the living room. "We want to look at Mr. Vincent's typewriter."

"His typewrituh? Oh—that. Well, Ah reckon y'all could do that," Astoria decided. "On account of it's right ovuh heah."

She dragged a battered portable from the lower shelf of a long table. "My, my! How dust do collect!"

"It doesn't look dusty to me," Prevost said.

He opened the typewriter, placed it on a table, and produced the sheet of paper Mrs. Cason had given Michael. He inserted it in the machine, quickly typed two lines, and nodded.

"It matches. We'll have to take this typewriter with us, Astoria."

"Ah cain't let y'all do that," Astoria protested.

"We'll explain to Mr. Vincent. You run on home," Prevost said firmly. "I'll talk to him later this evening. You don't want to telephone him, do you?"

"No suh! But Ah don't know," Astoria said mournfully, putting on a pair of long white gloves, "what things is comin' to with policemen in an' out all day long, askin' questions an' askin' questions. This keeps up, Ah don't know that Leroy—that's my husband—will think Ah should go on wo'king for Mistuh Vincent. Leroy, he don't 'prove of goin' ons like this."

"I'm sure he doesn't," Prevost said pleasantly. "May I use the telephone here? Where is it?"

"Right out in the hall, suh. Ah don't mind waitin'," Astoria said tragically. Michael looked at her, grinned, and put his hand in his pocket.

"The inspector can't give you this," he said. "But I am only a private citizen. For your trouble."

"No trouble a-tall, suh." Astoria whisked the money into a white oilcloth purse. "Ah sure does admire to see a gen'leman openhanded like—"

Prevost came striding back into the room, seized the typewriter, and made for the front door.

"Thank you, Astoria. Come on: we've got places to go in a hurry."

"Already?" Michael said, catching up with him on the front steps.

"Already," Provost said over his shoulder. "Just plain dam-fool luck. It might have taken days and it took less than two hours."

He dumped the typewriter into the car and slid into the front seat.

"Drive, will you? And fast. Yes, less than two hours, mainly because of a dog. They started over near Fleishhacker. The dog wouldn't be chased away, and he began digging, the way dogs do."

Michael had the car turned, and they were already approaching Polk Street. "Has this car a siren?" he inquired. "Oh yes. Then a lifelong ambition of mine is about to be fulfilled. I've always wanted to drive with an official siren wide open. Hold your hat, Inspector. . . ."

Less than half an hour later they stood in the waning light, ankle-deep in sand, in a section where houses were few and far apart. The salt smell of the sea was sharp and strong.

They looked into a shallow grave where a slight body lay, "wearing a brown skirt and sweater, an old brown coat, no hat." The hands were folded over the sweater, and there was a woman's fine linen handkerchief over the face.

PART SIX

This murderous shaft that's shot
Hath not yet lighted. . . .
MACBETH, ACT II, SCENE III

The siren was not going full blast, or at all, when they started back downtown. Michael drove carefully, even slowly, and it was some time before either of them spoke. Then Michael remarked:

"I'm beginning to feel that two hour sleep, a very light breakfast, two straight whiskies, and a cup of coffee are hardly sustenance enough for a day like this one."

"Hmm? I'm beginning to feel a little light-headed myself," Prevost admitted. "But I've noticed that the slim, wiry guys like yourself are still going strong when the beefy ones have wilted. Well, it's clear enough now. Margie was crossing the street—hurrying, I suppose—when Lydia's

211

car came speeding along it. Just where, we don't know. And we don't know that Lydia was driving. Well, you heard what the doctor said after just a superficial examination?"

"That the car must have struck Margie squarely? Her back was broken. That killed her even if she hadn't been—the doctor thought—hurled some distance along a street by the impact."

"Yes. Her head was injured so that it bled a little. Well, if anyone had been passing by, driving or walking along the street where it happened, Lydia Courtney would be alive today. But the general neighborhood out there is a quiet one where people are apt to be asleep before eleven-thirty."

"So they stopped the car and got out," Prevost went on. "They must have picked Margie up and carried her to the car, and that's how Lydia got blood on her coat and the car cushion. Also, they probably started driving on at once or someone would have seen them. But the girl was dead."

"And that," Michael said slowly, "is important."

"Naturally. If she— Oh." Prevost frowned. "You mean they seem to have been absolutely certain that she was dead?"

"I will give them the benefit of the doubt and say I don't think they would have buried the girl if they hadn't been sure she was dead."

"And the average person, with no great experience of death or injury, wouldn't be certain. Lydia wouldn't."

"Lydia wasn't. She still wondered if the girl had been past help."

"You're remembering what Miss Wendell overheard her say? That she kept seeing her and that sometimes she 'even wondered if—' She mentioned burial too," Prevost recalled.

"She also mentioned 'some of those awful stories of Poe's.' And premature burial did fascinate Edgar Allan, you know."

"Well," Prevost said, "someone knew the girl was dead. They'd been drinking. At least, according to Squiffy Bain, the car reeked of liquor. The police wouldn't miss that, and they'd killed a child."

"And the driver would be charged with negligent homicide or manslaughter," Michael said. "And tried by a jury that would be very unsympathetic."

"You can get one to ten years for manslaughter. And that expensive car of Lydia's would prejudice the average jury against her, and the fact that she'd killed a youngster would finish her with them.

"They must have realized all that," Prevost continued. "And no one knew what had happened. They could have left the girl's body in the street and run for it. But then the Accident Prevention Bureau would have started looking for the car that killed Margie."

"But if the girl simply disappeared it was doubtful that her disappearance would ever be traced back to them," Michael said. "So many girls like Margie vanish every year. And though we don't know just where the accident occurred, they were certainly in a neighborhood where all the sand dunes haven't been reclaimed. Probably, after putting her in the car, they drove several blocks before they made up their minds—or realized to what use the sand dunes might be put. Once they'd hidden Margie's body they were both in it up to their necks, whoever had been driving. Only silence would save their skins. But at the end of three days Lydia was ready to crack wide open, so she had to be disposed of."

"Yes, though at first she wasn't willing even to risk the minimum penalty, at the last, when she tried to see you, Lydia must have come to feel she could face it, that anything was better than sleeping with the light burning for the rest of her life—if she slept at all."

"But I doubt if she meant to come clean when she decided to try to see me. I think she still hoped she might wriggle out of it. I'd guess that first she would have tried to find out from me if she could get off by turning state's evidence and that I'd have had some trouble getting the truth out of her."

"Probably," Prevost said. "Well, you remember we were talking this morning about what was just a hypothetical situation then. But we agreed none of these people would want their lives interrupted."

"Even a short stay in jail certainly cannot be classed as a pleasant interruption in one's life. And people are inclined to look askance at anyone who's done time, regardless of why they've done it. The brand of jailbird would handicap the younger ones more than it would Kirk Vincent."

"But he wouldn't want his nicely arranged life interrupted. And he has some explaining to do. That letter to the Casons was written on his typewriter. I'm going to have it checked for fingerprints before I talk to him. And wouldn't I like to talk to Sally!"

"She should be able to tell you why Lydia came home fairly early Tuesday but left the cottage again."

"And you'd guess from what Miss Wendell heard that Lydia wanted Sally to go out with her."

"Have you given much thought to what Miss Wendell told us?"

"Of course I'm keeping it in mind. We just mentioned it. And what Lydia said then bears out everything we've been saying: that she couldn't forget what had happened Tuesday but wasn't prepared to face the consequences. She knew neither of them could talk without giving the other away."

"Yes. But," Michael said, "there was more than one reason why she couldn't bear to lie awake in the dark. And she said: 'It would be so much worse for me than you.'"

"She must have been driving the car," Prevost said wearily.

"No," Michael said flatly. "If she had been driving the car would she ever have decided to consult me? In that case she couldn't have wriggled out of it by turning state's evidence, could she? One will get you ten she was not driving the car when it struck Margie Cason."

"She may have meant she was a poor, weak woman, and a woman shouldn't have to go to jail because it would be so much harder on her than a man. Besides," Prevost pointed out, "when she started out to see you she may have meant to double-cross whoever was with her that night by claiming he was driving the car. It'd be his word against hers."

"That is possible—but I don't think so."

"I wish," Prevost said with commendable restraint, "that you wouldn't talk like a book detective. Lydia couldn't sleep because she kept seeing

Margie Cason—and no wonder. And she couldn't get that old poem about 'none shall know where he is gone' out of her head and—"

"That wasn't the only reason she kept the light on," Michael said irritatingly. "And remember that she said: 'I never have told anyone here. Only you.' It's eight o'clock. You'd better have dinner with me. Patton probably insisted that Valerie eat at the regular hour."

"Well—I will. I'll probably be glad I stopped for breath later on tonight. And I suppose," Prevost said rather wistfully as Michael headed toward Russian Hill Place, "that you'll catch up on your sleep? Unless you want to go with me to see Mark Shrader."

"If I pass that up to try to catch up on my sleep there is still Valerie to be reckoned with. She may stay me with flagons and comfort me with apples, but she will assuredly also pelt me with questions."

"I hope," Prevost said, "that her first question won't be: 'Who did it?'"

But when Valerie opened the living-room door her first utterance was simply a sigh of relief.

"It's about time you came. I've had a struggle to detain your material witness." She gestured toward Sally Rollins, sitting cross-legged on the chesterfield. "But there she is."

II

"All right, so I quit my job and so I caused you a lot of trouble," Sally said defiantly. "But how did I know—?"

"Of course you knew you shouldn't vanish for almost twelve hours," Prevost said with less than his usual patience. "Where did you go?"

"Out to old Aunt Mary's in Daly City. Sounds like a song, but I have an Aunt Mary and she is old and I'm very fond of her and so—"

"And so you chose the one day when the police were interested in your movements to go out to see your aunt?" Prevost said skeptically.

"It wasn't the way you make it sound! It—"

"Well, let that go now. Suppose we begin with Tuesday night around ten o'clock."

"Oh. How did you find out about that? But you wouldn't expect me to volunteer the information that Lydia came home at ten o'clock and I talked to her, would you?" Sally said reasonably.

"Why not?"

"Oh gosh, here we go again! Well, after you'd said Tuesday night was so important I wanted to think things over. I sez to myself: 'Sally,' I sez, 'don't talk too soon.' Then I thought maybe I'd never need to mention it at all, and that would save a lot of trouble. Because whatever happened to Lydia Tuesday must've happened after she went out again."

"You're sure of that?"

"She wasn't upset at ten o'clock," Sally said positively. "She sneaked into my room and woke me. I said something like 'I could kill you.' Well, she'd been drinking. She giggled and said she was good for hours yet and come on and go riding with Lydia, Sally."

"And you refused?" Prevost said.

"Yep. I love to drive fast at night in an open car, but the last time I'd gone with her we nearly had a head-on collision with another car that had right of way. That scared me, and I knew Marcia was right when she said we were damned fools. And I told Lydia so.

"She laughed like it was a great joke. And she was too nauseatingly cute for words. She said she'd had a little spat with her boy friend. I said: 'Who?' and she giggled and said: 'Wouldn't you like to know, Sally? Wouldn't you?' I said I wouldn't, and then I told her that wasn't going to get her any- where."

"Drinking, you meant?"

"Sure. But she wasn't tight enough that she didn't have some sense, Inspector. She'd closed the kitchen door so she wouldn't wake Marcia up. Or maybe she just thought it would be funny to put something over on Marcia. Anyway, I got up and shoved her into the kitchen, out of my room.

"I told her to go to bed quietly and not wake Marcia. She pouted, still being cute. Then she said she had to put her car in the garage. I couldn't stop her without a row so I let her go. I went back to bed. I told you she didn't wake me up when she came home, and that was the truth. She didn't really come home the first time."

Prevost grinned slightly and let this pass.

"And she never mentioned what had happened on Wednesday," Sally said. "And I didn't tell Marcia about it on Wednesday either."

"Why not?"

"Look, Inspector. If three gals are going to live together and get along at all, two of 'em had better not always be talking about a third behind her back. Though," Sally admitted, "I'd have talked plenty of times if Marcia had encouraged me to. And I guess she never let Lydia talk about me."

"And who did you think was the 'boy friend' she said she'd had a spat with, Miss Rollins?"

Sally hesitated. "Oh—oh, I guess you think I thought she meant Bill."

"And that gave you a very good reason for not wanting to tell us about your talk with Lydia Tuesday night, didn't it?"

"Yes," Sally said frankly. "I didn't want to get Bill into trouble. I wanted to think it over after I realized Tuesday night was so important. The way she said, 'Wouldn't you like to know?' made me think at the time she was dying to say it was Bill. But later I wondered if I'd coaxed her to tell me if she wouldn't have said it was Kirk. I mean, that would have surprised me, and maybe that was what she wanted."

"Why would it have surprised you?"

"He's managed to stay a bachelor, hasn't he? I never thought it was worth while to waste any wiles on him. He likes Marcia, but I can't see any reason why he should even dally with Lydia. However, you just can't tell about men."

"And you would also have been surprised if Lydia had told you that she had just left Mark Shrader?" Michael said.

"Mark Shrader? Gosh, I forgot all about him. But I would have been surprised," Sally said. "You didn't mention him this morning, but I guess you know about him being at the cottage once. Well, we understood his wife wouldn't like it."

"Did you see him again?"

"Me? No, though he hinted it would be nice if we went places some night when he managed to slip his leash again. I might have gone with him. He's a good Joe, and we might have had fun."

"And Lydia?"

"She talked a lot about him after we met him. She said wasn't it too bad if he had to marry money he hadn't found someone younger than Mrs. Shrader? Maybe she tried to see him; I don't know. But I didn't think he liked Lydia. She insisted on trying to talk art and about his work when he just wanted to have fun."

"And of course," Michael said, "it never occurred to you that Jay Stanton might have been Lydia's companion—who filled her with compliments, kisses, and gin and started her off on the road to roo-in—before ten o'clock on Tuesday?"

"You sound so heartless. And there's no reason Lydia should think that'd surprise or annoy me. Oh, don't look at me like that! I'd like to know how you manage to raise just one eyebrow."

"I practice ten minutes before a mirror every morning," Michael said. "And one personal question deserves another. Would you rather Lydia had been with Bill or Jay Tuesday night?"

"I haven't got any strings on either of them. But I don't mind telling you—I'm really old-fashioned. I'm as bad as Lydia. I want to get married. But all I expect is a square guy who'll put up with my faults if I'll put up with his. I haven't any romantic ideas about marriage. It's three meals a day and rings around the bathtub. And it's easy to fall in love."

Sally looked speculatively from Michael to Valerie and then at Nicholas Prevost.

"I know that with a few people it's 'this one or no other,'" she said shrewdly. "But with most people it depends more on propinquity than anything else. I've been practically in love lots of times, but I'm hardheaded enough to stop and ask if it's going to last, and so far the answer's always been no! Well, Bill is the knock-her-down-and-drag-her-off-to-your-cave type. Take me as I am or leave me—that's Bill. But if that's all there is to him it might get very tiresome after a while."

"I've only had one look at Mr. Kemper, but women are foolish enough to be attracted by excessive masculinity. As," Valerie added, smiling rather maliciously at her husband, "they sometimes are by simple unadulterated rudeness."

"Mr. Dundas certainly isn't a bit like Bill. But," Sally said thoughtfully, "he does give you the impression he'd just as leave sock a woman as not, if she annoyed him enough."

Prevost chuckled, and Mr. Dundas reddened. "Then don't, Miss Rollins," he said.

"Don't what?"

"Don't annoy me enough. I took off my hat when I entered the room."

"He means," Valerie translated, "that a gentleman never hits a lady without first removing his hat."

"Oh. Well, about Bill—I'd like to know if I'm really important to him and if anything is except getting ahead by hook or crook. And if he really does believe it's just that the breaks have always been against him or if he wonders sometimes if it's just *him*."

"What bad breaks has he had?" Prevost asked.

"Oh, having to go to work and help his mother, right out of high school. That was in '33, so you can see he had quite a time getting any job or keeping it for quite a few years. He's doing pretty well now. He is a hustler; I'll say that for him. He's got a nice enough business manner. But what he wants is a real-estate office of his own. And he's impatient."

"Aren't you all?" Michael said.

"Well, I'm twenty-four and sometimes I feel like I want to grab time and make it stand still. I have fun, but nothing much happens. I mean, I'm not getting anywhere. I guess Jay feels the same way: that time goes so fast and nothing worth while's happened to him yet. And then Kirk smiles and says: 'When you get to be my age you'll have something to complain about.' But Jay makes me so mad!"

"Why?" Prevost said.

"Oh, he's smart as a whip and hasn't any common sense. He's never even made a pass at me, but what he needs is a practical person like me to look after him. But, no: he has to think he's in love with Marcia because she seemed sort of mysterious. Well, it's in the evening papers about her being really Mildred Marcia Bondurant."

"Did that surprise you?"

"I knew already, but I wouldn't have told you, Inspector. It sort of came to me one day that might be who she was from little things she'd let drop. I mean, she knew too much about aviation and nursing. I looked up the crash in *Time*. There were little pictures of her and her brother.

"He was a swell-looking kid, but I gathered no one would have known that when they dug him out of the wreck. Marcia dreams about him," Sally said. "I've heard her muttering his name. So you couldn't have hired me to mention it or let Lydia tell me about it. She'd have loved to if I'd have given her an out by cross-questioning her.

"And I'd have loved to tell Marcia she was a fool not to get as far away from Lydia as possible. She's got guts enough that she'd have gotten back to normal by now if she hadn't had Lydia around to remind her of things. You can make a pest of yourself being grateful," Sally said.

"And though Lydia did buy that library for Marcia she barely makes a living from it, and Lydia wouldn't ever let anyone forget a favor she'd done them. She was always making suggestions about the library like she owned it. But one day when Marcia was half sick do you think Lydia would keep the library for her that day? Not on your life!"

"No, I don't suppose she would," Michael said almost dreamily. Prevost looked at him sharply, opened his mouth, and then closed it. "Did Marcia seem to expect that Lydia would?"

"N-no. Marcia didn't even ask her to."

For the second time that evening Patton entered the living room almost unceremoniously. Patton would never stoop to so plebeian a gesture as putting her hands on her hips, but the effect was the same as if she had.

"I beg pardon, Mr. Dundas! But you said that you would be ready for dinner in just a few minutes. So I did the best I could, hotting things up. And now they're dried out and I can't—"

"Coming!" Michael rose hastily. "If the ladies will join us perhaps Mr. Prevost would like to go on questioning Miss Rollins between bites."

III

Prevost helped himself to mint jelly and spread it over a lukewarm, overdone slice of spring lamb.

"I didn't have the nerve to bring up business while Patton was present or until I'd disposed of this salad," he confessed. "But—where did you have dinner Thursday night, Miss Rollins?"

"Dinner? I had a sandwich."

"Then why did you keep your six forty-five appointment waiting?"

"Who says I did? Dmitri? Look, that dame was never on time in her life until Thursday night. Yes, I took my time eating and got bawled out for it."

"Will they remember you wherever you ate?"

"I don't know. It was Wilson's at Sutter and Leavenworth, and a new girl waited on me. The place was full, but she might remember. Why? What happened Thursday night?"

"I haven't time to tell you. May I have the salt? Now, about that safe-deposit key."

Sally sighed. "I knew we'd get around to that. I was sorry I'd taken it the minute it fell out of my pocket. Especially when I saw it made Marcia suspicious of me. And I was going to put it back. . . . Well, I was! I'm always doing things on impulse and I almost always regret it. Which," Sally finished pertly, "is why I decided I'd better not be impulsive again and spill the works before I had time to think awhile.

"And I had plenty to think about. For one thing, Marcia was so icy toward Lydia after we got home from the Shraders' last night that I thought they had quarreled. Then this morning she made me sort of mad, talking about Bill like she did. Then she wouldn't tell you her right name or much about how she met Lydia, and I wondered why.

"I mean," Sally said, "I could see why she changed her name to begin with. And why she didn't want to talk about things if she could help it, but it seemed to me she was just inviting trouble by not coming clean with you this morning. Then there was that business of Lydia spilling coffee on her wrist that Marcia didn't seem to want to talk about. And I wondered why Marcia said she didn't think Lydia had been drinking Tuesday."

"That's all right," Prevost said. "We know Lydia had a shock between ten and midnight that would have sobered her up pretty well."

"Oh. I should have thought of that. But you can see why I was pretty much upset when I went to work. Then my nine-thirty appointment came in, wanting to know all about the nice murder. I blew up. I walked out of the place, had something to eat, and then tried to get in touch with Marcia."

"Why?"

"I'd decided I was a fool not to trust her. So I wanted to tell her what had happened earlier Tuesday night and explain about the safe-deposit key."

"Suppose you do, Miss Rollins."

"Oh, Costello let us fix ourselves up a little after he woke us and broke the news to us. I powdered my face at Lydia's bureau, and there was the key lying on it. I grabbed it without stopping to think. Then Costello hinted we'd better get back where he could keep an eye on us. So I didn't have a chance to put the key back before you came."

"But why did you take it?" Prevost said.

"I had a screwy idea I'd doll up in Lydia's fur coat and get a look in her safe-deposit box. I'll bet I could have pulled it off too. But then I sez to myself: 'Sally,' I sez, 'why stick your neck out for Bill Kemper? Would he do as much for you?' The answer was: 'No, he would not!'"

"Then you knew Lydia had loaned him two thousand dollars?"

"That much! Well, there's one born every minute, and I mean both Bill and Lydia. I don't blame him so much. One of the funny things about Bill is that he's really very fond of his mother. But do you suppose for one minute that Lydia wouldn't cast it up to me that she could do—and had done— more for Bill than I could?"

"I supposed she had," Michael said, smiling. "But apparently it didn't occur to Bill that Lydia would tell you about that little transaction."

"Bill thinks he knows a lot about women, but he's a babe in arms when it comes to figuring out how one woman's going to act to another woman. She didn't need to tell me: I got wise before she

did from the little digs she'd take at Bill that made
him so uneasy."

"Lydia could have set him up in business for
himself," Michael said thoughtfully.

"She mentioned that too. And—and I'll bet
Bill was tempted," Sally said drearily. "Only she
simply bored him to little bits. Well, I stood up
for him this morning, but Marcia was right about
him and so why should I try to break into Lydia's
safe-deposit box to get hold of his I.O.U.?"

"But Lydia didn't put the I.O.U. in her safe-
deposit box," Prevost said. "Did you think she
had?"

"Well, she said she had it in a safe place. So
naturally I thought that was what she meant."

"Kemper knew better. You haven't asked how
Miss Bondurant is."

"I was reading the afternoon paper when Sally
turned up, about six," Valerie said. "There is more
in it about Marcia's being Miss Bondurant than
about what happened to her at the library. But of
course Sally and I talked it over, and we called the
hospital. They were as soothing and noncommit-
tal as they always are. I made Sally stay here."

"I came here because when I still couldn't lo-
cate Marcia I wanted to talk to you, Inspector
Prevost, and not anyone else—except maybe Mr.
Dundas if he couldn't get hold of you for me. But,

look! Do you mean that Bill knocked Marcia out in the library?"

Prevost nodded. Sally sprang to her feet.

"Why, that—" She called Mr. Kemper a name no lady should know, let alone repeat. "So that's that, as far as we're concerned! If he'd do that to her—"

"I fancy your attitude is going to cause Mr. Kemper considerable pain," Michael said. "I imagine you will have a proposal of marriage from him in the near future."

"*That* proposal would be something new," Sally remarked cynically. "But do you—do you mean I inherit some of Lydia's money after all?"

"Why 'after all'?"

"Oh, when Lydia still thought I was one of the friends she'd been looking for all her life she did say she was going to leave her money to Marcia and me. But about—oh, a month ago, when we had a little row, she said: 'All right, if that's the way you feel, Sally Rollins! I can always make a new will.' And I said: "Okay, preshie, make the new will any time you want to.' So I supposed she had."

"And if her lawyer had made a new will for her it wouldn't do you any good to remove it from her safe-deposit box, would it?" Prevost said. "The lawyer would have a copy. But suppose Lydia had made a holograph will?"

"A—oh!" Sally clapped her hand over her mouth. "And have I put my foot in it! Well, it never occurred to me she'd just write another will without going to a lawyer, honest! But—had Lydia hidden Bill's I.O.U. in the library?"

"She gave Marcia a sealed envelope to keep there. I'm afraid we'll never know just what was in the envelope, Miss Rollins."

"He'd burn whatever was in it." Sally sighed and sat down again. "Give me a cigarette, somebody. I didn't think I had any illusions about people, but I feel like somebody had socked me in the stomach. It hasn't been long since Bill was telling me I really ought to try to be nicer to Lydia, not to cut my nose off to spite my face.

"But if Lydia would twit me with holding Bill's I.O.U. she'd let him know I wasn't going to get any of her money. And if she told him where his I.O.U. was she'd probably tell him where the new will was too. And he'd—well, here goes my mascara," Sally said, put her head down on the table, and burst into tears.

IV

Valerie came back into the dining room and announced that Sally was "putting on her make-up again, and when that's restored so will her morale be. And I want to tell you something before

she comes back. Squiffy telephoned this afternoon. Mr. Vincent has had work done on his car
at Squiffy's garage. He used to take it to the place
where Squiffy's mechanic worked before Michael
persuaded him to work for Squiffy. Mr. Vincent
has some sort of expensive foreign car, and this
man is a very good mechanic."

"He is," Michael agreed. "I can understand
Vincent following him from one garage to another. But has Squiffy ever talked to Vincent?"

"Yes, though he didn't know him by name. I
think Squiffy spends more time playing pinball
machines in a beer parlor than he does in the
garage. I didn't try to describe Mr. Vincent to
Squiffy because I didn't get a good look at him
last night. But Squiffy described Mr. Vincent to
me when he called.

"Squiffy said he'd only talked to him a few minutes, and that was about three months ago. Mr.
Vincent doesn't keep his car there or bring it in
for anything but a major operation. But—do you
suppose Mr. Vincent knows Squiffy's reputation?"

"The mechanic does. He is a law-abiding citizen, and I had to convince him that Squiffy didn't
want a garage merely as a front for extralegal
activities."

"Well then! The mechanic probably discussed
Squiffy with Mr. Vincent. And Lydia had a car,

too, and was new in the city, and while she hadn't needed any work done on the car yet—"

"She might have asked Vincent who kept his car in shape," Prevost finished. "And he told her and perhaps described Squiffy, just to make conversation. So when she wanted to have her car washed Wednesday she thought that a small-time crook like Squiffy could be depended on to keep his mouth shut for double pay. She thought she could buy almost anything. Just the same—"

He stopped and took a large white linen handkerchief from one pocket as Sally came back.

"Did you ever see this before, Miss Rollins?"

"It could be one of Lydia's." Sally took the handkerchief. "These cost about a dollar six bits at Livingston's, and she bought a half dozen like this lately. There's some grains of sand in it."

"Yes," Prevost said. "Around eleven-thirty Tuesday night Lydia's car struck and killed a young girl named Margie Cason. Instead of taking the girl to a hospital or going to a police station, Lydia and whoever was with her buried the girl in the sand out near Fleishhacker. That handkerchief was over the girl's face."

Sally, with a look of repulsion, dropped the handkerchief to the table. Valerie said sharply:

"They buried the girl in the sand?"

"Yes, Mrs. Dundas. Why?"

"Why—'why' doesn't apply in this case, does it?" Valerie said, smiling briefly. "Naturally it seems that if they—that it was a ghastly thing to do."

"So that was why Lydia couldn't sleep. And she was getting to the point where she'd spill the works one day," Sally said, "so she had to be killed. If I'd gone riding with her that night— But you don't know that I didn't, do you?"

"We won't go into that tonight," Prevost said. "It's after ten. Where do you want to spend the night?"

"I'm too tired to go way out to my sister's or brother's on the streetcar, and a taxi that far costs too much," Sally said thriftily. "I guess I'll go to the Y-dub. I'd like to get my pajamas and a toothbrush though."

"I'll take you to the cottage and on to the Y.W.C.A.," Prevost said. "But first, may I use the telephone again, Mrs. Dundas?"

He went out into the hall, and for several minutes they heard only the soft sound of his voice asking a question now and then. At last he said:

"All right; keep at it," and then: "Michael, could you come here?"

"What now?" Michael carefully closed the door into the dining room. "Is there a worm in the apple?"

"I'm afraid so." Prevost twisted his long legs about the telephone stool and leaned back against the wall. "I've been afraid something like this would happen, but there wasn't anything we could do to stop it. First, a fellow who owns a liquor store on Fillmore finally got around to letting us know that about a quarter of ten Tuesday night Lydia came into his place and bought a quart bottle of whisky."

"Which bottle, according to Squiffy, must later have been broken in her car."

"Yes, so that's one gap filled in. Costello went out to talk to the liquor dealer. And when he had he thought: 'Well, Lydia was in this neighborhood Tuesday night, and maybe she wasn't just driving through.' Costello's a good man. So he began going in and out of cocktail lounges on Fillmore.

"And in a place near Ellis he ran into something funny. The proprietor tends bar in the daytime, and he was sore because the fellow who works nights six nights a week hadn't showed up. Costello got the whole story out of him. This man Joe Tingley—was supposed to go to work at five.

"But," Prevost continued, "he came in then and told the proprietor he had to have a few hours off. He wouldn't say why. He worked until six-thirty, cleared out, and promised to be back by eight, but it was nine-thirty when Costello was in the bar. And the proprietor had found out Tingley isn't at his hotel. The proprietor has no idea Tingley's in danger. He's just sore and willing to talk about it.

"So he also told Costello that Tingley said he'd probably want time off next week to go up to Reno and get married. And, according to the proprietor, the reason Tingley hasn't married before is because he needed two hundred dollars."

"Oh?"

"Yes. Everyone who knows Tingley knows that his girl insisted he have two-fifty toward a nest egg and that he could never get that much together and hold onto it. It isn't much to go on."

"It's enough, when you also consider that Lydia was in that general neighborhood Tuesday night. And that she was fairly high at ten o'clock and, if Sally is telling the truth, had an escort before ten. I'd say the odds are that they did their drinking at some bar, and a bartender might remember Lydia and her escort. And Miss Wendell heard Lydia say, in some connection: 'I suppose he would remember.'"

"I know. She also said: 'It's too late now.' She may have meant Tingley would remember and testify that they had been drinking if they had to stand trial for manslaughter. That is, if whoever was driving did. So we've got to try to locate Tingley tonight."

Prevost uncoiled from the telephone stand. "Costello wants some pictures of the suspects. The proprietor of the bar says he never saw Lydia before, but Costello had no other picture to show him. He says there are some group pictures in Lydia's bureau."

Michael nodded. "I remember those. I imagine Vincent took them—in the living room at the cottage. And there was a sketch of Mark Shrader in a recent issue of the *Russian Hill Runt*. I'll see if I can find it, though he is easily described."

Prevost groaned. "You would bring that up. I wonder why I didn't go a-running to see him when you came to the hospital and told me what Miss Wendell said. Inspector Hunt would have. That is—"

"Don't let it worry you," Michael said. "Lydia did not address the person she was talking to as 'Mark' or even 'Kirk.' She really said, filling in the gap when she dropped her voice: 'I had to tell you that night at the Mark when you—'"

"The Mark? The Mark Hopkins Hotel?"

"Known to most San Franciscans as 'the Mark.'"

"Of course. It could be. But how would you finish that sentence?"

"I'd finish it: 'when you wanted me to go up to the Top of the Mark with you."

"Their sky room, you mean?"

"Yes. You go up in an elevator—nineteen floors. So," Michael said, "if I were you I wouldn't let that part of Miss Wendell's testimony worry me in connection with Mark Shrader."

"It's a good thing you're standing too far away to be conveniently kicked," Prevost said thoughtfully. "Well, Shrader and Vincent will have to keep until tomorrow. I'll take Sally over to the cottage and get those pictures. . . ."

Sally curled up beside Prevost on the front seat of the car with her head tucked down on her shoulder. He thought she was preparing to doze, but when they were away from Russian Hill Place she said in a very wide-awake voice:

"Why do you suppose Mrs. Dundas froze up there at the last? She'd been friendly all the time I was there, and I like her. But after you showed me that handkerchief I thought was one of Lydia's— No, I just don't get it."

"She was probably only tired," Prevost said quickly. "You must be too. And by the, way, I never let you finish telling me why you decided to visit your aunt Mary today."

"Oh, after I'd tried to locate Marcia and couldn't I called my sister in case she'd read the newspapers and was worried. But she hadn't, and her newest baby is teething, which means Sis is even less interested than usual in national or world events.

"She took the murder in stride and told me Aunt Mary was very poorly and one of us should go to see her. And since I'd quit my job, why didn't I? So I thought: why not? I was still in a dither and didn't want to be questioned again for a while or until I could talk to Marcia.

"So I told Sis to forget she'd talked to me if anyone asked and hiked out to Aunt Mary's," Sally ended cheerfully. "It takes a long time to get out there, and I didn't leave until five, except to call the cottage from the nearest drugstore to see if Marcia was back there. I just listened to Aunt Mary talk about her neuritis and had time to make up my mind about a lot of things."

"Next time you want to go out to Daly City to do your thinking let us know," Prevost said. He stopped the car in front of the wooden door on the street below the cottages. "I believe you have some photographs of all of you taken here," he added, following Sally through the door and up the first flight of steps. "I'd like to borrow them."

"You mean the ones Kirk took one night? Yes, he made copies for all of us."

"Then he isn't in any of the pictures?"

"He let Jay take one so he's in it. My copies are somewhere in my bureau. I'll— Well!"

Jay Stanton was sitting hunched up on the cottage steps, singing in an absent-minded sort of way. "'The garment makers' union is a no-good union,'" he chanted with a strong Hebraic accent. "'It's a company union by the boss. The Wallmans and the Thomases are making us promises And giving to us the double-cross.'

"Oh, hello, Sally. I wandered over this way, thinking you might be here, and I was resting awhile before I started home."

V

Once out of bed, Mr. Dundas had been known to shower, shave, and dress in ten minutes flat. But when it came to getting into bed there were times when he was a putterer.

So tonight it had taken him half an hour to remove shoes, shirt, and necktie, wind his watch, look over his small change, remove five books of matches from his pockets and stack them neatly on the bureau, read three old letters, and tear up two advertising circulars.

That done, he approached the mirror and gazed at himself thoughtfully. "Where," he said, "is my Christmas pie?"

"Little Jack Horner?" Valerie said. "Oh, what a good boy am I?"

"Exactly."

"Yes, so far you have cooperated beautifully with Mr. Prevost. And I'd continue to do so. If you stick in your thumb and pull out any plums you'd better show them to him."

"So far no plums have fallen my way. My theories are my own, based on evidence Prevost has too. I do want to talk to Marcia tomorrow."

"Shall I ask her to come here when they let her leave the hospital?"

"If you like," Michael said inattentively. He was looking at her reflection in the mirror as she lay in bed with her brown hair, curling and gold-tipped at the ends, spread out over the pillow. "You don't look twenty-four," he said abruptly. "You don't even look twenty."

Valerie giggled. "'Just a baby yourself,'" she said. "Oh, don't glare at me. I solemnly promise that if anyone ever tells me in those words what a young-looking mother I am I will make an impolite noise. Are you going to design me some beautiful maternity costumes?"

"You're an optimist, my dear. Even I can't design a garment that will hide your guilty secret four or five months from now. You won't be so well pleased with yourself then. But if you ever purchase one of these box-pleated jacket dresses that fairly shriek approaching maternity I'll put it in the furnace. You aren't listening to me."

"No. I— Come here, please. I want to ask you something."

Michael came over and sat down beside her on the bed. "Well?" he said when she hesitated.

"Well—is this going to be one of—of *those* cases?" She touched the scar on one of his lean, muscular shoulders. "I mean, one of the cases where someone takes a shot at you?"

"No, darling. I give you my word. You must see that it's very obvious to everyone that I've already told Prevost everything I know."

"Not your theories."

"You're the only one who knows I have a theory. And I promise you I won't give anyone reason to believe I have not confided in Prevost or that it would do any good to remove me from the scene. Will that do?"

"Um-hum."

"Well then." He bent down and kissed her. "Now, what else is worrying you?"

"Well, I liked Sally. But—Michael, if I hit someone when I was driving I wouldn't feel I was qualified to pronounce that person dead even if I was almost certain he was. You—you wouldn't bury someone if you weren't certain. At least, I can't think even the person who was with Lydia Tuesday night would do that. That first death wasn't really murder, and I think they just lost their heads. But—Sally started out to be a nurse."

"Oh, that's it?"

"Yes, she was in training for more than a year. She didn't finish because her mother needed her and she thought it was a pretty hard life, anyway. But she was certainly in the hospital long enough to have plenty of practical experience."

"Yes, in some hospitals they go on the floor when they've only been in training six weeks or so."

"And—suppose Sally did have a gun? Her father was in the army in the last war. He might have kept his service revolver. And she told me she slept in the same room with Lydia last night."

"So that Marcia could get some sleep—Sally said."

"She mentioned that and that Lydia kept a light burning. She said nothing could keep her awake. But suppose she insisted on sleeping in Lydia's room so she could watch her? Suppose she did watch and follow her? If she felt she had to kill Lydia it would certainly be better for Lydia to be found dead anywhere but in the cottage. Well?"

"We've talked a good deal about someone watching Lydia from the outside—but it would have been so much simpler for someone to have watched her from inside that cottage. Oh lord! What now?"

"Doorbell," Valerie said. "Perhaps the inspector had an afterthought—"

Michael sighed, shrugged into a dressing gown, padded through the hall and living room, and opened the front door to Mark Shrader.

"I hope," Shrader said diffidently, "that I didn't get you out of bed. If you want me to go away—"

"So long as you're here you'd better come in," Michael decided. "Though it is rather late, don't you think?"

"Couldn't slip out earlier without m'wife knowing it," Shrader said frankly. "She's gone to bed."

"But she does allow you to have a latchkey?" Michael said rather nastily.

Shrader stroked his beard and looked grieved. "Don't blame you for sayin' that. Pet poodle on a leash, that's what I am. Sold my soul for a mess of pottage. Oh, m'wife's a good sort. Don't know that I'd have been any happier married to a young woman I'd have been jealous of. Probably have quarreled all the time. Financial worries very trying to the temper, y'know.

"M'wife and I never quarrel. Married her so I could devote my life to painting without having to worry about the rent. So far it hasn't worked out too well. But if I live long enough I'll turn out my masterpiece yet. . . . But that's by the way. I've jumped a foot every time the doorbell rang this afternoon since Kirk telephoned."

"That was thoughtful of Mr. Vincent," Michael said.

"I'd do the same for him." Shrader chuckled briefly. "Kirk used to have a likin' for good-lookin' married women. The kind that know it's all a game and play it accordin' to the rules."

"But their husbands, unfortunately, didn't always know the rules or approve of them? And you'd warn him in time?"

"Something like that. Then he'd go fishin'. Saves trouble all around," Shrader said simply. "Well, Kirk warned me you and this police inspector had found out I knew Lydia Courtney and her friends better than I wanted to admit. Couldn't believe my luck when this inspector didn't appear while m'wife was around. Understood you're hand in glove with him, so when m'wife finally went to bed, decided to talk to you."

"Well?"

"Not very helpful, are you?" Shrader complained. "I don't know what you want to know."

"Miss Courtney referred to you as 'Mark' before we went to look at your paintings," Michael remarked.

Shrader raised his eyebrows. "Is that important? People use first names as soon as they're introduced—if they're introduced. But the girl called me 'Mr. Shrader' to my face. I think she was only trying to—well, to—"

"Impress me? That was my idea at the time," Michael admitted. "You might be called a celebrity, and she struck me as the type who refers to celebrities by their first names even if she's never met them."

"That's it. Immodest of me to suggest that, though. Well, Kirk told you I met the girl and her friends at her cottage."

"Yes. Did anything that happened that night stand out in your mind?"

"Nothing. Very pleasant evenin'. Seemed like a congenial group to me. Miss Courtney struck me as an unhappy sort of person. Always wantin' more attention than she was getting, y'know."

"Yes. But you saw her again?" Michael said.

Shrader eyed him speculatively. "Do you know or are you guessing? Well, I took a notion one day to do some work in that little park on Taylor. She happened to pass by and see me. Stopped and talked, couldn't get rid of her. Said she'd like to see my paintings."

"And hinted she might buy one?"

Shrader nodded. "Definitely. I told you m'wife bullies people into buying now and then. Always puts the money in the bank when she does. Tries to keep up the fiction that I help out with the household expenses."

Michael's grin was not wholly unsympathetic. "So when you do sell a picture you never see any of the purchase price?"

"That's it. Well, m'wife was going to a meeting one afternoon. This was—oh, two or three weeks ago. Arranged to let Miss Courtney in myself. Side door, y'know. Showed her over the studio. No one bothers me there. She bought a picture and gave me a check. I thought that was the end of it."

"Wasn't it?"

Shrader grimaced. "I happened to mention this party m'wife was planning. Miss Courtney wanted an invitation. Don't know why anyone would want to come to one of m'wife's parties, but apparently people do. The girl phoned me several times. Persisted. Couldn't have that, y'know. She didn't come right out and say what she wanted, but I finally realized what she was drivin' at."

"What did you tell her?"

"The truth. That m'wife wouldn't have approved of me going to that cottage with Kirk or sellin' a painting without consultin' her. But I promised to see that she and her friends got invitations to the party and left it to Kirk to get them."

"Then you didn't see Lydia a second time when any of the others were present—until last night?"

"No. Had hopes of seein' them all again. Took quite a fancy to the Sally girl," Shrader said candidly. "Anything else I could tell you?"

"Where were you Tuesday night? And on Thursday evening around six-thirty? What time do you have dinner?"

"Seven o'clock. And I was paintin' like mad all last week. Invitations for a party out, and m'wife decides there aren't enough canvases to make a good showing in the salon. Had to do three more in a hurry. That's art for you."

"And when did you do the sand dunes?"

"Hmm? Oh, Wednesday. Ran out of inspiration. Not my type of thing, but they filled a corner. Think you can live with 'em?"

"I think so. I'll tell Inspector Prevost what you've said," Michael promised. "He probably will still want to talk to you, but I'm sure he'll try, if possible, to talk to you without letting your wife know about your lapse from grace."

"Might make an excuse to see him at Kirk's," Shrader said hopefully. "M'wife doesn't approve of Kirk as a companion for me, but of course she is curious about this affair. She— but you want to go to bed. I'll take myself home. . . ."

Michael locked the front door, put out the lights, and went back to the bedroom, hoping to find it dark and Valerie asleep. But the bedside lamp was still on and her eyes wide open as she lay frowning at the ceiling.

"I know: it was Mr. Shrader," she said. "I got up and peeked into the living room. I heard you ask him where he was Thursday around six-thirty. Why?"

"Lydia had a conversation then with the person who later killed her. And most of Lydia's side of the conversation was overheard by Miss Wendell, who lives above them on the hill."

"Oh. Well, do you remember what you were doing on Thursday night?"

"I worked late and asked Patton to have dinner at seven-thirty instead of seven."

"And I'd been in all afternoon," Valerie said. "I hadn't had my exercise, so I decided to take some books back to Marcia's library. It was a little after six-thirty when I got there—maybe as late as a quarter of seven. But there was a sign on the library door: 'Back in ten minutes.'"

"Oh," Michael said bleakly. "And was she away from her dismal cloister only ten minutes?"

"I don't know. I waited about five before she turned up. She was very apologetic. She had a paper bag in her hand, so she must have been to the grocery store. She said that since she opened the library at eleven she got only one proper meal a day: breakfast."

"And Lydia had upset coffee over her at break-fast that day."

"Yes, I remember her wrist was bandaged. She said she'd gotten to the point where she felt she must have a cup of tea and something to eat. But when she got there—to her kitchen—the cupboard was bare, so she decided to run over to the nearest grocery store. There is one just up the street. I don't think it means anything, but I suppose you and Inspector Prevost have been taking for granted it couldn't have been Marcia who was talking to Lydia about six-thirty Thursday. So—"

"You should tell us these things," Michael said unreasonably.

"I could bear to be told a few things myself," Valerie retorted. "I didn't know—"

The telephone rang in the hall. Michael plugged in the bedroom extension.

"Why," he said, "couldn't Mr. Bell have left well enough alone? Yes? . . . No, I haven't gone to bed yet. . . ."

VI

Jay followed Sally and Prevost into the cottage and made himself comfortable on the big couch.

"Where," Prevost said, "have you been this eve-ning? How did you get here?"

Jay rubbed his big bony nose and grinned. "Was someone keeping an eye on me? I went to work after two-thirty, you know. I supposed I'd have to make up time by working until eight. But Uncle Job hauled me off about five-thirty to talk to me in a fatherly way about choosing my friends more carefully in the future. Meaning you, Sally."

"Hauled you off where?" Prevost said.

"Home with him. He lives on Pacific, not very far from the pharmacy. If I did have a little shadow you can't blame him for losing me, Inspector. Uncle Job's house has more than one door, and I didn't leave by the front one. I didn't stay to dinner—by request. Uncle Job and I had words. You'd think that I deliberately and with malice aforethought got myself suspected of murder. As I said to him: 'H.I.B.K.—'"

"What!" Prevost said.

"Had I but known. Don't you ever read mystery stories, Inspector?"

"I didn't know you ever read any modern ones," Sally remarked. "I thought when you weren't reading Saroyan, Hemingway, Faulkner, and stuff, you stuck to Edgar Allan Poe and Conan Doyle."

"But I do read Ogden Nash. As I said to Uncle Job: 'Had I but known what grim secret lurked behind that smiling exterior I would never have set foot within the door.' This door, I mean. And while I wouldn't say Lydia had exactly a smiling exterior—"

"You've seen tonight's papers," Prevost guessed.

"Yeah. After I walked out on Uncle Job I had dinner on Polk and then went into the Royal Theater. Anything was better than going back to my room too early. The evening editions of the morning papers were out when I came out of the Royal. They tell about you finding the body of that girl out in the sand dunes."

"You can't start a search like that and not have reporters get wind of it. And though I told them as little as possible they know I'm on the Court-ney case."

"Well, everything's clear enough to me now, and I don't like it. Though I don't know why, when people all over the world are dying like flies, we get worked up over Lydia's death. Or even that girl's. Think of all the trouble she's been spared. She was fourteen and she might be blown to pieces by a bomb before she's twenty-four. 'Duncan is in his grave—'"

"Come out from behind those boils, Job; we know you," Sally said impatiently.

"I'm not putting on an act," Jay said. "That's the way I feel. After I read the paper I felt less then ever like going to bed. I decided to walk it off. I thought maybe Kirk might still be up, but

his house was dark. So I wandered over here on
the off chance you might be home, Sally."

"Did you want to talk to her?" Prevost asked.

"If he has anything to say to me he can say it
right now, before you."

Jay raised his eyebrows. "Like that, is it? We
don't trust each other? Well, you asked for it, pet.
I'm afraid Lydia made another will."

"Is that all?"

"All, she says! A cool two or three grand a year.
Kirk tells me the will her lawyer has was drawn
up two or three months ago, and this happened
last month. Don't ask me what day or date. It was
March and it was raining, and when wasn't it raining in March?

"But we were all to have spaghetti here that
night. I suppose you and Bill were bowling or
roller skating, Sally. Marcia and Kirk hadn't come
in yet, so Lydia was alone. She'd been writing. Her
face was sort of flushed and she looked angry."

"I know: with her mouth drawn up tight. And
we had a row one morning when we were going to
have a spaghetti supper. She thought squabs and
wild rice would be nice. Go on, Jay."

"Well, she finished writing and said: 'There!
That's going to be a sad shock to two people.'
Then she laughed and asked if I'd like to witness

her will. I asked her what she paid a lawyer for. She said she was quite capable of drawing up a will that would hold in court, that it wasn't the first one she'd ever written herself.

"She said that while this one didn't need to be witnessed she'd like me to sign it. You know how she'd persist about some little thing she'd set her mind on? So I didn't argue. She put her hand over the last part of the sheet of paper, and I signed my name. All I saw of the top part was Marcia's name.

"I wanted to tell you about it, Sally, because I don't know what you'll want to do. Begin looking for that will or take a chance she destroyed it and it won't turn up. If it does and you aren't one of the legatees it's going to be—"

"I don't think she needs to worry. It's not likely that holograph will will ever turn up."

"No," Sally began, "because—"

Prevost frowned at her warningly. He felt that there was nothing to be gained now by telling Jay that Bill had broken into Marcia's library. He was not in a mood at this moment to listen to Jay's indignation or to restrain him from rushing back to the rooming house to try to avenge Marcia.

At least he supposed that was the line Jay would take, and another free-for-all in the rooming house at this hour of the night was an unnecessary complication.

"Since there are no close relatives to contest the will Dawson made for Lydia, it will probably never be questioned," he added. "Miss Bondurant won't object to sharing with Miss Rollins. You didn't even read the will Lydia wrote, and even if you had, Mr. Stanton, I don't know that your testimony would be enough to deprive Miss Rollins of her legacy."

"So I'd better forget all about it?" Jay said. "I will—and that's all, Sally."

"But I want to ask you another question, Miss Rollins," Prevost said. "When Lydia decided, after all, that she didn't want to put her car in the garage around ten Tuesday night or come home and go to bed, would she have been apt to get in touch again with the person she'd quarreled with before ten? That is involved."

"Oh, I get it." Sally frowned. "And I just don't know. Lydia was fairly high and feeling kittenish. If she got her feelings hurt when she was sober she was usually dignified for a while."

"But then she'd decide to ignore it and act as if nothing had happened, though that didn't mean she'd forget it," Jay said. "I didn't know she came home and then went out again Tuesday night."

"She did. And when she said she'd had a little spat with her 'boy friend' she seemed to think it was more funny than anything else. That was because she'd been drinking. So she might have taken a notion to make up with the 'boy friend' before she went to bed. You just can't say."

"And," Jay said gloomily, "if it was that way she might have hunted up someone else to finish out the night with. Me or Bill. I might as well say the front door of our place isn't ever locked until eleven o'clock, and she knew where our rooms are."

"She'd think tiptoeing upstairs to Bill's room— or down the hall to Jay's—was 'daring.' I told you that when she was drinking she wanted to do things she thought were. And," Sally said impersonally, "I suppose to keep her quiet and from waking up the rest of the house, you and Bill might have given in and gone out with her. Well, shall I hunt up those pictures for you?"

"If you would. How far did you get in medicine, Stanton?" Prevost said as Sally left the living room.

"Medicine? How did you know—? Oh, I flunked out my second year. Second year after I graduated from college, that is. I took my B.S. first. And Uncle Job says the only reason I didn't make the grade was because my heart wasn't in it."

"Is that true?"

"Well, I don't wear my key, but I'm a Phi Bete," Jay said, flushing. "If that answers your question.

My father always said I wasn't cut out to be a doctor, and he was one so he should have known. But when he died Uncle Job was determined there was still going to be a Dr. Stanton. It's too bad he didn't have Bill for a nephew."

"Did Kemper want to be a doctor?"

"Not having enough money even to go to college, he never even considered it. But if he'd had Uncle Job to foot the bills he might have thought it would be a good money-making racket. And Bill is the sort that others' pains would never bother. He drove an ambulance for a while."

"Oh, did he!"

"Why does that interest you?" Jay inquired. "He's done a lot of things since '32 or '33. Someone who had a pull with some hospital got him the job. I guess that's where he got to driving the way he does. And he saw a lot of nasty accidents and apparently never turned a hair. He— What's the matter with you, Sally?"

"You wouldn't know, would you, preshie?" Miss Rollins said venomously. "Mother's little helper! Can't you think up a few interesting details about my past to tell the inspector? And you've seen at least one nasty accident yourself."

"I don't know what it's all about, Sally."

"You know what the inspector is driving at! And so do I. And that time when you went up—"

"Telephone," Jay interrupted. "Is someone supposed to be here?"

"I'll get it," Prevost said. "There was a man here until we located Miss Rollins. Then I sent him off. Hello! . . . Yes, this is Nick Prevost. . . . What? . . . Where? . . . Then I'll be there in a few minutes."

He put the receiver down, lifted it again, and dialed a number.

"Get your things and those pictures, Miss Rollins," he said over one shoulder. "I'm taking you to the Y.W. as quickly as possible and I'll finish talking to you two tomorrow. Michael? . . . Have you gone to bed yet? . . . Then I'll be by for you in about ten minutes. They've located Joe Tingley. . . ."

PART SEVEN

. . . bear welcome in your eye,
Your hand, your tongue: look like the innocent
* flower,*
But be the serpent under't.
MACBETH: ACT I, SCENE V

"Do you," Inspector Maxon inquired genially, "want to view the scene of the crime?"

He was a round, brown bear of a man with a big, furry voice. A cigar stub resided permanently in one corner of his mouth, and his derby was always one size too small for him. But he was a shrewd, hard-working police officer and he liked and admired Nick Prevost.

"Do we need to?" Prevost said wearily.

"I don't see why. It was like this. There's a small park less than a block from this hotel, you know."

Prevost nodded. "At Steiner, you mean?"

"Yeah. About ten o'clock a guy was walking through there. He saw this fellow sitting on a bench, hat down over his eyes, head on his chest, like he was asleep. The first guy was tired so he sat down, too, hit against the arm of the man he thought was asleep, and he toppled: just like that. Come to find out, someone sitting beside him on that bench had stuck a gun in his ribs and let him have it.

"They sent me out before the precinct men had moved him and looked through his pockets and found out he was Joe Tingley, a bartender, and lived in this joint."

Inspector Maxon waved a hand about the lobby: small, poorly lighted, furnished with four cracked leather chairs, two tarnished spittoons, a small desk, and one lanky avocado plant in a large pot.

"I came right over here. I knew you'd wanted to locate Tingley, but I'd hardly got here before Costello came in. Came back, that is. Seems Tingley was his discovery, and he was still looking for him. He said he knew where to get in touch with you. From what he told me, I'd say this is part of the Courtney case, though you can judge that for yourself. Costello went to bring in Tingley's boss. The woman's upstairs. We might as well go up there.

"She came in right after Costello," Maxon explained as they went up the thinly carpeted stairs to the second floor. "Tingley's girl friend, Babe

Johnson. The hotel manager—he acts as desk clerk too—knows her. She went to pieces when I told her Tingley was dead, so the manager brought her up here. She knows something."

He knocked perfunctorily and opened a door near the head of the stairway. A plump blonde woman was sitting on the rickety bed, her small blue straw hat pushed to the back of her head. What had been a crisp, perky veil was limp and bedraggled, as if she had wiped her eyes on it. A small man with a sallow face that was all unhappy vertical lines perched uncomfortably on the edge of a very uncomfortable chair, watching her anxiously. Seeing Inspector Maxon, he cleared his throat warningly.

"Uh—Babe? Maybe you feel like talking now."

"She'll talk," Maxon said. "She'd better. Come on, sister—what did you mean when you said: 'Oh, I shouldn't have let him'? Who were you and Tingley blackmailing?"

"Who were we—?" Miss Johnson squared her shoulders, sat erect, and finally got to her feet. "What do you mean: who were we blackmailing?"

"Now, sister! Don't try to tell us you and Tingley weren't in this together," Maxon said. "You've called here twice, trying to locate him since eight o'clock. You knew what was cooking and wanted to find out what had happened."

"Wise guy, hunh?" Miss Johnson said unpleasantly. "Well, I was all set to play ball, but no flat foot can talk to me like that and get away with it. I'm going home."

"We can't let you do that, Miss Johnson," Prevost said in his softest voice. "Not until you've told us what you know."

Miss Johnson picked up a heavy glass water pitcher and flung it at his head. No batter ducking a bean ball ever hit the dust more quickly than Nicholas Prevost did the floor. The pitcher broke against the wall, and a piece of flying glass nicked him on the temple.

Maxon made a snorting noise like a bull pawing the dirt and charged Miss Johnson. He got her flat, heavy purse across his face before she kicked him neatly in the shins and drove her elbow into his middle. Inspector Maxon said: "Oof!" and wrapped his arms about his belly.

"That," said Miss Johnson, "will teach you to insult a self-respecting working girl." She eyed Michael, who was standing in the doorway, scornfully. "Out of my way, you little squirt," she said and reinforced the command with a sweeping side-arm slap.

Mr. Dundas' head snapped back, and he bit his tongue. His pupils dilated until his eyes looked black. He caught the woman's arm as she started through the door, spun her around, and connected with a straight left to her chin. Miss Johnson staggered back to the bed, cast herself on it, and wept.

"Well," Prevost said after a minute, dabbing at the scratch on his temple, "that's done it."

"Yes," Michael said calmly, massaging his knuckles. *"Por Dios,* must you call out a riot squad to detain an important witness? Where's what's-his-name? Under the bed?"

"M-me?" said the hotel manager, venturing out from where he had taken shelter to one side of the bureau.

"You. If you've any liquor handy, suppose you produce it now. Miss Johnson! I am a private citizen, so if you want to sue me, more power to you—though I'm sure we can settle this amicably out of court. Just now nothing is so important to me as hearing your story so that I can go home and to bed. And I'm sure you don't often act like this. It's the shock of learning that Mr. Tingley has been murdered, coupled with Inspector Maxon's completely unwarranted accusations."

Maxon had finally recovered his breath, but he only grunted disparagingly and let this pass. Miss Johnson hiccupped twice, sat up, and laughed shakily.

"You're right: I just went haywire. I was all primed to go off half cocked, and what he said did it." She looked at Michael admiringly. "Can you beat it? Though my dad was a little, dark guy like you, and did he make Ma stand around! No hard feelings?"

"None," Michael said.

Inspector Maxon muttered something that sounded like: "Generous guy!" and the hotel manager came trotting back with a bottle of muddy-looking whisky. They took turns drinking from the bottle. Then Miss Johnson wiped her eyes on the back of her hand and said grimly:

"All I really want is to get my hands on the dirty bastard that got Joe. I know Joe was up to something fishy, but he didn't mean no real harm. He just wanted two hundred bucks, and that was my fault. He couldn't hold onto money. I wouldn't ever stop working, but I wanted some furniture, paid for, and a little extra in the bank for rainy days before we got married. I had two-fifty and wanted him to match it. And he only had fifty that I know of."

"Do you mean," Michael said, "that he was only asking two hundred dollars for—well, what did he have to sell for two hundred dollars?"

"I don't know. He talked to me about eleven from Ted's lunch counter, where he always ate breakfast."

"Did he read a newspaper with his breakfast?"

"Hmm? Oh, sure, an afternoon paper."

"There's an afternoon paper with that picture of Lydia Courtney in his room," Inspector Maxon said.

"Well, he told me he thought he knew where he could get two hundred bucks," Babe Johnson said. "He said he was just going to do somebody a favor, and there's no sense in asking for more than you can get, and almost anyone can raise two hundred bucks if they got to."

Michael looked at Prevost. The inspector sighed.

"It doesn't help," he said. "Go on, please."

"Well, I guess most people can borrow that much from a loan shark if they got a job, but I asked Joe if this person he was going to do a favor for had that much money. Joe said he didn't know. He might have to settle for less or be able to raise the ante, but he couldn't explain over the phone at the lunch counter. And he had to scour around to find out how to get in touch with this person. He never said 'he' or 'she' that I remember. He said he didn't even know if he could do it by phone, but the drugstore up the street had a city directory."

"We'll check on that—and whether he used their phone," Maxon promised.

"He didn't use our telephone," the hotel manager said. "I saw him come back in around eleven-thirty this morning. He went up to his room and changed his clothes and went right out again. I don't know what time he came back—if he ever did. Somebody sitting in the lobby this afternoon might know."

"That can wait," Prevost said. "Had Tingley ever gone in for—for this kind of thing before?"

"You can call it blackmail," Babe said wearily. "But how could he? Oh, things happened when he was working. Like he'd see some floozie pick up a well-dressed guy that was half seas over, and Joe'd wonder what the poor dope would think when he woke up."

"Did he ever tell you about seeing some couple quarrel in the cocktail lounge until one of them walked out on the other one?" Michael suggested.

"But that happens all the time."

"Well, did Tingley have a good memory for names?"

"Joe? He always remembered names. That's one reason he was popular with the customers."

"But he hadn't mentioned anything that happened Tuesday night and stuck in his mind?" Prevost said.

"Not a thing, and I saw him Wednesday. I work from eleven to seven, so I didn't see him today. I went back where I live and waited for him to call me up. Come eight o'clock I begun to get nervous. I called here and the bar and finally came over here."

"I know. And you can go home now, Miss John-son." Prevost turned to the hotel manager. "If Costello has arrived with Tingley's boss, suppose you send them up here. It's a better place to talk than in the lobby."

Michael sat down on the bed. "We don't live right."

"No," Prevost agreed. "Since Tingley didn't know how much money his prospective victim had or even if he could get in touch with him by telephone, we have no idea who he was going to blackmail."

"I think Tingley was strictly small-time," Max-on said. "He read in the paper that you wanted information about the Courtney girl's movements on Tuesday and recognized her picture. Well, say she and somebody was in his bar Tuesday night—"

"And Lydia took one drink too many and she and her companion quarreled," Michael said. "One of them walked out on the other."

"The only thing is, how'd Tingley know her companion's name?" Maxon objected.

"I think Lydia called her companion by name. When Sally spoke of a disagreement she'd had with Lydia she said that Lydia said: 'All right, if that's the way you feel, Sally Rollins!' It's a rather childish way of speaking that some people revert to when they're angry."

"Yes, some people do call you by your full name when they're mad at you or laying down the law," Prevost said. "Say Lydia walked out on her companion and said—well, maybe she used the same phrase she did to Sally. And spoke loudly and Tingley heard this person's name and remembered it. And he figured it was worth two hundred dollars to someone for him not to tell us about it."

"But he was dead before he could have read in the papers about you finding that girl in the sand dunes," Maxon said. "I think when he realized how serious the thing was he'd have come to us."

"He might have. As it was, he could argue that maybe the fact Lydia quarreled with someone in his bar Tuesday night had nothing to do with her being killed Friday. But that that person would be glad to pay him two hundred bucks just to avoid publicity or being questioned. So of course Tingley had to be killed before he did learn what else had happened Tuesday night."

"Or before he decided his information was worth far more than two hundred dollars," Michael said cynically. "He might have wanted far more than anyone but Vincent could pay—and more than Vincent cared to pay. Besides, only a fool pays blackmail."

"I'm surprised Lydia didn't try to bribe Tingley before she was killed, the way she tried to cover up. Of course Miss Wendell did hear her say something about 'The man won't tell if he does remember.'"

"There was more than one man who had something to remember—and tell," Michael murmured.

"Hmm? Oh, you're right. But it does look now like Lydia had only one companion Tuesday night. If she'd been with A before ten o'clock and B after ten, when Tingley approached A—well," Prevost said, "A might have wished Tingley would keep his mouth shut, but I don't think he would have killed him."

"So A equals B," Michael said. "Do you know yet if Lydia was alone when she bought that whisky?"

"Yes. That's another reason I'm willing to argue she walked out on her companion, not vice versa. The proprietor of the liquor store told Costello she came in alone and he saw her get into her car and is sure there was no one waiting in it. He even described the car. . . . Hello, Costello."

"I did my best, Inspector," Costello said glumly. "It makes me feel better to know Tingley was dead before I knew he was missin'. This here's O'Rourke."

II

O'Rourke was pink and hairless with one extra chin in front and two in back. He looked as if he

had been born in a starched white coat and, without a bar in front of him, only half finished.

He repeated what he had already told Costello:
that Tingley had insisted he must have several
hours off this evening and had left the cocktail
lounge at a little past six-thirty.

"I tried to pin him down as to how long he'd
be gone, but he said he couldn't tell me, only he'd
try to get back by eight and he'd sure be back by
eight-thirty."

"Probably had an indefinite date to meet someone in the park between seven and eight," Maxon
said. "Much earlier than that there'd be too many
people around. And the doc says Tingley was killed
between seven and eight, and I can tell he favors
the later time."

"And I know at least one person who could have
met Tingley between seven and eight without anyone knowing it," Prevost said. "Jay Stanton. Sally
couldn't have had anything to do with this killing—directly."

"Sally was in training once," Michael said without opening his eyes, which he had closed because
he had the beginnings of a violent headache.

"To be a nurse? Oh, was she! And she didn't bother to mention it when I asked young Stanton how
far he got in medicine," Prevost said. "Am I right in
thinking you work one night a week, O'Rourke?"

"Fridays, though sometimes I drop in to help out on Saturdays if there's too many for Joe to handle alone. Though I didn't need to do that often."

"Is there any reason why a person who just happened to drop into your bar the first time should return to it a second time?" Michael asked.

"If you happened to try my special fizz and liked it," O'Rourke said. "People come back for it. It's my own invention. I show the guys that work for me how to mix it, and then they quit on me and set up in business for themselves and feature it."

"Isn't there a place somewhere near here where you can go roller skating?"

"Sure thing. Upstairs, at Geary."

"Who roller-skates?" Prevost asked. "Oh; Bill and Sally. Well, O'Rourke, here's some pictures I want you to look at. Tell me if you ever saw any of these people before."

Mr. O'Rourke took the pictures Sally had given Prevost into his pudgy hands, drew a pair of old-fashioned spectacles from his pocket, and moved nearer to the light that dangled from a chain in the ceiling.

"This guy," he said, putting a stubby forefinger over Kirk's head. "Hasn't he got a kind of little scar near his mouth that makes him look like he was smilin'? Besides, there was a funny little duck with him in pants too large for him and a big tie, and he had a red beard."

"Mr. Shrader must have slipped his leash more than just one night recently," Michael observed. "When were they in your place?"

"Jeez, I don't remember. Maybe a month ago, maybe longer. It was the guy with the beard that caught my eye, and I only remember him the once. If this guy"—O'Rourke indicated Kirk again—"come in alone again I mightn't remember. Of course they may've come back nights often. But poor old Joe ain't around to tell you if they did.

"And I think I've seen this young fellow." He pointed to Bill Kemper who, in the photograph, was sitting on the floor in front of Sally. "At least, seein' him and this girl together here makes me think I've seen 'em together in my place. The kind that breeze in, buy one drink, and beat it. But these other two dames and this lanky young fellow—" He shook his head.

"That's more than I'd hoped for," Prevost said. "I suppose you'll be working for Tingley now?"

"Yeah—and breaking in a new man. These young sprouts I get don't take no pride in their work besides takin' too many drinks with the customers an'—"

"I wanted to speak about the customers," Prevost broke in. "I want you to try to find out if any of your regulars were in the bar Tuesday night. If you'll make a point of finding that out from anyone that you know at all you'll get results quicker than we ever would."

"I'll give it a try," O'Rourke promised. "There is guys that drop in reg'lar every afternoon and night. Only trouble is, they mostly mind their own business. If this Miss Courtney and whoever was with her was sittin' at one of the tables toward the back they might never have noticed her. And Tuesday's a quiet night. But I'll do my best."

"Well," Prevost said when O'Rourke had left them, "is there anything more to be done here tonight? You've looked over Tingley's room, Maxon, and made all the routine inquiries that can be made tonight. Tomorrow we'll start making door-to-door inquiries along Fillmore."

"Unfortunately," Michael said, standing up, "while a good many very respectable and estimable citizens live in this neighborhood, there is also a lot of riffraff on and around Fillmore."

Maxon nodded. "Yeah. Folks that wouldn't come forward to tell anything they know to the police, just on general principle. Well, Nick, you get some sleep. You look deadbeat. I'll wind up loose ends here and see you tomorrow morning. I'll handle inquiries here as far as they concern Tingley directly. You concentrate on the suspects you already got. I'll take another look through Tingley's things, just in case. . . ."

He started up toward the third floor while Prevost and Michael went downstairs and out of the hotel. Fillmore was not a block away; in this district a roistering, free-and-easy, cheerfully mongrel street. Fillmore is at once dingy and colorful, bedecked at every street intersection with garish arches of lights running from each corner to a point above the intersection. It had not, even at this hour, settled down to sleep.

But a block away in the other direction the little park where they had found Joe Tingley was quiet and deserted. From where they stood the two men could see a graveled path and a park bench in the light spread by a street lamp, but the green of trees and shrubbery beyond that was black in the night.

Michael stood for an instant looking across the street at a Jewish synagogue and the enormous colored window that adorned its front. Its grape leaves and the letters of its Jewish inscription seemed to twist and turn before his eyes.

"Aspirin, Anacin, Bromo-Seltzer—or all three— are indicated," he decided. "Take me home, Nicholas, gently and carefully. If your murderer begged me to listen to his full confession right now I'd tell him to go away and let me sleep. And speaking of sand—"

"We weren't," Prevost said, getting into the car.

"I am. 'Round the decay Of that colossal wreck, boundless and bare The lone and level sands stretch far away.'"

"What colossal wreck?" Prevost said obligingly.

"Me. Famous wrecks—me and No. 9. Not to mention the Hesperus."

"I begin to see why even Jim Sullivan admits there are times when you are 'trying.' What would you do if you didn't have a straight man?"

"Go home and inflict my bright sayings and snappy retorts on my wife. What a pity you haven't a wife, Nicholas. You could shake her awake and growl at her. Then you would feel much better."

Prevost grinned wearily. "I won't try to get the last word—not with you. But can I tell you what happened at the cottage after Sally and I got there and found Jay Stanton sitting on the doorstep?"

"The Wedding-Guest he beat his breast, Yet he cannot choose but hear.' Proceed, *amigo*. I'll listen."

Prevost brought his story to a close as he drove up to Russian Hill Place. "And then the telephone rang. Costello telling me they'd found Tingley. So I hadn't time to ask Sally what she meant when she said Jay had seen at least one nasty accident. She knew what I was driving at though. We'll work on the Tingley angle tomorrow, and I won't call you early—unless you want to go with me to talk to Kirk Vincent."

"Thank you, no." Michael got out of the car. "I told you about my conversation with Mark Shrader on the way out to Fillmore Street tonight."

He hesitated briefly, and decided not to inform Prevost now that Marcia had been out of her library at some time around six-thirty Thursday night.

"I think that's all. Good night. I'll see you some time tomorrow—not too early," he said, let himself into the house, took three aspirins, and got into bed without waking Valerie.

In five minutes he was asleep, only to wake in a foggy dawn because Valerie was shaking him.

"Darling, I hate to wake you when you're so tired," she said. "But you make my blood run cold."

"Oh." Michael turned over on his back. "Talking in my sleep?"

"You do when you're tired, you know. Though you never say anything incriminating or interesting. But you kept muttering: 'a rope of sand to hang them.'"

"Oh," Michael said again. "I was a little confused. If I was trying to recite *Lord Randall* it should have been 'a rope of my hair to hang her.' However, Miss Wendell heard Lydia tell the person that killed her that they were bound together, too, with a rope of sand."

"Oh." Valerie shivered. "It still makes cold worms crawl down my back. And then you muttered: 'But the rope broke.'"

"Did I?" Michael said inattentively, brushing her hair out of his eyes as she put her head against his shoulder. Then: "Did I?" he repeated. "Um-m. Could be."

"Could be what?"

"She did say 'too' if Miss Wendell reported that half a conversation correctly. Go to sleep, my love. Tomorrow morning, before we go over to see Marcia, I'm going to visit a morgue."

"The kind of morgue where Joe Tingley is or what they call a morgue in a newspaper office?"

"You guess," Michael said irritatingly. "Lullaby and good night. Remember, you're sleeping for two now."

III

Kirk Vincent looked, as usual, as if he were half smiling, but his bright, dark eyes were angry. Mark Shrader, who had been with him when Prevost arrived, pushed his chair into a corner and was very much the little man who wasn't there though he produced a conciliatory smile whenever Prevost glanced in his direction.

"So you calmly helped yourself to the typewriter?" Kirk said. "I'll have a word with Astoria."

"I'll have a word with her too," Prevost said coolly. "You've read the morning papers and you know now why Lydia Courtney was killed."

"There are still gaps, but the general outline is clear," Kirk admitted.

"Well, she tried to make amends for having killed Margie Cason by sending her parents fifteen hundred dollars in twenty-dollar bills."

"She sent— Good lord! Well, I suppose that is the kind of thing Lydia would do."

"Of course when she had read in Thursday's paper that the girl was reported missing she also wanted to make the Casons think Margie was all right. She was lucky because Margie's stepfather was anxious to believe the girl had gone off with some man. But Lydia sent a short typewritten note with the money."

"Oh. Written on my typewriter?"

"Yes, and Lydia's fingerprints are all over this typewriter case, Vincent."

Kirk scowled at the battered portable. "I see. When would this note have been written?"

"Sometime on Thursday, and since Lydia went to a movie with Marcia after the library was closed, probably the letter was mailed before seven-thirty."

"Well." Kirk walked into the hall and shouted: "Astoria! Come here!"

Astoria was slow in answering and eventually came in, wiping her hands on her apron, protesting:

"Mistuh Ki'k, Ah just sta'ted your waffles."

"Never mind the waffles, and don't look so blasted innocent," Kirk said. "You're only making waffles because you know you shouldn't have let the inspector carry away my typewriter. But never mind that. What time did you go home on Thursday?"

"Why—'long about five-thi'ty, suh."

"I thought so. I played golf that afternoon."

"Yes suh. Y'all went off right after lunch and got back 'bout five, suh."

"Well, was Miss Courtney here while I was away?"

"No suh. What'd she want to come back again fo' when y'all was gone an' she'd been heah in the mo'nin'?"

"In the morning?" Prevost turned and looked at Vincent with raised eyebrows. "So Miss Courtney was here Thursday morning? What did she say when you let her in, Astoria?"

"Ah didn't let her in, suh. Mistuh Ki'k—"

"I didn't let her in! What time was this? And if you didn't let her in, how do you know she was here?"

Astoria began folding her apron into an elaborate arrangement of pleats. "Ah've did fo' you and other bach'lor gen'lemen a long time," she remarked majestically. "And Ah reckon Ah've learned not to talk. A lady comes to see a gen'lemen, and he don't say nuthin' 'bout it; Ah reckons Ah knows enough jus' to ignore it."

Kirk looked at Prevost and shrugged. "Your witness. I think I know what happened, but I don't want to seem to be prompting from the wings."

"Well, what time did Miss Courtney arrive, Astoria? And where were you then?"

"Ah couldn't say jus' what time she got heah because Ah wasn't heah myself. But it would've been 'round about ten to one, suh. On account of lunch was at one and Ah didn't have butter 'nuff, so Ah just stepped out to the grocery store to get some."

"Leaving the front door open," Kirk said. "And I've asked you a number of times not to do that."

"Why?" Prevost said.

"Because a sweet young thing calmly walked in one time when Astoria did that. She arrived at the foot of the stairs just as I was crossing the upstairs hall from the bathroom to my bedroom, completely *au naturel*. She was not disconcerted—but I was. And I didn't relish having a full description circulated among her friends."

"A very full description," Mr. Shrader said thoughtfully from his corner.

Prevost grinned. "Well, Astoria?"

"Ah was in a hurry," Astoria said sulkily. "So Ah didn't take my keys an' Ah did leave the door open. But Mistuh Ki'k was upstairs, shavin' and dressin', Ah thought. He'd lazed 'round all mornin'.

"Anyhow, Ah come back with the butter, walkin' soft like Ah do in my house slippers. The livin'-room door was open when Ah went through the hall. Ah could jus' see the pa't of the room over there by them windows. Ah s'posed Mistuh Ki'k was in heah too. But all Ah seen was Miss Cou'tney, bendin' over with her back to me an'—

"Well, Ah declare! She was at that table Ah took the typewrituh off'n the bottom shelf of last night. Ah remember now Ah thought she was lookin' for a magazine. But Ah didn't stop. Ah went on to my kitchen and kind of took my time. Givin' Mistuh Vincent time to get rid of her," Astoria admitted.

"Astoria is not fond of having to lay an extra place at the last minute," Kirk said. "And she didn't like Lydia."

Astoria sniffed. "Ain't my place to say who Ah likes an' don't. But when her and them other young folks was heah it was her that wanted a powerful lot of waitin' on. But Mistuh Vincent was in this room when Ah finally called him to lunch, so Ah s'posed he'd let her in."

"And do you answer the telephone for Mr. Vincent?" Prevost asked.

"Only when he ain't heah or Ah jus' happens to be passin' by when it rings. When Ah'm in the kitchen Ah don't like to drop things."

"You left here soon after noon yesterday, didn't you, Vincent?"

"Didn't I talk to you at the hospital around one-thirty? I know I had lunch earlier than usual because you woke me so early. When we left the hospital I took Jay back to his rooming house and came home. I stayed here until about four-thirty, I suppose."

"And then you went out to see some friends. How many times did the telephone ring while Mr. Vincent was gone, Astoria?"

"Ah don't remember answerin' the pesky thing a-tall, Inspector. Nobody what left any message, anyhow."

"She wouldn't remember the messages or the party's name in any case," Kirk said disparagingly. "But isn't this a new line of inquiry, Inspector?"

"Yes. A man named Joe Tingley was killed last night. His death hasn't been linked with Lydia's in the newspapers—yet. But Tingley got in touch

with one of you yesterday. He didn't come to see
you, Vincent."

"Here, you mean? How do you know that?"

"I had a man keeping an eye on this house.
No one called on you yesterday, but you could
have received a telephone call. We can't prove you
did or didn't," Prevost said pleasantly. "The same
thing goes for you, Mr. Shrader, except that your
home wasn't being watched."

Mr. Shrader seemed to grow smaller. "We've
maids to answer the door and telephone," he said
unhappily. "Even if someone asks for me m'wife
usually knows it before I do. Kirk's the only one
who tells her to mind her own business and let
him talk to me."

"I've sent a man over to talk to your maids
again. I told him to be discreet, not to take your
wife into his confidence. Tingley was killed between seven and eight. Where were you at that
time?"

"Should have had dinner at seven," Shrader said,
still more unhappily. "But Cook wanted to go to
her sister's silver wedding anniversary. M'wife let
her serve dinner at six-thirty. All through by seven-
thirty. Went up to my studio. Stayed there till
m'wife went to bed and I could slip out to talk to
Dundas."

"And what time did your friends, the Preedys, have dinner, Vincent?" Prevost asked.

"Around six-thirty. Why don't you ask them? But I suppose you will," Kirk said resignedly. "The Preedys won't mind being questioned by the police again. They think it's 'too exciting.' But the Dunlaps didn't like being dragged into this investigation."

"That," Prevost said dryly, "is too bad. What time did you leave the Preedys' last night?"

"Don't you know? Wasn't I being shadowed?"

"You were in your car, and the man watching your house didn't have a car available," Prevost said. "I didn't consider your movements yesterday afternoon that important—then. Of course I do know that you got home at about eight-five last night."

"I couldn't have sworn to that myself. But in that case I must have left the Preedys' about ten of eight. And who was Joe Tingley?"

"You can go back to your waffles, Astoria. . . . Tingley was a bartender at a cocktail lounge on Fillmore, near Ellis. They feature a special fizz."

"Oh, that place. Remember, Mark?"

"What? No, I don't."

Kirk grinned. "Well, I don't suppose you do. The bartender was the old-fashioned, pink-jowled type. Was that Tingley?"

"No," Prevost said. "Go on."

"But there's nothing to tell. We tried his special fizz. It's one of these delayed-action drinks. It slips down very smoothly and then explodes half an hour later."

"I didn't think you were a drinking man."

"What a charming, old-fashioned phrase, Inspector," Kirk said rather mockingly. "I can go without drinking all day and all week. I can also lap it up with the best of them, given the right companions. Lydia wasn't the right companion. Neither is Kemper. Give him three drinks and he picks a quarrel with whoever's handy. And liquor upsets Jay's sensitive digestive apparatus."

"He was rather under the weather on Wednesday, wasn't he?"

"That isn't unusual. The food in the sort of café Jay usually patronizes is enough to give anyone indigestion," Kirk said hastily. "Where were we? Oh yes. Mark and I only stopped in at the bar you were speaking of. We went on from there—"

"Until Kirk poured me into bed around midnight," Shrader said gloomily. "Ended up in one of those dime-a-dance places—he told me. I don't remember. But of course m'wife saw I had a hangover the next mornin'. And a girl's compact in my pocket. Besides, she was home from her meetin' before Kirk got me home."

"That was about six weeks ago," Kirk said. "And I've been back to that bar, but not at night again, though the same bartender was on duty every time."

"He usually works days. Didn't young Stanton see—or wasn't he in—some rather bad accident once?"

"Accident? Jay? I don't know what you have in mind unless you— I've never heard him mention anything of the sort," Kirk said flatly.

"Keep thinking and try to remember," Prevost advised. "The only reason I don't take you in on suspicion, Vincent, is because I doubt if Lydia's— well, call him her partner in crime—knew she sent that money to the Casons."

"If he did there were two fools in partnership."

"Yes. So the fact that Miss Courtney used your typewriter doesn't mean you were her partner. On the other hand, if you had been with her Tuesday night she might not have minded involving you through the typewriter, if her scheme for quieting the Casons didn't work out. Against that is the fact that she couldn't have known, when she came here, that she'd be able to use the typewriter without you knowing she had."

"Oh, she might have made some excuse to get me out of here so she could use it," Kirk said impersonally.

"Yes. And there's something else I nearly forgot."

"Well?" Kirk said wearily.

"You've had work on your car done at Bain's garage out in the Mission, haven't you?"

"Why—yes. His mechanic used to work in a larger garage, and he's a wizard with engines."

"I know," Prevost said. "The thing is, did you ever mention Squiffy or his garage to Lydia?"

"Squiffy?" Kirk laughed. "I thought his name was Algernon. But I've only talked to him once. The mechanic we're speaking of said he didn't know if he'd done the right thing, going to work for Bain at a larger salary, because Bain has a criminal record."

"Squiffy has only been in the county jail for short periods: nothing worse than that."

"Well, I told Lydia about his garage, but I didn't think she'd taken her car there. For a woman, she took good care of a car. She said hers should be gone over and asked where I took mine. I told her."

"Did you tell her anything about Squiffy?"

"I described him. And told her my friend the mechanic says Bain is a natural pickpocket but doesn't dare work at that trade in San Francisco. We had that conversation the night I took Mark to the cottage, because then he told us about some crooks he's known."

"Bunco artists," Mr. Shrader said sadly. "Used to have quite a bit of beautifully engraved stock in non-existent gold mines. Remember Kirk tellin' us about Bain, but I don't see why you—"

"Never mind," Prevost said. "And that really is all—now."

IV

It was eleven o'clock when Prevost left Kirk Vincent and Mark Shrader. He went back to his office and called Michael, but it was Valerie who finally talked to him.

"I'm waiting for Michael to come back so we can go over to the hospital and ask Marcia to come home with us for a while."

"I'm glad you're doing that," Prevost said. "I imagine she'll want to clear out of there as soon as they'll let her go, and I've been wondering where she'd go. But where is your husband?"

"I think he is doing some research in a newspaper office. He got in touch with a reporter he knows."

"A reporter!"

"Oh, he won't sell out to the opposition," Valerie said. "Could he want to find out—well, something more about that plane crash? But of course you can't tell me. Do you want Michael to call you? Because we unfortunately have a dinner engagement for four o'clock."

"Oh, he needn't bother unless he thinks he should. I'll be busy."

"Well, if you aren't too busy drop by around seven or eight tonight," Valerie said. "We'll be home by eight, anyway."

"I'll do that," Prevost promised, hung up, and began checking over the results of the morning's inquiries.

No results so far on Fillmore. No one had been found and no one had come forward who remembered having seen Lydia Tuesday night. It was too early to hope for any word from O'Rourke. He wasn't apt to see any of his "regulars" in the bar before late afternoon.

One of Mrs. Shrader's maids remembered having called Mark Shrader to the telephone around two o'clock yesterday afternoon to talk to Kirk Vincent. But no strangers had called at the house yesterday if you counted out policemen. However, Shrader had been downstairs all morning until after lunch, and they'd been a little disorganized, what with cleaning up after the party and the police there asking questions too.

So, though the phone was part of her job, she couldn't say for certain that it couldn't have rung without her hearing it. That is, if someone answered it before it rang very long. . . .

Unluckily the telephone at the Pine Street rooming house was no one's particular care. It was in the lower hall, but the landlady admitted that when it rang anyone who happened to be handy or was expecting a call at a certain time answered it. At night, that was. All of her roomers worked, so they were only home nights, Saturday afternoons sometimes, and Sundays maybe. And she had plenty to do all over the house all day.

However, Mr. Stanton had been home yesterday morning, and she had called him to the telephone to talk to a Miss Rollins who'd called before—for Mr. Kemper, usually. No, she hadn't called Mr. Stanton to the phone again: him or anyone. Because she went upstairs after that to clean a vacant room. Mr. Stanton's room was on the first floor. He could hear the telephone and answer it if he wanted to. He quite often did.

She'd seen Mr. Kemper come in some time after one o'clock, but naturally she couldn't say if he'd had any phone calls. Or if any strangers had turned up at the rooming house yesterday, though if she'd seen any wandering around she certainly would have found out what they wanted. She'd like to keep the front door locked, but too many people forgot their keys and called her from her work to let them in when she'd tried it once.

But Miss Jessup on the second floor complained that she'd almost run into a strange man in her bathrobe around one o'clock Saturday. Miss Jessup had rushed home from her office to get a bath before all the other women in the house got home and wanted the bathroom too.

Miss Jessup, when interviewed, described the stranger as tall and fairly thin. She'd been so startled she hadn't taken a really good look at his face. He was wearing a brown sports outfit. So had Joe Tingley been, when he was killed.

But, as Miss Jessup had remarked, that outfit was "just the kind of thing half the men in the city are wearing now." And she had whisked into the bathroom, so she couldn't say who the man was looking for. Yes, he was near Mr. Kemper's room, but she didn't hear him knock or speak after she was in the bathroom.

The Stanton Pharmacy was open on Sundays, and Jay was working today. He had told the landlady to tell anyone who "might want to know" that he would be home by one o'clock.

Bill Kemper had eaten dinner at a small restaurant on Bush Street at Jones around six o'clock last night. He was back at the rooming house by

VIRGINIA RATH

seven and had not been seen leaving it again that night. However, the building did not lack fire escapes or a back door. Mr. Kemper had gone out to breakfast around nine this morning and come straight back to his room. . . .

Nicholas Prevost sighed. He had given orders that Bill was to be left for him to question, but what, he thought wearily, was the use of questioning Bill—or anyone—just now?

The only questions he could ask were too easily answered: with a blank look or one of injured innocence or with a flat denial. No one was going to admit having been with Lydia Tuesday or to having had any dealings with Joe Tingley.

He couldn't, Prevost reflected, prove anyone had lied to him. If you detected a suspect in even a relatively harmless lie you could make capital of that. And sometimes, trying to justify himself, a witness ended by telling more than he intended to.

If Sally hadn't quite lied she had certainly withheld evidence. But she hadn't lost her head when she discovered that Prevost knew that. She'd merely insisted she'd already made up her mind to tell everything she knew. As to Kemper . . .

Thinking of him, Nicholas Prevost began to whistle softly. Kemper had certainly broken into Marcia's library, found and destroyed his own I.O.U. and, very probably, the holograph will Jay

Stanton said Lydia had written in March. But, Prevost admitted, there was nothing he could do about it.

Kemper hadn't left any fingerprints in the library. There was no blood on what glass was left in the doorframe. While he had certainly scratched his arm on the glass, the scratch evidently hadn't been deep enough to spurt blood or begin bleeding for a minute. Kemper, as he probably realized this morning, could think up some story to account for that scratch on his arm.

Prevost sighed again, but he got to his feet. He would question the Preedys himself. He wanted to see this couple who considered it "too exciting" to be questioned by the police. Vincent's alibi depended on them. Though it was no alibi at all, and Vincent hadn't claimed it was.

He had gotten home at eight-five last night. But Tingley could have been killed any time between seven and eight. By fast driving Vincent could have made it from the park to his home in ten minutes. And if it should turn out that he had left the Preedys' home as early as twenty of eight he could have made it out to the park to meet Tingley.

Prevost smiled rather sourly. "Well, at least I finally have something that slightly resembles an alibi to try to break," he muttered. "I'll talk to Kemper first, though. . . ."

Bill was lying on his bed with his shirt and shoes off, reading the Sunday papers. He greeted Prevost with a pugnacious sort of affability.

"I've been thinking, Inspector. I've been thinking that if you forget what I admitted yesterday in the can at the bowling alley I'll forget you hit me. That's a fair exchange, isn't it?"

"Is it?" Prevost said warily.

"Well, you can't prove I broke into Marcia's library. And I can't prove you hit me. But you wouldn't like me to even accuse you of it—publicly. I mean, it hasn't been so long since some of you coppers got into trouble for beating up some guys and raised a stink that hasn't died down yet. Right now people aren't liking coppers that beat up on guys," Bill said cheerfully.

"I see your point. You're quite right," Prevost said pleasantly. "Have you talked to Miss Rollins this morning?"

"Jay told me where she went last night. But she checked out of the Y-dub before I got around to phoning her. But if you mean Sally may be sore about—well, some little thing, I can talk her out of it. You can't take what Sally says when she gets mad too seriously."

Prevost set his teeth and let this pass without comment. "How often do you go roller skating on Fillmore?"

"Oh, once or twice a month. I'd rather bowl, but Sally likes to skate."

"And do you always get a drink afterward?"

"We usually get a malted milk at a place right under the skating rink. Why? Once in a while we take on a real drink—not often."

"But you have been in a small bar near Ellis."

"Maybe. There's all sorts of small bars along Fillmore. What are you driving at, Inspector?"

"Haven't you read your newspapers?"

"Just the comics and sports so far."

"Well," Prevost said, "a bartender named Joe Tingley was killed last night, probably because he knew who Lydia Courtney was with Tuesday night and tried to blackmail him."

"You can't get blood out of a stone," Bill said with unusual mildness. "I haven't any money to pay blackmail with. Now Kirk is what I'd call a first-class prospect."

"No one paid Tingley blackmail. He was killed," Prevost pointed out. "And a Miss Jessup who lives here did see a stranger—who could have been Tingley—near your room around one o'clock yesterday."

"He could have been a bill collector too," Mr. Kemper said indifferently. "A lot of people here are always one jump ahead of collectors. I may have been in the bar this Tingley worked in, sometime.

But the only bartender I remember on Fillmore Street is a fat bald-headed guy."

"He remembers you and Miss Rollins too. You don't," Prevost remarked, "seem to be at all surprised to learn that Miss Courtney was out on Fillmore Tuesday night."

Bill shrugged. "She got around."

"Did you talk to anyone here or did anyone see you here between seven and eight last night?"

"I didn't talk to anyone, and my door was closed. I went out to the can several times, but I didn't meet anyone in the hall. But there aren't many people in the house on a Saturday night, you know."

"I suppose not. I wanted to talk to Mr. Stanton, but I know his uncle wouldn't like it if I turned up at the pharmacy. Perhaps," Prevost said casually, "you can tell me the circumstances of that accident he witnessed."

"What accident? Jay's father was a doctor, you know. He had offices in his home over in Berkeley. Jay's been called in to help out in emergencies, if that's what you mean. Or—seems to me he saw a woman fall and break her neck once."

"Or perhaps her back?" Prevost suggested.

"I don't know," Bill said uneasily. "He just mentioned something of the kind once and then shut up. Maybe he saw one of these women who're always jumping out of tall buildings I know he's one of these people who don't like heights. But I think Kirk knows about that. I mean, I think he was connected with it someway. And—well, Jay and I don't always agree, but he's not a bad guy. He's just kind of—well, moody.

"I talked to him this morning," Bill went on. "I hadn't seen last night's papers, and he told me about you finding this Margie Cason. We decided Lydia must have been drinking Tuesday night. Is that right?"

"That's right," Prevost said.

"And at the bar this Tingley worked in, I suppose, from what you've just said. So Tingley could have said she was tight if they ever discovered she hit this Cason girl and killed her. And it's a wonder to me Lydia hadn't tried to buy Tingley off and shut his mouth before she was killed."

"She would have been very foolish to do that—to approach him or ever let him see her again—as long as no one knew what had happened to Margie Cason," Prevost said. "However, she did several foolish things because she couldn't let well enough alone and—"

Prevost stopped abruptly and for so long a time that Bill Kemper finally broke the silence with:

"You act like you might have had a brain storm. If you've got any more questions to ask—"

"'More than one man who had something to remember—and tell,'" Prevost muttered. He looked
at Bill benevolently. "No," he said slowly, "no
more questions, Mr. Kemper—just now."

V

"So while I was very glad to see Sally and she was
very sweet, I told her I didn't think they would let
me leave the hospital tonight," Marcia said. "And
she decided to spend tonight with her sister. She
says her brother-in-law is tough enough to handle
Bill if he tries to see her there. She says she never
wants to speak to Bill again."

Valerie sat down on the guest-room bed. "Don't
you believe her?"

"I'd like to. But Jay came to see me this morning
too. He told me he was certain Lydia made a new
will. It must have been in the envelope she gave
me to keep in the library. And if Bill knew about
it he might have told Sally—or it could have been
the other way around and Sally told Bill about it."

"You know it was Bill who broke into the library?"

"Sally told me. And I can see that she and Bill
might have been working together without ever
intending to do *me* any real harm. So I'm glad you
asked me to come here, because if I went back to
the cottage Sally would insist on going with me."

"I wish we didn't have this dinner engagement," Valerie said. "I hate dinner at four o'clock. But the Keiths would like to have you too. You shouldn't mind meeting them. Nora and Roger know what it is to be mixed up in a murder investigation."

"I'd like to meet Roger Keith someday. I like his books. But not today."

"Well, we won't be late getting home. Because Roger is, as he says, 'with book,' and we know enough to leave by seven or eight so he can get in several hours' work before bedtime. Patton will feed you whenever you're hungry, and we'll have to eat again before bedtime. You'd better sleep this afternoon, because Inspector Prevost promised to try to come by around eight."

"I hope he does."

"Do you?" Valerie said. "Michael's been saying he would like, just once, to encounter a perfectly straightforward murder minus love interest. Most critics will tell you it doesn't belong in detective stories. But Michael says that people choose the damnedest times to fall in love. And that the older a man is and the more certain he is that he's absolutely immune, the harder he falls."

"Is Mr. Dundas speaking from experience?"

Valerie laughed. "He is. And if you consider the question impertinent, just say so—but what do you think of Mr. Prevost?"

"Maidenly modesty should forbid my saying," Marcia said with an exaggerated pretense of primness. "But I don't think of him as Mr. Prevost. Nick suits him. Maybe he'd even let one person in the world call him Nicky on special occasions."

"Nicky? No," Valerie said. Marcia laughed.

"But you're not me. And why do you suppose I borrowed Sally's rouge and lipstick? I was afraid yesterday that maybe I was just feeling grateful to him."

"Which would be disastrous," Valerie said.

"Yes. But I knew it wasn't that when he didn't come to see me at the hospital this morning. I know he hasn't time but—well, it is ridiculous. I suppose with me it began when he told me he'd been left on the steps of an orphanage when he was five weeks old. That fact means so much—when you look at him now."

"Yes—and probably only the woman he marries will ever know just how much."

"Well, whatever happened to me afterward, I did have a perfectly happy, normal childhood. When my father and mother died I still had my brother and hosts of friends. Well, I can't see now why I've acted as I have for a year. I didn't use to lack guts."

"You should never have humored Lydia when she insisted on repaying you for saving her life."

"No, I shouldn't. Have you ever noticed how sometimes he just skirts on the edge of saying 't'rough!' or 't'ought'?" Marcia said irrelevantly. "He sounds a little like James Cagney. I mean, Cagney's voice is soft, too, and—"

"No, it's not gratitude," Valerie said. "And you don't even want a quiet and peaceful life, as one might expect you would."

"I suppose if one is married to a detective— Does this sort of thing worry you?" Marcia asked.

"Well, I tell myself that if it wasn't this it would be something else. I mean, life with Michael would never be dull. And I'm not immune to the excitement of a man hunt. I've done my share of snooping and pulling strings. But I know it's dangerous, though Michael's tried not to worry me this time. He says he isn't in any danger, and I believe he believes that.

"But murderers are so apt to get jittery, waiting," Valerie added, "and not leave well enough alone. Besides, I think Michael thinks he knows who the murderer is—though he hasn't any sort of proof, even if he must have gone looking for some this morning before we came to the hospital. But he hasn't explained yet."

She looked at her wrist watch. "Well, I'd better dress. If we get to the Keiths' by three then we can

politely leave around seven. If you don't want to
lie down now Michael is in the living room."

When she had finished dressing she went looking for Patton to tell her there might be a fourth
for Sunday supper. As she passed through the hall
she heard Marcia saying, in the living room:

"Of course I guessed, though she never admitted it. And it's not as unusual as you might think.
I'd come across it before when I was an air-line
hostess. She didn't mind being in the air."

Now what, Valerie thought, going on to the
kitchen, can have inspired Michael to discuss
that plane crash with Marcia? Though I suppose
we should refer to it matter-of-factly sometimes
instead of always side-stepping the subject. And
Marcia only sounded as if he'd given her something to think about. Oh well . . .

Valerie talked to Patton for several minutes
and started back to the living room. As she came
through the hall again Marcia was speaking.

"Of course I see that in one way it's important," she said. "It does explain her actions. But
why do you think it's important for other reasons?
You do—"

"Something your neighbor on the hill, Miss
Wendell, overheard gave me that idea." Michael
stood up as Valerie came into the room. "You're
ready? Then let's make an early start so we can

return early. I'm not exactly in the mood for Roger Keith's airy persiflage today. . . ."

It was just five minutes past seven when they came back into their own living room. Valerie tossed her coat on a chair and sat down on the chesterfield.

"Nora would be so much happier if she didn't feel she should reform Roger just a little," she remarked tolerantly. "She takes life, and him, so seriously. It's fortunate he never listens to her— any more than you're listening to me."

"I heard what you said. But I was wondering what Nick Prevost's found to do this afternoon. I rather expected he'd be waiting for us here."

Valerie leaned back, yawning. "I'll wake Marcia in a minute so she can primp. I wonder . . . Why, Patton! What's wrong?"

Patton's sleek, well-behaved hair was rumpled, and that was nothing short of phenomenal.

"I just ran up to the back yard to see if she might be there," she gasped. "But she—"

"Who?" Michael said sharply. "Marcia?"

"Yes sir—and you told me to watch her. But she said she was going to try to sleep, and—and you know I've the habit of an afternoon nap on Sundays myself. I tried not to drop off, but I did for a bit. It was the telephone woke me."

"How long ago?"

"It was right on seven. A man's voice asked if you were here. No one I know, though it might have been Inspector Prevost, as I've never heard his voice over the telephone. When I said you weren't here he thanked me, said he'd call later, and hung up. So then I passed by the guest room, and it was so very quiet I edged the door open and—"

"She was gone," Michael said. "And we don't know how long or where."

He was across the living room, in the hall, and speaking into the telephone before it rang a second time.

"Yes. . . . Where are you? . . . I'm on my way."

He slammed the receiver down on the table without taking time to replace it in its cradle.

"Marcia," he said. He was in the bedroom now, yanking open the drawer of the bedside table, taking out the gun he kept there. "Valerie."

He caught her arm and pulled her through the hall and living room with him, talking as they went.

"I have to go, darling. This is my fault. Try to locate Prevost and send him over to Marcia's library." He wrenched the front door open. "And thank God I didn't put my car in the garage!"

VI

Her hands were shaking now so that the telephone clattered against the desk when she put it down. She stood still, biting her lip, looking about the dimly lighted book-lined room. The green enameled alarm clock on the desk ticked away importantly, and water dripped monotonously into the sink in the tiny kitchen.

I've cut it too fine, Marcia thought. I've got to make time now. If I seem frightened I can't. Sit down then. Take a book, adjust the reading lamp. Act as if you were trying to read.

Her hands fumbled with the book, trying to open it. No, she decided suddenly, I shouldn't be reading. I'm not supposed to be too calm. I'm not even supposed to be very happy. If I put my head down in my hands as if I were thinking or even crying a little . . .

She closed her eyes, pressing her fingers hard against the lids. This is best, she thought. This way I can't watch the door or the street. There's the cable car going by—clank-clank, jingle-jangle. Now there won't be another for a long time.

She jerked erect. There was something hard and cold pressed against the back of her neck. A voice behind her said:

"You didn't think I'd come so soon or so quietly—or by the back door? We learn something new
every day, don't we? No, don't turn around. I don't
want you looking at me. Find a sheet of paper."

Her hands were steady now. She opened the
middle drawer of the desk, took out a sheet of letter paper, reached for the pen in its holder.

"Yes?" she whispered.

"If this was a trap you're caught in it. If it wasn't
it will work out very well just the same. Write: 'I
can't go on. I thought that if I had Lydia's money everything would be all right. The money was
what I wanted. I always meant to kill Lydia when
I'd thought of a safe way to do it. It was just bad
luck that I was with her the night her car struck
Margie Cason. . . .'"

VII

"Please!" Valerie said. "I must have this line. . . .
I know it's a free country. I know you pay your
telephone bill too. But this is a matter of life and
death. I swear it is! Listen in and hear what I have
to say if you want to. I don't care, but please give
me the line."

"Mrs. Dundas! The inspector—"

Valerie flung the telephone aside and herself
into Nicholas Prevost's arms.

"The library," she sobbed. "Marcia's. Michael's gone over there with a gun, and those awful people on our party line were talking about Aunt Susie's operation and wouldn't believe I had to use the telephone."

The latter part of this explanation was breathed into Patton's percale shoulder instead of Prevost's tweeds. Prevost was already down the front steps. He turned his car in the middle of the street and set the siren going. He took the sharp turn into Jones on two wheels, righted the car by main force, and headed down Jones.

Hours afterward he remembered the cars he passed very clearly. One had an Indiana license plate; another was from Texas. There was a battered Ford crammed to capacity with a large Italian family and a shiny Packard with a Negro chauffeur.

He even recalled faces: that of a plump, pink woman on the curb, clutching a child with one hand and the leash of a small yapping dog with the other, and the apoplectic countenance of the gripman on the Clay Street cable car.

But at the time these were only so many obstacles glimpsed through a shifting fog: to be avoided if possible and smashed through if they did not give way. He slid his car to a stop at Jones and

Sacramento, its front wheels on the sidewalk, set the brake, and jumped from the car in one movement.

Half a block down on Sacramento the painted sunflower that marked Marcia's library rocked gently in the wind. The great bulk of Grace Cathedral was gray in the gray evening. Lights were appearing in the hotels and apartment houses of Nob Hill. They shone softly through the fog, but the window of the little library was dark.

Inside a reading lamp lay on the floor, still burning. There was no other light in the place and no sound but the ticking of a clock and the dripping of water in the kitchenette.

Nicholas Prevost leaned back against the front door for an instant. Telephone, he thought confusedly. Use the telephone to call someone. No, look in the kitchen first. You can't put that off. . . .

Beyond the swinging door into the kitchen someone spoke. "All right now? More water—or do you want to faint or cry again?"

Prevost crossed the room and kicked the door open. Michael was standing with one arm about Marcia, a water glass in one hand. He smiled wearily when he saw Prevost.

"And the Guards came through?" he said, put the glass down on the sink, shoved Marcia into

Prevost's arms, and sauntered past him into the library. "What delayed you?"

"What— Here!" Prevost's hands closed over Marcia's shoulders. "You're all right? Sure? Then what t'hell goes on here?"

"Marcia has just kept a little rendezvous with a murderer," Michael said.

"Oh, has she!" Prevost released Marcia and followed Michael. "And whose idea was that? Who t'ought up this little scheme? I warned you yesterday morning—"

Michael looked up, saw danger approaching in the form of one very angry inspector, and seized the nearest chair. He flung it in front of Prevost. Nine men out of ten would have fallen headlong over it. Prevost only barked his shins.

"Count ten," Michael advised. "And then if you still want to knock someone's teeth out let it be Marcia's. I believe that amounts to a declaration of love in some primitive tribes. And this was her scheme. She didn't consult me."

"That's the truth," Marcia said, clinging to Prevost's arm. "I only sent him an S. O. S. He's been lecturing me severely."

"Oh." Prevost rubbed his shins and finally grinned. "That's a good trick," he said, indicating the chair. "I know it but I didn't know you did. Well, your plan didn't work."

"Who says it didn't work?" Marcia managed a shaky smile "Mr. Dundas got here in time. I hadn't guessed I'd be required to write a confession to dictation."

"Confession?" Prevost came as near to roaring as the invariable softness of his voice would permit. "Whose confession? Where is he?"

"Mr. Dundas hit him over the head with a gun."

"And I don't think he will regain consciousness very soon. It was no love tap I gave him, and I hit him again for good measure. But I had to look after Marcia, so in case he did recover quickly I shoved him into that closet."

Michael pointed to a narrow door between bookshelves at the back of the room. Prevost strode over to the door, yanked it open, and bent over the man huddled on the floor.

"Out colder than a dead mackerel," he said.

"Close the door again. I don't want to look at him," Marcia said. "Do you want me to explain? And you don't seem surprised."

"I'd figured it out, though I didn't have evidence enough for an arrest. And don't explain. Just let me guess," Prevost said grimly, picking up a sheet of paper, half covered with Marcia's writing, from the desk. "You were to write and sign this confession and then have your brains blown out and your fingerprints planted on the gun to make it look like you'd done it yourself."

Marcia shivered. "Yes," Prevost said more gently, "I want to scare the living daylight out of you so you'll never try another stunt like this. Now, explain."

"Well, you see, Lydia was a claustrophobic."

"I tried to tell you that," Michael said. "So many things pointed to her having a dread of confined spaces. There was her open car, those unusually large rooms in the cottage she rented, the fact that while she'd go to night clubs she soon became restless and wanted to move on—so many night clubs being small, crowded places. Even when she went to the theater, if the picture didn't hold her attention she'd become restless and refuse to sit it out. And she wouldn't use an elevator if she could possibly avoid it."

"How can you know that?"

"I only guessed that. She wouldn't go to Vincent's dentist though she asked him to recommend one. And his dentist is on the twenty-second floor. You can't walk that many flights of steps. And Bill Kemper had never taken her to the sky rooms at either the Empire Hotel or the Mark, though a person who wants to see San Francisco usually goes to them at once. But you have to use an elevator to reach them."

"And Michael guessed right," Marcia said. "Lydia never got into an elevator if she could avoid it. And I told you that she was hysterical after our plane took off, when she decided to see if she could travel by air. And it was having the doors locked and being shut into the plane that upset her."

"Yes, you told me that," Prevost admitted.

"And she was never in this library for any length of time," Michael said. "It's a small, low-ceilinged room, made to seem smaller by the shelves of books—which might seem also to press in on you. She wouldn't even relieve Marcia here one day when Marcia wasn't well.

"And that brings us to Miss Wendell's testimony. She heard Lydia say: 'I know—I know! I'd go mad in a month. It would be so much worse for me than you.'"

"I get it. I see now why you insisted that, in spite of her saying that, she hadn't been driving her car when it struck Margie Cason. She meant that because she had a morbid fear of confined spaces, being in jail even a short time would be worse for her than it would for a perfectly normal person."

"What is normality? Who is perfectly normal?"

"Let's talk about that some other time," Marcia said, smiling. "And lots of people do suffer from a mild form of claustrophobia. But the fact that

Lydia did helps account for her consenting to hide Margie Cason's body, doesn't it? Even if she hadn't been driving the car and wasn't the one who'd be charged with manslaughter she would be held in jail overnight at least.

"And she'd been drinking and wasn't exactly rational. The idea of going to jail even for a little while must have thrown her into a panic. And he took advantage of that fact to persuade her to conceal Margie Cason's body. And once she'd helped him do that she couldn't ever talk—he thought."

"Admirably stated," Michael said. "Well, it was the fact that, according to Miss Wendell, Lydia said that the walls pressed in on her if she didn't have a light burning that first made me wonder if Lydia was a claustrophobic. I decided that she was for the reasons already stated. Going on from there, after she said: 'It would be so much worse for me than you,' she added: 'You do seem to understand.'"

"Yes," Prevost said, "and then she said that she had never told anyone here, 'only you.'"

"And she hadn't," Marcia said. "She did fight that fear and she never discussed it with me, the person she'd have been most likely to confide in."

"But Lydia added, 'I had to tell you that night at the Mark when you wanted to go up to the Top of the Mark.'"

"That's guesswork," Prevost said. "But you're probably guessing right, so go on."

"Well then, according to Lydia herself, she'd admitted her fear only to one person. Do you know the derivation of the word claustrophobia?"

"I don't think I do."

"Cloister plus phobia—fear of a cloister. Lydia didn't like to stay in this library for any length of time. Everyone knew that but not why, though Marcia could guess. But who was it that spoke of this place as a 'dismal cloister' instead of as a cubbyhole or hole in the wall?

"And later on I was trying to find out if Lydia did avoid being shut into elevators. So I asked what dentist or doctor she went to, if any. Vincent said he had recommended his but she hadn't taken his recommendation. And Jay said that Lydia had gone to his man instead: one who had offices in his home instead of one of the large medico-dental buildings.

"But not before Vincent had volunteered the information that his dentist was on the twenty-second floor of the four-fifty Sutter Building. I hadn't asked him what floor his dentist was on. But Lydia's little peculiarity was on his mind then, just as it had been when he called this library a dismal cloister."

VIII

"And that was what first made you suspect Vincent had killed Lydia? Well, I missed that," Prevost said generously.

"It wasn't much to go on. Marcia saw in fifteen minutes what it took me twenty-four hours to figure out. I asked Marcia about Lydia's phobia this afternoon. And when she asked me why it was important I very foolishly said that something Miss Wendell had overheard Lydia say gave me the idea that it might be."

"And I know Miss Wendell," Marcia said. "She does a sort of mental shorthand that records what people say down to the last 'I sez' and 'he sez.' I couldn't sleep after you and Valerie left. I finally decided to go over to the cottage and talk to Miss Wendell."

"And she was quite willing to tell you what she knew?" Michael said.

"Yes. She was letter perfect. Well, after I'd listened to her I began working backward. It had already occurred to me that whoever was with Lydia must have had some experience of death to be certain Margie Cason was dead. I couldn't believe anyone would bury her if there was any chance she was alive. Not then, when no real murder had been done. Later on, once Kirk had deliberately killed two people, he probably wouldn't have hesitated at a little thing like that. Murder does have that effect on people, doesn't it?"

"More often than not it does," Prevost agreed.

"Well, from what Miss Wendell heard Lydia say it was plain that sometimes she tortured herself by wondering if Margie Cason might have been— been buried alive. She mentioned Poe, you remember, and he wrote so many stories about premature burial. I remember Jay giving us goose flesh one night, telling us some of them when the lights were low.

"That's how I worked backward: from Poe and premature burial to Lydia's saying: 'I keep seeing her and sometimes I even wonder if—' Then Kirk must have tried to reassure Lydia. He would, naturally. And then Lydia said: 'And no one could do anything for her, *either?*' Is that right?"

"Yes, that's right," Michael said. "I worked backward too."

"Then Lydia said that they were tied together, *too,* with a 'rope of sand that won't break.'"

"And that's what threw us off. It was natural enough that she should say a rope of sand. But we, knowing from the beginning how that painting of sand dunes had affected her and, later on, the reason for her reaction, concentrated on the word 'sand' instead of 'rope.' But Vincent is a mountain climber. People who are foolish enough to climb mountains are sometimes roped together, and ropes do break. Lydia said: 'We're tied together *too*.'"

"And Kirk had evidently just been trying to convince her he was perfectly certain Margie Cason was killed outright when the car struck her," Marcia said. "What would be more convincing than for him to tell her he'd seen another death similar to Margie's? Whatever he said led Lydia to say: 'And no one could do anything for her, either?'

"Well, Kirk's seen more than one death and accident when he's been off in the wilds. And Margie Cason's back was broken. Well, several years ago Kirk was with a party in the mountains, doing some difficult climbing. They were roped together —but the rope broke. Two of them fell. One was a woman, and her back was broken."

"And," Michael said, "'no one could do anything for her, either.'"

"No. Jay told me about that. It was the first and last time he went with Kirk on one of those expeditions. Naturally he was a rank amateur and wasn't climbing with Kirk, but he saw the woman fall and he saw her afterward. Jay doesn't forget things like that. He told me about it and maybe he told Sally. I mean, it's the kind of thing he'd tell a sympathetic woman."

"I learned the details of that accident by consulting the file on Vincent in one of our local newspaper offices this morning," Michael explained. "He is prominent enough that they do have a file on him. And I'll have to ask you to give Sam Hadley a break, Inspector. He made it possible for me to consult the file and he promised to keep his mouth shut. I didn't explain, but naturally he is curious."

"I'll give him a break. Well, you settled on Vincent as the murderer, Marcia, but Jay Stanton was with him on that expedition, so—"

"But Jay never did any climbing that was dangerous enough for him to be tied to anyone with a rope. Besides, I knew Jay didn't kill Lydia for a very simple reason you two seem to have overlooked."

"What was that?"

"Why, you agreed whoever murdered Lydia was watching her and trying to keep her in line and coaxing her to forget what had happened. But Jay was so rude to Lydia—or sarcastic—Friday night at the Shraders' that she flounced away and left us. He'd have been very careful not to antagonize her or to drive her to going off by herself if he'd thought she needed watching."

"Damn!" Prevost said. "You're right."

"Of course I am. Well, I called Kirk. I told him I'd gone over to the cottage to get some clothes and that Miss Wendell saw me and came down to talk to me. I told him everything she told me: everything she'd heard Lydia say Thursday evening."

"The poor fool," Prevost said. "Oh, it must have been a shock. But he should have realized Miss Wendell would probably never be allowed to tell that story in court. That kind of thing helps us, but it's not good legal evidence."

"Isn't it? I didn't know that. And when I'd finished there was a rather awful silence," Marcia said. "So I rushed right on. I said I had no idea where you were and hadn't decided yet whether I wanted to talk to you. And that the Dundases had gone out to dinner and wouldn't be back until late, and I simply had to consult someone.

"'Because,' I said, 'you see, don't you, that everything Miss Wendell heard Lydia say points to Jay?' I made a great deal of Lydia's having mentioned Poe and Jay being a Poe reader. I dragged in the fact that Jay had studied medicine and that his father had been a doctor."

"You didn't overlook one bet, did you?" Prevost said.

"I tried not to. And then I got to the rope of sand and 'We're tied together too' and 'No one could do anything for her, either.' I told Kirk how I'd reasoned things out, just as I have you—but I put Jay in his place.

"When I'd finished Kirk said: 'It's pretty damning, the way you put it.' And I said: 'Yes, but perhaps Jay can explain. Perhaps he isn't guilty.' I put a sob in my voice," Marcia said. "That wasn't hard to do. And I went on: 'Shouldn't we give him a chance to explain? Would we be doing a terrible thing if we warned him? You're fond of him too.'

"And Kirk was very regretful and soothing. He asked where I was. I said I'd come here because I was afraid the telephone wire at the cottage might be tapped. Then he suggested that he come here and we'd go to Jay together."

"*Señorita, te saludo,*" Michael said. "And he fell for it."

"I wonder if he did? But the thing was, I let him know what I knew. And he knew that if I told Jay everything Jay is clever enough that he'd immediately make the same point I have—that *he'd* never tried to climb mountain peaks roped to other climbers. Of course," Marcia said in a tone of mild wonder, "I must have been a little crazy."

"You were completely off your nut," Prevost said flatly. "And why did you—?"

"Oh, I thought it was too bad that Valerie should be worried, wondering if Michael knew

too much for his own safety. Maybe I just wanted to cut clean and quick and have it over with.
Or perhaps I wanted to prove to myself that I'm
Marcia again and not just a reasonable facsimile
thereof. And to prove it to you too, Nick.

"But," Marcia said before Prevost could speak,
"I very nearly gave Kirk too much time and
Michael not enough. I called Kirk about ten of
seven. Valerie had said you'd try to leave the
Keiths' by seven, which would get you home about
ten after. And, you see, I counted on Kirk's calling
your home to find out if I was lying when I said
you weren't there."

"Mr. Prevost and Mr. Dundas will now slink
quietly into back seats and join in the applause,"
Michael said.

Prevost smiled ruefully. "You even thought of
that?"

"But that's what I would have done if I'd been
Kirk. So I gave him time."

"And he did call and Patton told him I was not
at home, which made him feel it was safe to come
here."

"Yes. And when I thought it was safe and that
you would be home, Michael, I called you."

"She told me to come armed and to come quietly by the back door. And to listen as long as I
thought I should if Kirk Vincent was with her."

"And then I was frightened," Marcia admitted. "I was so rattled, trying to decide how I should look and what I should say when Kirk arrived, that I didn't stop to think he might come in by the back door too. I sat down at the desk and—"

She pointed to the chair behind the desk. "Of course that put my back to the kitchen door. He was behind me and had that gun against my neck before I could even get up. But he set me to writing that confession. Would people have believed that?"

"No!" Prevost said angrily.

"Yes, my dear, I'm afraid they might have. In view of your—er—"

"My depression for the last year?" Marcia finished for Michael. "And my past history? Yes, I suppose they might have believed that confession. Well, I wrote. And when the letters were swimming in front of my eyes Kirk gave a funny little grunt and slumped down. Michael can move as quietly as Kirk did. He hit him over the head with his gun. He hit him again while I was watching. You didn't look very nice when you did it," Marcia said thoughtfully. "I have an idea now how you'd look when you're angry. And—well, that was that."

"Except for the fact that it didn't do my heart failure any good. And why did you decide that you'd settle for Vincent as the murderer, Inspector?"

"Because of something else that Lydia heard Miss Wendell say. You remember that twice Lydia spoke of someone who might remember something? I supposed, at first, that both times she was referring to Tingley. I still imagine it was Tingley she meant when she said: 'I suppose he would remember. No, it's too late now.'

"But, as you remarked after Tingley was killed, more than one man—besides the murderer—had something on Lydia that he might remember and tell. You meant Squiffy Bain, didn't you?"

Michael nodded. "Well," Prevost said, "Squiffy had remembered and told. But we'd agreed that if Lydia knew his reputation when she took her car to his garage to be cleaned she probably took it there deliberately because she reasoned that Squiffy was the sort who would keep his mouth shut, especially if she paid him double for the job.

"And Vincent admitted to me this morning that he had recommended Squiffy's mechanic to Lydia and that he had discussed Squiffy with her— and the rest of the gang at the cottage—because Squiffy is quite a character. All right! Approaching the end of her conversation with Vincent on Thursday evening, Lydia told him that she was glad he'd come to see her though she knew that he was watching her."

"Yes," Michael said, "and probably he then pointed out that neither of them could weaken without involving the other. And perhaps that neither one should do anything without consulting the other first. At least, Lydia said something to this effect: 'We shouldn't, but how do I know you won't?'"

"And she laughed, which might make Vincent uneasy," Prevost said. "And probably he asked what she'd been up to, if anything. She'd sent money to the Casons that morning, but she couldn't have been referring to that when she said that there had been one thing that had to be done the *next morning.*"

"No," Michael agreed. "The next morning after the accident would have been Wednesday. And Miss Wendell thought Lydia said something about 'washing' after that."

"Well, Lydia thought the car had to be washed and cleaned Wednesday morning. I suppose Vincent protested and asked Lydia why the hell she hadn't cleaned the car herself. Because she said angrily: 'I couldn't do it myself. And the man won't tell if he does remember.'"

"Lydia wouldn't have thought she could wash and clean a car, even in an emergency," Marcia said.

"Evidently not. And then Vincent must have guessed she'd taken the car to Squiffy's garage and

protested some more. Miss Wendell said she sounded sulky when she spoke again. And she said—
which was the pay-off, with what Vincent admitted
this morning—'You can't blame me for thinking
that after what you said.' In other words, you can't
blame me for thinking it was safe to let Squiffy
Bain clean the car after what you said about him."

"Nice going, Inspector," Michael said.

Prevost shrugged. "At least one half of it is guesswork. I couldn't arrest him. We'd have watched
him day and night: got him up in the morning
and put him to bed at night. But our best bet
would have been that one of O'Rourke's regulars
saw him in that bar with Lydia Tuesday night. We
still want to locate someone who did. But you
take Marcia home and leave Vincent to me. I'll try
to bring him to now. And your wife was crying."

"Valerie was!"

"She'd been trying to get the use of your telephone, and the other people on your line wouldn't
let her have it. So she was a little overwrought."

"And Patton's manner toward me for the next
week will be one of frigid reproach," Michael
prophesied. He took Marcia's arm. "We used to
have that line to ourselves. And tomorrow, though
the shades of all my thrifty Scottish ancestors
whisper that a one-party line is an unnecessary
expense, we are going to have one."

IX

Michael watched his wife hand Nicholas Prevost a very potent highball, then glanced from Patton, offering coffee and sandwiches, to Marcia, setting cigarettes and matches at Prevost's elbow.

"'They roused him with muffins—they roused him with ice,'" he remarked. "'They roused him with mustard and cress.' Shall I remove your shoes and bring you my carpet slippers, Inspector?"

"He is dreadfully tired," Marcia said reproachfully. Michael grinned.

"'Honey and milk are under thy tongue,' but not for me. And I'm tired too; tired of waiting for the inspector to appear. Well, 'They roused him with jam and judicious advice—they set him conundrums to guess.'"

Prevost groaned. "Don't go whimsical on me and I'll answer your conundrums. Thank God there's not much we don't know already. Vincent ran into Lydia when he was walking along O'Farrell after he'd had dinner at Omar Khayyam's. She was just getting her car out of that parking lot farther down the street. We asked about her at that parking lot, and they should have remembered her car but they didn't.

"Well, she offered to take Vincent home and then suggested they get a drink somewhere first. She was set on it, and he gave in. They went out to O'Rourke's joint on Fillmore. They sat at a table in back. One drink led to another, and Lydia got out of hand. Vincent got fed up and told her off. She fired up. She said very loudly: 'All right, if that's the way you feel about it, Kirk Vincent!' Then she got up and left the place. And went off and bought a bottle of whisky before she went on to the cottage.

"Vincent paid the bill and left too. There weren't many people in the bar, and probably only Tingley paid any attention to him. He took his time going home: didn't call a taxi and walked part way. Lydia went home, talked to Sally, couldn't get her to help her finish out the night, and said she'd put her car in the garage.

"But Lydia decided the quarrel was her fault and drove over to Vincent's to make up, instead. He'd just gotten home and had to let her in to keep her from making a scene on the doorstep. She wanted to ride for a while and turned stubborn about it.

"Since she'd sobered up a bit he went with her. They got out to the avenues, and she produced the whisky. Vincent wasn't having any. They struggled for the bottle and managed to break it. Then he said he'd drive and changed places with her.

"He was irritated and liked to drive fast too. Lydia egged him on. They struck Margie Cason a few blocks from where they buried her. Vincent knew the girl was dead; that her back was broken. Lydia was half crazy with fright at the idea of being locked into a cell even overnight and ready to do whatever he said.

"He knew he'd be charged with manslaughter and that the average jury wouldn't treat him kindly. He'd been drinking; the car stunk of liquor, and he'd be labeled a 'wealthy playboy.'

"Which, to the average citizen, is synonymous with 'wealthy waster,'" Michael remarked.

"Yes. He wasn't willing to take the consequences. He figured if they left Margie's body on the street the police would start looking for a hit-run driver. And they might catch up with him. But if a young girl, out alone late at night, simply disappeared, who'd connect her disappearance with a recklessly driven car?

"So"—Prevost shrugged—"they buried the girl. And then it was up to Vincent to keep Lydia in line. He didn't know until Thursday that she'd taken her car to Squiffy to be cleaned. His disapproval of that must have kept her from telling him she'd sent money to the Casons. She didn't have to tell him because he really didn't know she'd written the note she sent with the money on his typewriter.

"His conversation with Lydia on Thursday was as we reconstructed it even when it was just flagrant guesswork. He had no idea they were overheard. He didn't know about the peculiar acoustics of that hill where the cottages are. When he got there, there were no lights in Miss Wendell's place. He did hear her door open as he was leaving and dodged into the doorway of that vacant cottage so she couldn't see him.

"By Friday night he saw Lydia was going to break and that she might throw him to the wolves and hope to get of lightly herself. She'd come to feel there are worse things than being shut into a cell.

"When he learned she had fainted and knew she'd been talking to you at the Shraders', Michael, he thought she had better be watched that night. He did watch and follow her, and when she started up the steps from Taylor to this block here he was certain that she was coming to talk to you. So he shot her as she saw him coming up the steps behind her and started to run. He used an old gun of his father's that he'd never had on display with the guns he was known to have.

"Then about eleven-thirty yesterday Joe Tingley called him. Tingley asked if he remembered his 'girl friend who's been killed' walking out on him Tuesday night. The police might like to know

about that, Tingley said, since they wanted to
know what Lydia was doing Tuesday.

"Vincent guessed that Tingley had no idea what
had happened later on Tuesday night. Tingley remarked that 'these little spats happen all the time.'
And he said he wouldn't want to inconvenience
Vincent by telling the police about an unimport-
ant thing like that—if Vincent happened to have
two hundred dollars to spare."

"The poor fool," Michael said compassionately.
"He asked for chicken feed."

"But Vincent argued that once Tingley knew
what had happened later on Tuesday night he
wouldn't ask for chicken feed. In fact, just from
talking to him over the telephone Vincent was
afraid Tingley couldn't be bought off at any price
once he learned what had happened to Margie
Cason.

He still hoped we'd never learn about her, but
he wasn't willing to take the risk of letting Tingley live.

"So he told Tingley he'd meet him that night.
Tingley suggested that park near his hotel since
naturally he didn't want us to know what he was
up to. They agreed to meet last night between
seven and eight.

"In the afternoon Vincent took his car and
went out to see friends. He purposely made the

Preedys' his last stop. I discovered this afternoon that the Preedys are two-fisted drinkers. Vincent was with them several hours, and they did have dinner, as he claimed. But it was a pick-up meal of scrambled eggs, and so on, and they didn't stop drinking because they ate.

"When he left they were in no state to say what time it was. He said he left them at about ten of eight, though he was too wise to insist on it. We knew he was home at eight-five. But he left the Preedys' at seven thirty-five, though they could never testify to that. He had plenty of time to get out to that park, locate Tingley sitting on that bench, kill him, and drive back home by eight-five."

"And why," Michael said, "did he tell you all this?"

"He's dead," Prevost said bleakly. "I should have searched him. And I should have remembered that amateur photographers sometimes have cyanide available. I suppose he always expected to escape that way if he was caught. I got some of the boys over to the library after you left. Vincent was still pretty groggy for quite a while. That's one reason I didn't handcuff him."

"I'm glad there won't be a trial," Marcia said. "Is that all?"

"I suppose there's nothing to be done about Bill Kemper's activities. The will Lydia's lawyer has will have to stand. I hope Sally meant it when she said she doesn't ever want to see Kemper again. That is, I hope Kemper doesn't profit by her inheritance."

Michael laughed. "I doubt if he does, and that is going to be very funny. If Sally tells him he can't play in her back yard his first instinct will be to pay her back by announcing that Lydia made a will that disinherited Sally. And then he'll realize he doesn't dare admit he knows that."

"He should have thought ahead and kept the will to hold over her head," Valerie said. "Though if he had I think I know what Sally would have told him to do with it."

"Little ladies shouldn't be familiar with phrases like that one," Michael said. "And it's time you were in bed."

"Oh, I'm sorry." Prevost got to his feet. "I'll be on my way."

"Why? Opportunity may never knock again. Marcia is staying with us for a while, and we will be glad to see you at any time, but we don't promise to make tactlessly tactful excuses and fade away to leave you two alone in the living room."

"We like to have our friends married," Valerie said. "But don't pay any attention to Michael."

"We like stories in which we leave 'them all in couples a-kissing on the decks, All the lovers loving and the parents signing checks.' You two have no parents and don't need checks signed, but we will give you our blessing. And a bit of advice, Nick. 'That man who hath a tongue, I say, is no man, If with this tongue he cannot win a woman.'"

"You go to—to blazes!" Nicholas Prevost said. "I—" He looked at Marcia. She leaned forward, smiling.

"Are you a mouse, Nick?" she said. "Or are you a man?"

"Good night, all," said Mr. Dundas.

COACHWHIP PUBLICATIONS
CoachwhipBooks.com

VIRGINIA RATH

DEATH AT
DAYTON'S FOLLY

COACHWHIP PUBLICATIONS
COACHWHIPBOOKS.COM

VIRGINIA RATH

THE ANGER
OF THE BELLS

COACHWHIP PUBLICATIONS
COACHWHIPBOOKS.COM

VIRGINIA RATH

AN EXCELLENT
NIGHT FOR
MURDER

COACHWHIP PUBLICATIONS
COACHWHIPBOOKS.COM

THE DARK
CAVALIER

VIRGINIA RATH

COACHWHIP PUBLICATIONS
CoachwhipBooks.com

MURDER

with a theme song

VIRGINIA RATH

COACHWHIP PUBLICATIONS
COACHWHIPBOOKS.COM

DEATH OF A
LUCKY LADY

VIRGINIA RATH

COACHWHIP PUBLICATIONS
CoachwhipBooks.com

VIRGINIA RATH

FERRYMAN,
TAKE HIM ACROSS!

COACHWHIP PUBLICATIONS
CoachwhipBooks.com

POSTED
FOR
MURDER

VIRGINIA RATH

COACHWHIP PUBLICATIONS
CoachwhipBooks.com

COACHWHIP PUBLICATIONS
CoachwhipBooks.com

A DIRGE FOR HER
VIRGINIA RATH